DEATH AT THE HUNTING LODGE

LAURA STEWART

BLOODHOUND
BOOKS

First published in 2024 by Bloodhound Books.

www.bloodhoundbooks.com

Print ISBN: 978-1-916978-80-5

A man travels the world over in search of what he needs and returns home to find it.
George Moore

TWO WEEKS BEFORE BELTANE

Moira Ballantyne cut the tarot cards, then carefully fanned the pack out on top of her deep-purple silk cloth. Tonight, she was only using the twenty-two cards of the Major Arcana, but that would give her enough information for the answer she sought.

'Should I go back?' she asked, then picked a card out with her left hand. Repeating the action another two times, Moira then turned all three cards she'd selected face up, studying the beautiful illustrations of the classic Rider Waite deck she'd been using for forty years.

For the past week she'd read her cards each sundown. No matter the layout she used or the question she asked, while it wasn't always the exact same images that appeared every time, the meaning was constant.

She paused to take a sip of her oolong tea, the white candles on the table flickering slightly with the disturbance in the air. Nursing her cup, she looked up, momentarily distracted by the view out the window at the front of her house, watching waves roll in towards the French shore. There was no need for a television as the ever-shifting scenery of Mother Nature was all the entertainment she desired. The sun was setting, slightly later than the previous night, which was later than the night before that. Winter was in retreat. Draining her tea, she put her cup aside to read the leaves later.

Turning back to her three tarot cards, Moira smiled. First up was The Lovers. In the broad sense it represented all love and relationships but it also signified making mature decisions that involved the heart more than the head.

The second card was The Moon, which was all about heeding dreams and using intuition rather than logic. It also reflected deep emotional conflict and a decision to be made. She gave a little laugh; more decisions! The Moon also was a time for self-reflection and for facing emotional vulnerabilities.

Finally, The Sun. This card immediately followed The Moon in the tarot and symbolised light after the preceding darkness. It denoted energy and growth; of being reunited with old friends, partners and family. It was also very auspicious, especially for the question she'd asked.

Collecting the tarot together, she cut the pack once, then, with a little tremor of anticipation, turned the top card over. The High Priestess.

She felt a little tingle in the tops of her arms and the base of her skull when she saw the image. The High Priestess had repeatedly appeared to her throughout most of her readings. She touched it thoughtfully knowing the key elements signified secrets, intuition, and the spiritual world.

Moira understood what the cards were telling her loud and clear.

Packing up her deck, she wrapped it gently in the silk cloth, then blew out each candle, leaving a smoky haze in the air. Glancing down at her finished cup of tea she decided to forgo reading the leaves tonight. She knew it would be the same message. Just as the tarot, runes and the dreams all pointed her to the same conclusion.

It was time to go home.

Walking over to the window, she rested a palm on the cool glass, her breath leaving a little circle of condensation as she watched the waves break in the dimming light.

Home.

A small word, but the implication was huge.

It was time Moira Ballantyne went home to Glencarlach.

ONE

Amelia Adams stood behind the reception desk of Stone Manor, the luxury boutique hotel she owned and managed, looking at the colour charts and paint swatches spread out before her. She debated the merits of warm golden yellows, calming greens and sophisticated inky-blue-toned paints, wondering which one she'd like adorning the walls of her new house.

The book she'd been lovingly filling for months with décor and furniture ideas for her new home with her fiancé, Jack Temple, was bulging and she'd soon need a bigger scrapbook. But although she had dozens of suggestions for sofas, beds and kitchens, the one thing she was still lacking was a new house to put them in.

Finding their 'forever home' had sounded so romantic. Amelia had been certain she would walk into a house and get that instant 'feeling' like so many couples did on *Location, Location, Location*. Unfortunately, very few houses came up for sale in the picturesque coastal village of Glencarlach in the north-west of Scotland and her search was further hampered by a slow housing market. Of the handful of properties the local estate agent had found for them to view, none of them had been suitable and the only 'feeling' Amelia was getting was one of despondency.

It wasn't that she didn't love the little Gatehouse she and Jack lived in; she did. It was a cosy little whitewashed, thick stone-walled cottage that sat on the grounds of Stone Manor. But it soon became apparent that its bijoux room sizes were woefully inadequate for Amelia and Jack, especially as Jack, who was six-foot two and muscular, banged his head so regularly on the low-set wooden beams that Amelia was concerned he lived in a state of perpetual concussion.

She picked up another colour card and a new shade caught her eye; caffe latte crème. Not because she particularly liked the beigey tones of the paint, but it reminded her it had been at least two hours since her last mug of coffee.

But before Amelia had a chance to sneak through to the kitchen for a welcome shot of caffeine, the front door of the hotel opened and her best friend, Sally Bishop, hurried in, engulfing Amelia in a rib-squeezing hug.

'I had to come and see you; I have news!' Sally gushed, her lovely Cornish accent full of warmth. 'Hamish's cousin... or maybe second cousin, I'm really not sure of that family's dynamics... well, some sort of cousin-like relation is coming back to the village in time for Beltane!'

Never having heard of Beltane before moving to Glencarlach from London, Amelia had been surprised at how important the pagan festival was for the locals. Preparations had been in place for months for the parade, dancing, feast and symbolic bonfire to herald the beginning of summer. Houses throughout the village were adorned with floral wreaths and there was a definite frisson of excitement building throughout Glencarlach as May 1st approached.

Sally flicked her long glossy auburn hair over her shoulder as she continued, quite breathless with excitement. 'So, this relative,

Moira, grew up in the village but moved away years ago. She lives in France now and has only popped back to the village a couple of times over the years to see family. Moira's totally into all this Beltane stuff. Very into her spiritual side and a bit of a practicing white witch by all accounts. She's also a humanist celebrant and has offered to carry out a handfasting ceremony for me and Hamish!'

'A what?'

'Handfasting. It's when a couple get their hands bound together in a symbolic gesture. Traditionally it was for a year and a day, after which they'd decide if they wanted to stay together or go their separate ways. A kind of pagan *try before you buy* scenario.'

'Wow. It sounds... nice, if a little intrusive.'

'Oh, it doesn't mean *literally* tied together for over a year, I double-checked before I agreed. I mean, I love Hamish very much but even I don't want to be frontline while he milks his dairy herd and I'm sure he wouldn't want to be attached to me while I'm setting perms and doing leg waxes. I also confirmed the *fasting* bit has nothing to do with food deprivation.'

'Will you still be having your actual wedding ceremony in the summer?' Amelia asked, thinking of the amount of planning that had already gone into Sally's 'big day', the reception of which was due to be held at Stone Manor.

Sally laughed. 'Oh yes! We're still having the official ceremony and massive party! My parents would never forgive me if I cancelled that. This handfasting thing is a lovely, natural way for Hamish and I to express our love for each other.'

Amelia couldn't agree more. Despite previously having led a jet-setting, cosmopolitan lifestyle as a freelance make-up artist, Sally had slipped into Scottish country life remarkably easily since arriving to help Amelia renovate Stone Manor, the grand, if dilapidated Georgian mansion Amelia had inherited.

As well as helping Amelia with the refurbishment, Sally had also met and fallen in love with the local farmer, Hamish McDonald. Leaving her job to stay permanently in Glencarlach, Sally had opened up a hairdressing and beauty salon on Main Street and was Stone Manor's in-house beauty therapist for any guests wishing a spa treatment during their visit.

Glencarlach had a way of enticing people to stay as it seemed to weave its own special magic, due to the warm, friendly locals as much as its beautiful setting; often named as one of Scotland's prettiest villages with its quaint, cobblestone streets leading away from the harbour and Main Street. Having been welcomed into the community so heartily Amelia couldn't imagine living anywhere else. Which made it all the more frustrating not being able to find a slightly bigger house to move to!

'It's going to be so romantic,' Sally carried on. 'We're hiring a boat for the ceremony which will be at sunset. I know it's rather last minute but please say you can come.'

'Of course!'

'Oh good. And I can't wait to meet Moira, she's seen as a bit of a character; part of Hamish's Great Aunt Betty's side of the family,' Sally added.

'Ah!' Amelia said, needing no further explanation. Having met the delightful, if eccentric and bohemian Betty previously and hearing stories of her wild past, Amelia understood how the elderly lady had shocked the more conventional side of Hamish's family.

'We were going to ask if she wanted to stay with us but she's already made a reservation.'

'We have a Moira Ballantyne due to arrive today.'

'That's her! And Betty called last night to say she's coming here for Beltane too and wondered if there would be room for her here? Arriving Wednesday?'

'Yes, we've got a few reservations but we've definitely got space for Betty,' Amelia said, bringing up the booking screen on the front-desk computer.

Amelia had become very fond of Hamish's relative when she'd stayed at Stone Manor over Christmas. Luckily Betty hadn't been put off by an intruder appearing in her room during the night or having a dead body turn up on Christmas day. In fact, the older lady had revelled in the drama.

'Right,' Sally said, 'I need to get a move on. I've to find some hawthorn and birch for the ceremony. Moira sent me a list of things to get to make into wreaths.'

'Hawthorn and birch? Where'll you get those?'

'Haven't a clue. I thought I'd ask around. Or download a tree-recognition app and go wandering through the woods.'

Wee Davey, the night porter and general helper around the hotel chose that moment to carry a crate of beer out from the staff door which led to the kitchens and storage areas. He paused.

'Hawthorn and birch? My dad's got some growing in the back garden of the pub. He was talking about trimming back the branches, so he'll give you some, no bother,' he said and continued on into the bar, the bottles clanking together.

Having lived in Glencarlach for a couple of years, nothing surprised Amelia about the owner of the village pub; the Whistling Haggis. As an instrumental member of the community, the owner and landlord, Big Davey, was on the winter fair committee, the summer fair committee, the Beltane committee, and any other committee that could be dreamt up, especially if it led to a knees-up. He was also always in the centre of village activities, including the much-anticipated annual panto, where he regularly threw himself into the role of ugly sister, Widow Twankey, fairy godmother; any role that showed off his deep baritone voice and involved wearing a big hooped dress, make-up and wig. With an ear always open for passing gossip, he had a way of knowing everyone's business. The apple didn't fall far from the tree with regards to his son, in either looks or personality. Wee Davey worked part-time at Stone Manor while studying for a hospitality degree and was a popular staff member, and also quite the gossip and more than once Amelia had had to gently remind him about guest confidentiality.

'Off to the Whistling Haggis I go!' Sally said. Glancing down, she noticed the colour charts in front of Amelia and turned them towards her to have a better look. 'Ooh, go with the strawberry parfait cream!' she said, then gave a chuckle. 'But I may just be saying that because I really fancy a creamy strawberry cake.' She winked. 'Right! I'm off. I also need to pop into the gift shop for some red ribbon.' And in a flurry of air kisses, Sally hurried away.

Amelia turned back to the booking page and finished filling in the details then went into the kitchens to seek out her brother, Toby.

The main running of Stone Manor was down to Amelia, but as head chef, Toby kept all culinary matters under his domain which Amelia conceded was for the best as she was first to admit she couldn't navigate her way around a recipe book or kitchen and had a rather unhealthy reliance on Pot Noodles.

Resplendent in his chef's whites and red durag to keep his dark-brown quiff in check, Toby stood at one of the burners stirring a delicious-smelling sauce. Despite them not having many people staying, Stone Manor was still open for lunches and dinners to non-residents and they were often fully booked. Toby glanced over his shoulder at the clock. 'Caffeine time?'

'Yup!' Amelia confirmed as she headed over to the coffee maker in the corner.

She poured herself a mug as Toby's phone rang on the worktop beside him. He reached over and pressed the hands-free button and continued to stir the sauce. 'Hey, Gideon, Ames is here too, in case you're about to talk dirty to me!' he said and gave a laugh, but instead of Gideon there was a moment's pause and then,

'Is this Toby, Gideon's partner?' an unfamiliar voice asked.

'Yes.' Toby looked up at Amelia worriedly, as her stomach gave an anxious lurch.

'I'm filming with Gideon... I have to inform you, there's been a bit of an accident...'

TWO

'Don't you worry, my agent will have something to say about all this!' Gideon Fey's voice rose dramatically as he looked from Amelia to Toby as he struggled into the drawing room at Stone Manor with a bandaged foot and crutches. 'The lack of safety on set was *utterly* appalling. I'm surprised no one has died since the film started shooting. Why we had to have the chase scene on quad bikes, I have no idea! The original script had called for it to be on horses. I know horses. Horses *like* me! A horse wouldn't have had a faulty handbrake, engaged its engine, or whatever, then hurtled full-throttle towards the catering tent and tried to mow me down before bursting into flames moments after I leapt out the way when I was sitting quietly, going over my lines as I ate my quinoa and chia-seed porridge!'

Amelia thought it sounded like a lucky escape from an uninspiring breakfast but didn't like to say, as Gideon Fey had been in full rant mode since Toby had picked him up from hospital at lunchtime and brought him back to Stone Manor.

'Gideon, we may have a bit of a problem,' Toby said. 'You won't manage in the cottage. There's no way you'll be able to manoeuvre up and down our narrow spiral staircase to the bedroom and bathroom.'

Amelia realised her brother had a point. The cottage Gideon and Toby lived in was situated at the top of the village, accessible by one of the zigzagging cobblestone streets, and neither home nor approach were crutches friendly.

'Oh my God! Are you saying I'm homeless as well as a cripple?' Gideon gasped, pressing his hand to his high, Slavic cheekbone theatrically, his golden-brown eyes darting from Toby to Amelia.

'You'll have to stay here, at Stone Manor while you recuperate,' Amelia said. 'We're not fully booked so we've room. And, obviously we have the elevator...'

'Ugh! The old biddy express. It has come to this!'

'The elevator isn't just for our more elderly guests,' Amelia chastised lightly. 'It's to allow our less mobile guests—'

'The old and infirm ones!'

'—to move around more easily. For this exact scenario.'

'I suppose,' Gideon said grudgingly, but then his face lit up. 'Amelia, why don't you move back in too? It'll be like old times when you and I arrived. Remember that first night? We had such fun!'

Either Gideon was wearing his rose-tinted nostalgia glasses or the painkillers he'd taken were having an effect on his memory. Amelia remembered the first night she stayed at Stone Manor. Shell-shocked at discovering she'd inherited such a grand and imposing house, she'd also been freezing due to the lack of heating and every time a light was turned on, the whole system fused and they were plummeted into darkness. Amelia distinctly recalled feeling completely overwhelmed and out of her depth. And that was all *before* she'd discovered Gideon had organised a documentary crew to come and film her 'transformative' story.

'And imagine, if you moved in too, you could be like my own personal nurse, attending to my every need! It'll be lovely!'

'*Wouldn't* it!' Toby echoed with a mischievous grin aimed at Amelia.

'But surely Toby will be moving in with you too,' she said with a desperate look at her brother. 'You are his boyfriend, after all!'

'Of course I will, but we're booked up for dinners for the foreseeable so I'll be working a lot. And I'm helping out with the food for the Beltane feast too, that's going to keep me busy long after service is over. And speaking of dinners, I need to get on!' Toby said, then bolted through to the kitchen before he could get roped into anything else.

'Let me have a think,' Amelia said. No matter how cramped she was finding the Gatehouse, she wasn't sure moving in to tend to a demanding Gideon was the answer. 'Guess what? Betty will be staying with us,' Amelia said, changing the subject.

Gideon's eyes lit up.

'Yes, and I need to do a quick stock check of the bar.' Amelia knew how much Betty loved a dry martini cocktail.

'Ames, darling,' Gideon called out when Amelia was barely out of the drawing room. 'I don't suppose you could plump up my cushions a bit, and I'd *love* a choccie biccie to go with my tea.'

'I'll get James to bring you one in. I need to pop out.'

Gideon's face fell. 'Where? That means I'll be all alone.'

'I need to go and see a couple of folk in the village.'

Gideon gave her his hurt puppy look.

'But, we can always go to the village hall later this afternoon, there's a big meeting about the archaeologists excavating the Pictish site and abbey ruins. Some locals aren't happy,' she said to appease him.

'Oh, do you think there might be some drama?' Gideon said, perking up considerably.

'Definitely! So you'd better get some rest now, as it would be such a shame if you had to miss out.'

'Very true, darling, very true,' he said, sinking back into the cushions.

THREE

Embracing the spring day, Amelia walked the mile or so from Stone Manor into the village. The sun was valiantly attempting to warm the sky, as fresh April winds blustered along Main Street causing the red, yellow and green bunting that had been hung up between the intricate Victorian lampposts to flap enthusiastically. Amelia could see the water was choppy; the bright blue reflected from the cloudless sky crested with foaming crowns of white as boats bobbed about in the harbour of Loch Carlach, which led directly out to the more turbulent North Atlantic.

The harbour area was a hub of activity. More decorations had sprung up for the Beltane festival which was now four days away. Although Beltane wasn't until the Sunday, the Beltane committee had decided to celebrate with the parade, feast and bonfire the day before, on the Saturday. Amelia knew the official line was so the villagers didn't risk a hangover at work on the Monday, but unofficially it was to elongate the festivities for those who wanted to party all weekend.

Walking along Main Street Amelia headed straight to Drew

McAvoy's estate agents, but when she tried the handle found it to be locked. She checked her watch. It was five past two. Although they closed for lunch, they were usually open again by now. She peered in through the glass door but the place was empty and in darkness.

Moving on to the next item on her 'to-do' list, Amelia crossed the road, stopping briefly at the newly-erected maypole to where a group of council workers, having set it up, were trying it out by skipping gaily between each other with their hi-vis vests and tool belts. Chuckling to herself, Amelia walked down the stone steps to the lower part of the harbour and made her way along the jetty, where a few little dinghies and smaller boats had been berthed.

Not being a working commercial fishing harbour for many years, the boats that bobbed up and down belonged to the locals or those who'd arrived for a day trip or holiday. But the one she was looking for was at the very end of the dock and considerably larger.

The *Amber Dram* was painted a deep golden brown and had *'Rory's pleasure cruises'* emblazoned along the side in scarlet. The captain himself was lounging, feet up, on the storage-bench seating as he chatted to his best friend, Johno Davis, the local water sports and scuba instructor and owner of SeaShack for those swimming trunk, snorkel mask or tadpole-net emergencies. Johno waved and hollered a greeting at Amelia as she approached. Rory turned and smiled when he saw Amelia, stretching out his hand to help her across the gangway, onto his boat.

'Afternoon, gents!' Amelia said, seeing her reflection in Johno's mirrored sunglasses a second before he pushed them up to sit on the top of his unruly mop of blond hair. Always tanned and looking as if he'd moments earlier been balancing on a surfboard, Johno seemed impervious to the cold as Amelia had never seen him wearing anything other than summery-type clothes, no matter the gale that was blowing or how low the temperature dropped. And today, despite the spring sunshine, Amelia doubted the temperature had risen much into double figures.

'How are things?' Rory McAvoy asked as he lowered his feet and slid along the bench to let Amelia sit.

'Good, thanks. Bookings seem to be going well for you,' Amelia said, gesturing towards the chalk A-board sat on the dock beside the boat with that week's cruise times where Rory had crossed out a couple and written 'sold out' notices beside them.

'It's the Beltane effect. Folk fancy a bit of a jolly,' Rory said with an easy shrug, leaning back against the side of the boat, holding his face up to the sun and repositioning his denim bucket hat. 'The free glass of Prosecco on boarding doesn't hurt the bookings either. And there are a few more visitors berthing up for a night or two. Aye, I've been busy in the office.' He gave a little bemused laugh. As the part-time harbour-master, he kept an eye on the comings and goings of the boats in Glencarlach and his 'office' consisted of a ramshackle hut next to where he berthed the *Amber Dram*, his 1930s 'gentleman's motor yacht', for his cruises.

'That's good to hear. Think I could get more of your leaflets for the reception area? We're running low.'

'Sure, I've got another batch due from the printers. I'll hand a pile in.'

'I've been thinking about organising some sort of tie-in package we could offer between us, incorporating a meal at Stone Manor and a cruise on your boat.'

Rory rubbed the dark stubble on his wide chin. 'That sounds good. Anything to boost bookings is always welcome.'

Despite Rory only running the cruises between April and October, Amelia knew he worked very hard for those months, offering the dolphin-watching and scenic tours by day and the more grown-up party cruises in the evenings. Out of season, in the winter months, in between working as a handyman, Rory also took the boat over to the Isle of Harris where Johno organised surfing tuition around the Hebridean island. Amelia could think of nothing worse than getting into the sea in anything other than warm sunshine, preferably in the Mediterranean or Caribbean, but Johno had assured her many times that winter was the best surfing season in Scotland and the water was surprisingly warm due to the North Atlantic Drift which moved in from the Gulf of Mexico. Despite this, Amelia had no intention of donning a wetsuit any time soon, no matter how well-insulated it was meant to be, especially coming from a man who wore shorts and flip-flops in a hard frost.

Johno clapped his hands together and leant forward keenly. 'I don't suppose any of your guests would fancy a bit of snorkelling or scuba-diving, or even a bit of kayaking and paddleboarding?'

Amelia smiled. 'I was hoping you'd ask that. I think it would be a great thing to offer. We should sit down and work out a plan for the summer season. When are you free this week?'

'What's today? Monday... Tuesday?' Johno said.

'Tuesday. All day,' Rory said with an indulgent smile to his friend.

'Cool, maybe tomorrow or Thursday?'

'Great.'

'So, what are you up to now on this fine day?' Rory asked, squinting up at the sun. 'Off to see my big brother in case a house has appeared on the market overnight?'

It was well documented through Glencarlach that Amelia was house-hunting and she'd been a regular visitor at Drew McAvoy's estate agency on Main Street.

'I went there first, but it's shut.'

'Really?' Rory darted a glance over to the row of shops.

'Drew probably saw me coming and hid,' Amelia joked. 'I think your brother is close to taking out a restraining order on me if I keep pestering him about houses for sale.'

'It's more likely Drew and Lily are in the back partaking in a little afternoon delight,' Johno said with a wink.

It was also well documented that the estate agent was seeing his co-worker Lily Wu, but considering Amelia had walked in on the couple more than once when they were in the middle of a heated argument, she wasn't entirely convinced romance was the reason for the closed office.

Rory glanced over towards Main Street. Judging by the worried expression on his face, it seemed Rory also had concerns.

'I'm sure it's nothing sinister,' Amelia said, hoping she was right. 'Probably just a long lunch.'

'Aye,' Johno leant over and punched his friend on the shoulder, 'he'll be schmoozing some potential customer with his full-on charm offensive. Or having a quickie with Lily. Oh, heads-up, you've got customers,' Johno said, looking over Amelia's shoulder.

Amelia turned to see a group of tourists making a beeline for Rory's boat.

Rory stood up, ready to greet them as Amelia carefully disembarked. Heading back along the dock and climbing the harbour steps, she breathed in the fresh salty tang of the sea air, feeling the Beltane buzz having an effect on her too.

A deep thud bass coming from inside a car disrupted the peaceful afternoon and Amelia turned to see Drew McAvoy speed along Main Street before screeching to a halt in an empty parking space outside the estate agency. Cutting the engine, Drew got out. With a thunderous expression on his face, he unlocked his office and went inside, slamming the door closed behind him.

FOUR

The village community hall was packed when Amelia, Toby and Gideon arrived just before four o'clock, that afternoon. After struggling through the doors and almost knee-capping the local minister with his crutches, Gideon bulldozed his way towards the front row of seating, loudly stating he didn't want to make a fuss, then proceeded to do just that by getting everyone to shift their chairs so he could find a comfortable position where he could elevate his leg but with maximum visibility so everyone who arrived would instantly see the renowned actor and come over to express their concern.

Amelia had just sat down when local artist Lorcan Flyn and his girlfriend Evangelina Wilde sat in the row behind them.

'Gideon! What happened?' Evangelina exclaimed, looking at his bandaged leg.

'What happened? I barely got away with my life intact, darling! *That's* what happened!' Gideon's well-modulated, RADA-trained voice rose dramatically over the chatter in the hall.

Toby rolled his eyes as Gideon gave Lorcan and Evangelina

a blow-by-blow account, which he had managed to embellish slightly with every retelling.

'Is it badly broken?' Evangelina asked.

Gideon evaded the question whilst behind him, out of his line of vision, Toby shook his head and mouthed '*sprained*'.

'The pain is intolerable,' Gideon said, closing his eyes and breathing in deeply through his nose.

'It's not the only thing that's intolerable,' Toby muttered to Amelia.

'...and clearly the NHS is on its knees as they didn't even have a spare wheelchair they could give me,' Gideon carried on. 'I was just left grappling with these crutches, *abandoned* on the street to fend for myself.'

'I picked him up from the hospital,' Toby added for clarity. 'Right, I'm going to have to head back to Stone Manor and get on with prep for tonight. Will you be okay?'

Amelia nodded and shooed her brother away.

'Is Jack coming along to this?' Lorcan asked Amelia.

'No, he's meeting us in the Whistling Haggis later.'

Just then, Andy McAvoy, Rory and Drew's father and one of the local councillors, stood up at the front of the hall. Andy raised his hands for silence.

'Hope you're feeling better soon, mate,' Lorcan whispered, patting Gideon on the shoulder and Gideon shifted round slightly in his seat to face the front, wincing at the movement.

Amelia had a quick glance behind her, realising the room was now full, with stragglers having to stand at the back as all the folding chairs had been taken.

'Thank you all for coming,' Andy said. 'Um, we didn't expect quite this turnout. Jolly good, jolly good.' He gave a little nervous chuckle as he peered out at the audience. He then accidentally dropped his piece of paper and spent a moment trying to catch it as it fluttered to the floor and glided under someone's chair. The audience shifted and coughed and started a low murmur of chat until Andy eventually retrieved his notes and stood back up, red-faced and flustered.

'Yes, so, um, we thought it best to call this village meeting due to the archaeological excavation as it has raised some, ah, some, concerns.' Not a natural public speaker, Andy McAvoy blinked at everyone and tapped his fingers on the back of his bald head. 'Without further ado, I'd like to pass the floor over to the project director, Isobel Aitken, who is happy to discuss the plans and will answer any questions.' Andy finished speaking then rushed off to the side as the archaeologist stood. Tall and slim, Isobel had eschewed her customary look of black combat trousers and indie-band T-shirt for a pair of jeans and a linen shirt. Her dark-brown hair which was normally tied back was, this afternoon, hanging loose in a heavy curtain to her shoulders. Her freckles and usually slightly sunburnt skin was camouflaged with a touch of foundation and she'd bothered with mascara and a slick of lip gloss. Clearly, Isobel had made an effort.

'Ooh, she's staying at Stone Manor, isn't she?' Gideon stage-whispered to Amelia. 'I saw her in the bar earlier. She was interested to hear about my accident. *Very* sympathetic.'

Amelia nodded, keen to hear what the archaeologist had to say.

Gideon sat forward slightly, to get a better look at the other side of the hall. 'Are those the other archaeologists?'

Amelia glanced to her right and saw field supervisor, Tim, and the two field technicians, Gus and Maja.

She gave a slight nod to Gideon.

'Thought so, they look a bit dirty. Like they've spent too long in a muddy trench.'

Amelia widened her eyes in warning and held her index finger up to her lips, trying to concentrate on Isobel.

Gideon, not taking the hint, continued. 'Are they staying in Stone Manor too?'

Amelia ignored him but Gideon nudged her arm.

'Yes,' Amelia whispered.

'I hope you get them to wash and change before they sit on the furniture.'

'Shh, I want to hear what she's saying!'

Gideon sat back in his chair with a harrumph, as Amelia tuned back in to Isobel.

'...and I truly believe we're on the cusp of a tremendously exciting excavation. Especially as the abbey ruins are pretty much on top of the Pictish site. There could be a link as to why, in the twelfth century, an abbey was built on the previous Pictish burial grounds four hundred years before. Our findings suggest there may be spiritual reasons as well as practical- and agriculturally-based decisions.'

'Like ley lines?' someone asked from the back.

There was a peal of laughter from Gus who was sitting, arms folded, slumped in his chair.

'Well, um, not really,' Isobel said, clearly trying to be diplomatic.

'Ley lines? Don't they attract aliens?' someone asked.

'I saw a documentary on Area 51 and all those dodgy government folk that covered it up!' another woman added.

Isobel had to raise her voice considerably to be heard over the chatter this last remark caused. 'The idea of ley lines was suggested by Alfred Watkins in 1921, that was based on ancient societies aligning their buildings to create some kind of earth energy. It grew to be a popular theory during the sixties through to the eighties but we archaeologists don't really think there's anything to them. But, in Glencarlach, there does seem to be a connection with the main Pictish stones and large ceremonial stones from the abbey. But definitely no alien lifeforms.'

Although quiet and a little breathless with nerves, Isobel continued to speak with passion. 'We believe the burial cairns and carved stones we've already identified are just the tip of the iceberg. And I, *we,* are quietly confident in thinking we've got a Pictish site that could rival those that have so far only been discovered on the east coast of Scotland. I know how precious the landscape and environment are to you all. To me too. And we want to allay your worries about our presence here. Does anyone have questions? Yes?' The project director nodded at someone in the audience.

Amelia turned to see Christine McGuthrie, owner of the outdoors shop and active member of the Glencarlach Wildlife Society take to her feet.

'We're worried about the wildlife,' she said and quite a few folk nodded and made murmurs of agreement. 'We've had reports of rare types of moths in the area and we don't want bright floodlights at night to disturb them. Plus, spring is a crucial time for new life and we're concerned about habitats being damaged.'

'Yes!' Someone from the Glencarlach Ornithological Society stood a few seats away. 'We have many species of birds nesting at the moment. It's a fragile ecosystem and any disruption to the environment could have devastating consequences. And of course, we have bats and they're protected.'

Gus turned in his chair to look at the audience. 'Surely the moths are more at risk from being eaten by the birds and the bats!' he said with mock horror. 'Nature can be very cruel.'

Isobel threw the field technician a warning look before she carried on addressing the room.

'We won't be carrying out any work at night so large floodlights won't be used.'

'But how can you tell from those large lumps of rock that

there's anything there?' someone else shouted. 'My garden's got masses of big stones in it, are you going to come and say my veg patch has got archaeological relevance too?'

There were a couple of laughs from the crowd as Tim, the field supervisor stood up. Tall, skinny and with a buzz cut, he went over to Isobel and whispered something and she smiled and took a step back, giving him the floor. Tim cleared his throat.

'Hi, everyone, thanks for coming today, I just wanted to add a couple of things,' Tim said with a slightly apologetic air. Although not loud, he had a commanding voice and his strong Manchester accent echoed throughout the hall.

'We've taken painstaking care to check the ground.' He started off a little haltingly. 'We are keeping to the small area our aerial photography and GPR has identified as a place of interest. That's been highlighted in red.' He pointed over to the wall of the community hall where boards had been hung. 'I've put up a detailed map of the area we're excavating and I invite you all to study them. You can see clearly the furrows and ridges. The highlighted site we believe to be of relevance is the area south of the standing stones, in the slight dip in the field, which runs onto the grounds the abbey was built on. The second board has a reconstruction of what the abbey looked like in its heyday and you can see just how close it is to the Pictish site. What looks like plain lumps of rock to you tells me a story from the past. And, in a rather exciting development,' his face became more animated as he continued speaking, 'Gus believes there's the potential of a secondary site, situated on the north side of the abbey ruins. And we hope to look at that if we can secure extra funding.'

Gus stood up. Short and heavyset with a shaved side undercut, the long piece of hair tired up in a topknot which still had traces of pale-pink hair dye, he cut an imposing figure with his tattoos, multiple piercings and stretched earlobes.

'Now, Tim, we don't want to be giving anyone here an apoplexy. Let them get to grips with the original site first, eh? The secondary site was meant to be our little secret.' Although Gus spoke lightly, Amelia caught the flash of warning in his eyes.

Tim reddened.

'And,' Gus added in a stage whisper, 'we need to save something for them to complain about in a few weeks' time, don't we?'

There was a rumble of conversation and Amelia saw Isobel give Gus a look and lightly touch his arm, gesturing for him to sit down.

Gus rolled his eyes at Isobel. 'Come on, we all know how this plays out. Whilst it's a lovely show of village solidarity, we all know it's a tick-box exercise. They complain, we appease, they have a petition, we show them all the permits and legal papers. They clutch their pearls and have a mump and a moan. We carry on regardless.' He turned back to face the audience. 'Let's face facts,' he said chummily, 'I know you are all secretly thrilled about us being here. We must be the only exciting thing to have ever happened in this sleepy little backwater.'

'He *clearly* hasn't read up on Glencarlach,' Gideon said sniffily as an aside to Amelia.

'Sit down, Gus,' Isobel said sharply.

'Why are you pandering to all this! Get a backbone, Izzy! And all this fake humility, Tim, about *maybe* being able to secure extra funding. Of course there'll be extra funding. We have a stupidly rich benefactor. Or maybe he's just stupid and rich, who knows? Makes me think someone here is screwing our patron. All I know is, it ain't me!' He laughed. 'Ooh!' he exclaimed in an overly camp manner as he turned to Isobel. 'I hope to God it's not you.' He raised his eyebrow and laughed.

'*Gus!*' Isobel hissed, her face reddening.

But Gus was on a roll. He looked back up at the hall. 'Trust me, you don't want to stand in the way of breakthroughs and progress, complaining about your birds and beavers and not seeing the bigger picture. What looks like plain lumps of rock to you, tells me a story. I already know so much, just from looking at these photographs. I can interpret the secrets of the past. *All* your secrets,' he added with a wink.

There was a ripple of dissent in the hall.

Gideon leant in to whisper to Amelia. 'If they're still here at Christmas, Gus would make a very good pantomime baddy.'

Amelia saw a flash of blond and the bright-green and pink of a Hawaiian print shirt as Johno stood up.

'Don't claim to know all about us, making us out to be pathetic country bumpkins,' the owner of SeaShack said. 'You've come to where we live, imposing your vision on our environment. We're not idiots. We understand the cultural significance of what you're doing but we also want reassurance that you're not going to bulldoze your way across our land. The fields and forests and shoreline are part of us, where we grew up and live. For many it's our livelihood. Can you guarantee you won't be using heavy diggers? And what if you decide to open up your investigation site and move closer to the cliff face? Natural erosion is already a problem and our shores are losing a lot of its diverse marine life, and it doesn't need you speeding up the process. You can't expect us to just roll over without asking some questions first.'

There was a smattering of applause at Johno's impassioned speech.

Gus feigned shock. 'Get you and your big talk, Johnny boy. Playing the hero. You and your precious shoreline, I know how much you love your shoreline.' He winked then placed his hands over his heart and said with an air of solemnity. 'I will give you my personal oath I won't mess that up.'

Gus turned to Isobel. 'I'm going for a drink.' He picked up his leather jacket from the back of his chair and strode up the middle of the room waving and smiling at everyone despite the stony reception he received.

'You need to rein in that cockiness,' Johno said as Gus got nearer to him.

Gus paused, less than a foot away. 'I don't *need* to do anything. Suck it up and go cry to your girlfriend.' He made a sweeping gesture with his arm. 'Do these good people know you're sleeping with the enemy?' Gus turned and blew Maja a kiss. 'We've all been there anyway.'

Maja screamed something which Amelia took to be a swear word in her native Swedish.

Johno stepped out into the aisle. 'Apologise for that!'

'Make me.'

They squared up to each other.

'I'll make you, all right. And I'll make you regret ever coming here,' Johno said passionately.

'Will you, now?' Gus laughed. 'I seriously doubt it,' he added as he continued heading out the door. 'Later, dudes!' he called out, putting on a Californian twang.

After a second's silence the hall erupted into chatter.

Isobel looked on helplessly. 'Excuse me... Hello!' She tried to be heard.

'God, what a rabble!' Gideon remarked.

Then Amelia saw Isobel raise her fingers to her mouth and give out a very loud whistle.

Everyone stopped talking.

Isobel smiled. 'I'm so sorry for that. I will speak to Gus

about his rude interruption. I want to stress that his views are not mine, *ours*.' She gestured to Maja and Tim.

'But what guarantees can you give us that you won't be disturbing the land?' Christine asked.

Isobel took a breath. 'We will be moving around on electric golf carts so we have as little a carbon footprint as possible. We won't use diggers, or any machinery which could cause damage. It'll be a slower process but one that will have minimum impact, and we will have a selection of students coming on weekly rotations. They'll be camping out in the field next to the site.'

Tim cleared his throat. 'I'll hang on here throughout the evening so I can answer any questions on the tech, as that's my speciality.'

'What about leaving the poor dead souls to stay at rest?' someone else called out. 'That land is sacred.'

'We are always respectful and we won't exhume any human remains. We will take photographic evidence then cover the body as it was. We hope what we find will benefit everyone and give more insight into this fascinating period of history. If we are successful in our findings there are plans to create a cultural heritage centre which will bring in an interest to the area.'

'And have even *more* people stomping all over our land!' someone shouted.

'The only people that'll benefit will be the shops, the Whistling Haggis and Stone Manor. And they all seem to be doing fine at the moment, anyway,' a man with a scarlet bobble hat shouted.

'But money spent in the area will benefit everyone!' the local butcher retorted.

'Stone Manor's already making plenty of money from this,' Bobble-hat Man called out again. 'That lot are staying there!'

Gideon turned to Amelia. 'Oh my, are you now a figure of

hate? Placards tomorrow, lynch mob by the weekend. I've seen things like this escalate!'

Amelia felt very uncomfortable as the attention was turned onto her.

There were quite a few murmurs of agreement from the hall but before Amelia could say anything, a voice piped up from the back.

'I do think any annoyance at my dear neighbour, Ms Adams, is wholly misdirected. She's just trying to run her business and, in these difficult times, who is in a position to turn paying customers away?'

Intrigued, Amelia turned to see the owner of the rich, plummy tones that filled the room. There was one of her neighbours she'd never met. Could this be Hector Bain, the elusive landowner who possessed pretty much most of Glencarlach and the surrounding fields?

A man stepped forward. Tall and quite broad, with a wide, open face, he had a small, pointed soul patch beard and collar-length salt-and-pepper hair. He wore tartan trews and a rather threadbare woollen jumper, which Amelia would have put money on coming from the local shop due to the jaunty asymmetric design and rather jarring pink, orange and green colour combination the local knitter favoured. On top of this he wore a long tweed cape and riding boots.

'If you're going to be angry at anyone, save your ire for me, good people. I'm the one funding this excavation which also happens to be on my land.'

Amelia looked back to the front where Isobel stood, flushed of face, as she stared at Hector Bain.

'Now, to show my deep affection and to encourage you all to be a little more understanding towards these good scholars, I've put money behind the bar in the Whistling Haggis. Quite a lot of it, in fact. I wish you all a very pleasant evening.' Hector gave a slight bow then plonked a lilac fedora on his head, which topped off the eccentric fashion mish-mash spectacularly. With a dramatic swish of his cloak, he left.

Apart from one dissenting voice that shouted, '*Hoity-toity bastard*,' which Amelia would have sworn came from Bobble-hat Man, most of the villagers seemed mollified and cheerful as they filed out the hall, the danger to rare moths not quite as worrisome a problem in light of the prospect of free drinks.

FIVE

'He might not be as bad as you think.'

Amelia turned to look at Jack, who'd uttered the ridiculous statement as they stood at the bar of the Whistling Haggis, where everyone had piled into after the meeting in the village hall.

'I have a horrible feeling he might be worse!' From past experience Amelia knew Gideon was a dreadful patient, overdramatising the slightest ache and pain, googling every symptom if he so much as sneezed, often convincing himself he had dengue fever or a strain of the bubonic plague.

'Maybe I *should* move into the hotel for a few nights,' Amelia said. 'Toby will be busy and won't have time to run about after Gideon and you've got your novel to finish and send off.'

Jack threw his head back with a groan. 'Don't remind me. I still need to work out how a bloodied murder weapon could have remained hidden in plain sight for the best part of twenty-seven chapters without having someone accidentally discovering it. It's why I ended up missing all the drama tonight. I keep writing myself into a corner with this novel.'

'If I'm staying at Stone Manor, you won't have me getting in the way of your creative process.'

As Jack worked from home as a bestselling thriller writer, his laptop, notebooks and plethora of Post-it notes were constantly littered over the kitchen table and cupboards, and more than once Amelia had accidentally covered some of his crucial plot scribblings with a coffee-mug ring or strawberry-jam splodges.

'I like you getting in the way of my creative process,' he said, kissing her.

'Not the week of your deadline you don't,' she pointed out lightly, kissing him back. 'Don't worry, it'll be very temporary. Just until Gideon's back on his feet and you've sent off your manuscript.'

'What's it to be tonight?' Big Davey asked as he sidled over to them, hands poised over the beer taps.

'Pint of Export for me and–'

'An orange juice, thanks,' Amelia said. 'Were you at the meeting earlier?'

Davey shook his head as he pulled the pint. 'I heard it was a good turnout. And that it got a bit heated.' Davey gave a knowing nod.

'Yeah. The excavation site does seem to be dividing the village. I hadn't realised who was funding it.'

'Aye, Hector Bain.' Davey raised his eyebrows. 'And not just funding the archaeologists. He's man of the hour in here thanks to his benevolence,' he said rather cynically.

'Do you know him?'

'Many moons ago. Well, until he got packed off to a fancy boarding school.' Davey put Jack's pint down then got a little bottle of juice and a glass for Amelia.

Jack thanked Davey then asked, 'Does he own the big Scots baronial place that you can only see from the water?'

Davey nodded as he opened the crimped lid of the juice. 'Gull Point. And he also owns most of the land from the edge of Stone Manor halfway to Ullapool. As a rough rule of thumb, anything bordered by thick trees you can't see past is his estate.'

'Most of Stone Manor backs onto the Grant farm, there's only a small section of our woodland beyond the folly that borders Hector Bain's land,' Amelia said, recalling the documents she'd received on inheriting Stone Manor.

Big Davey nodded. 'And he owns the rest of the land as far as the eye can see. I'd say three-quarters of the farmers around here are his tenants. It's only really the Grants, the McDonalds, and the McDougalls who have the big farms that still own them outright. A couple of smaller ones too. Not that Hector has much to do with any of them as he has estate managers like Andy McAvoy to handle everything.'

'I thought Andy McAvoy was a local councillor,' Jack said before taking a sip of his pint.

'Aye, he is. Some of us wear a couple of hats in a small place like Glencarlach.'

'It was the first time I'd even seen Hector Bain,' Amelia said.

'He lives in London for the most part. Probably spends all day in a fancy club counting his money. Comes up for the Glorious Twelfth in August, you know, to mark the start of the grouse-shooting season. Brings a host of MPs and business folk with him as a networking exercise. He'll maybe appear the odd day here and there. Rarely mixes with the locals though. I can't remember the last time he came in here. He has a housekeeper to get everything in for him and the only way you'll know he's here is the sound of helicopters flying overhead, usually at antisocial times.'

Amelia was aware that the pub had suddenly became quieter. She looked around to see Gus making his way up to the bar.

He squeezed in between Amelia and Jack. 'If I'm not persona non grata, am I able to get a drink?'

'You are,' Davey said. 'Hector's put money behind the bar.'

'Ooh!' Gus rubbed his hands in glee. 'How many drinks can we get each?'

'Hector didn't specify.'

'Well, then...' Gus clicked his tongue, the stud piercing clacking against his teeth as he perused the wall of spirits. 'I'll have a rum then. That dark one, the Gosling's.'

'Single? Double?'

'Bottle. I'm sure good old Hector won't begrudge me that.' Gus drummed his fingers on the bar as Davey reached up and got it from the shelf.

Isobel pushed her way towards them.

'Gus, that was really uncalled for back there.'

Gus clutched the bottle to his chest. 'Oh, Isobel, don't be a spoilsport,' he pleaded in a sing-songy voice, 'let me play with the locals. I love to tease them and see them getting all annoyed and indignant. It's my only pleasure. Okay,' he rolled his eyes, 'it's not my *only* pleasure. You know me well enough!' He winked. 'But, Isobel, if it isn't protestors here, it's the threat of lack of funding somewhere else. It's always the same. It gets so repetitive. I've wondered about packing it in altogether, going back into academia. Ooh, what if I do a moonlight flit! Then what'll you do, hmmm? You know I hate it when I feel under-appreciated,' he said as he turned and schlepped out the bar.

Isobel made eye contact with Amelia.

'Don't worry, he's always doing this. Annoyingly, he is very good at his job which is why I entertain his moodiness.' Isobel sighed. 'I'll buy him a bottle of rum and fluff his ego for a bit and he'll be fine in a day or two. I just wish he didn't take such delight in winding people up.' She gathered her long hair up in a ponytail and secured it with a bobble. 'I think I'll sack off the rest of the day and take up Hector's offer and have a drink. Although I don't think I'd have any protestors to contend with, it seems they're all in here,' she said wryly. 'I'll have a gin and tonic, please, Davey. Best make it a double.'

Amelia knew most mornings since the archaeologists had set up the gazebos and pegged out the area for excavation, they'd been met with at least one person holding up a protest sign. Red paint scrawled out variations of 'Keep our ancestors sacred' or 'Protect our animals'.

On a positive note, the joint dislike of the excavation had united the wildlife and ornithological societies who were usually sworn enemies. And a new sub-genre calling themselves 'Picts in Peace' had also sprung up. They objected to the sacred land being disturbed. Luckily the protests were silent and had never led to any trouble. And Tim had confided in Amelia that he'd let a couple of the more elderly protesters pop into the gazebo when it rained, even giving them a cup of coffee to warm them up.

Isobel took her drink and threaded her way through another crowd of people entering the pub, to join Maja. Amelia wondered if Gus had a point. Maybe the good folk of Glencarlach did just like having a mump and a moan.

At that point Gideon hobbled over with a pair of binoculars round his neck, clutching a clipboard with papers attached.

'What have you got there?' Amelia asked.

'The means to stopping the besmirching of your reputation, poppet.'

'I wasn't aware I was being besmirched,' Amelia said wryly.

Gideon leant in closer and nodded over to the man in the scarlet bobble hat who'd been vocal earlier. 'There are rumblings you're getting some financial bonus whilst fraternising with the enemy.'

'What? That's ridiculous! And there *is* no enemy! I had

reservations when I heard about the excavation but I studied the plans and heard what Isobel had to say and they're not going to be digging up chunks of ground willy-nilly. I think it will be of great value from a historical and cultural point. As George Santayana said, *"to know your future you must know your past".*'

Big Davey nodded his support. 'Well said, Amelia.'

Gideon patted her arm. 'I didn't know you were a fan of Santana! I quite liked their cover of "Black Magic Woman".'

'No, *Santayana*. He was a philosopher and poet.'

'I feel the same about David Bowie, darling.'

But before Amelia could clear up the misunderstanding, Gideon carried on. 'Now, as I was saying, I have selflessly sacrificed a few hours for you.' Gideon puffed out his chest, looking pleased with himself. 'I'm taking one for the team.'

'What are you doing?' Jack said, trying to take a peek at the clipboard which Gideon had pressed tightly against his torso.

'The Glencarlach Ornithological Society asked if we could do a survey, a bird count, to make sure there aren't any dwindling species numbers during the dig.' He flipped the board around to show a printed sheet with thumbprint-sized pictures to help with identifying the birds. 'There's even a picture to show the difference of the male and female as they need to know nesting figures.'

Jack raised an eyebrow. 'There's a Glencarlach Ornithological Society?'

'Yes, and it seems they're in quite heated competition with the Glencarlach Wildlife Society. I have a feeling they'll also be approaching you, Amelia, as I heard one of them talking about placing heat and motion cameras on parts of your property to check the badger population.'

'I would never have had you down as a keen twitcher,' Jack said. 'You're a constant surprise.'

'It's not as if I've anything better to do at the moment, is it? The least I can do is smooth out some ruffled feathers.'

'Well, thank you, Gideon,' Amelia said sincerely. 'The atmosphere does seem to be turning a little tense. I'll drop you back at Stone Manor and then I'll go and pack up a few things. I've decided to move into Stone Manor too.'

Gideon looked delighted. 'We're going to have an absolute blast, poppet!'

Amelia wasn't quite as certain. But, seeing as Gideon was going out of his way to help Amelia by taking part in the bird count, the least she could do was be on hand to help during his convalescence.

Amelia clocked Jack raising his eyebrows in surprise as he took a swig of his pint but diplomatically said nothing.

SIX

'I'm going to kill him!'

These were the first words Toby greeted Amelia with a couple of hours later when she walked into the kitchen at Stone Manor, pulling her small case behind her.

Her brother was brandishing a rolling pin with a grim expression on his face, and Amelia gave him a wide berth.

'Who?' she asked, although she had a pretty good idea who her brother was referring to.

'Take a wild guess! Gideon's called down pretty much every few minutes since you dropped him back here. First, he wanted a cup of tea, then a snack. Then another cup of tea, then he wanted a chat. Then his pillows needed plumping. Then he couldn't find his remote control for the television, which was down behind the pillows he'd just had plumped!'

'Breathe!' Amelia reminded Toby. Normally so laid-back, Toby very rarely let anyone ruffle his chilled demeanour.

'I'm so behind on tonight's prep I had to get Ben to come in early.'

'Yo!' Ben, the sous chef, greeted Amelia as he appeared from the storage room with large bunches of herbs and a bag of icing sugar which he plonked down beside Toby.

'I've not had a chance to get back to the cottage and pack. I'll stay there tonight and bring my things in tomorrow. I've said to Gideon,' said Toby.

'I'll go upstairs and quickly unpack and don't worry, I'm on hand to help with everything,' said Amelia.

She left as Toby turned up the volume on the radio, no doubt to drown out any more attempts made by Gideon to get in touch.

Out at the reception desk, Amelia was slightly surprised to hear the phone ringing and James, the usually highly conscientious deputy manager, making no move to answer it.

James blushed pink to the roots of his sandy hair when he saw Amelia, just as the phone stopped.

'I'm sorry, Amelia, but it's Gideon calling. I've been up a few times already and I needed five minutes to get on and sort out the rota. Ruth's meant to be waitressing tomorrow but she forgot she's got a rehearsal for the parade. She's the Beltane Queen, you see.'

'Don't worry, I'll step in. I'll be staying here for the next few days while Jack finishes his book.'

'That's great!' James said, scribbling Amelia's name on the chart in front of him.

The phone started ringing again and they both looked at it. It was the McDermid Room.

Gideon.

Taking a deep breath, Amelia picked it up.

'Hi, Gideon!'

'Ames! Thank goodness it's you. It's hell sitting here. *Hell.* And painful. And I'm so *bored!*'

'Okay, I'll be up in a minute.' She hung up and went to get a key for the room she'd be staying in. She hovered over the one for the PD James Room but that would be directly next to Gideon and she thought it might be wise to have a little distance from him. She plumped for the Nesbo with its lovely pared-back Scandi design. When refurbishing Stone Manor, Amelia had wanted the rooms and suites to embody her favourite authors in her much-loved and much-read mystery and crime-fiction genres.

Updating the booking page she noticed Sally's future relative had booked in.

Amelia tapped the screen. 'Oh, did you see Moira Ballantyne?'

'Yes, she seemed nice. Quiet. Said she was tired and I suggested room service and gave her a menu, but haven't heard from her since.'

Taking the key with the tasselled fob, Amelia headed for the first floor. Leaving her case on the bed to unpack later Amelia went along the corridor and knocked on the door to the McDermid Room.

'Come in,' Gideon said in a rather pathetic voice.

Amelia opened the door. Gideon was sitting on the two-seater sofa by the window, his bandaged foot elevated onto the table in front of him which was littered with mugs, chocolate-bar wrappers, empty packs of Haribo and an assortment of magazines. He turned around, lowering his binoculars.

'Thank God you're here to relieve me of the boredom! Bird watching is so dull! Oh and you may want to check the hotel phones as I don't think they're working properly. I've been ringing James for the past twenty minutes with no response.' He picked up the hotel-room handset from the cushion beside him and waved it accusingly at Amelia.

'James has been busy.'

'What! Standing at the reception desk, waiting to greet people as they arrive? It's hardly skilled,' he said huffily.

It constantly astounded Amelia that Gideon could still have such little insight into what their jobs consisted of in the running of Stone Manor.

'How's the bird counting going?' she asked, taking a peek at his chart.

'Well, you've an inordinate amount of starlings. They're cheeky buggers too, causing all sorts of fights. And there was a bit of a surge in chaffinches just after seven. I got a bit muddled with my tits though. I think I may have marked a couple of extra great ones instead of blue. I hope that won't matter too much.'

'I'm sure it will be fine.'

'I have to say, these are a pretty swanky bit of kit.' He waggled the binoculars. 'This button here,' Gideon pointed to the one he meant, 'switches them on to night vision so I can check owl numbers once it gets dark. I'll feel very like James Bond staking out a secret nuclear bunker. I've often thought I'd make a very good 007.'

'Were you wanting anything?'

'Um, I can't remember now. Don't worry, I'll let you know.'

'Okay, I'm off to unpack, see you later!' she called out, making a quick exit.

Being just a few rooms away from each other, Gideon decided to bypass phoning Amelia and now shouted whenever he wanted anything; a blanket, a glass of water, his painkillers. Then Amelia had to nip downstairs to help with dinner service. She'd barely managed to unpack anything and that which she had, she was sorely tempted to bundle back into her case and drag back to the Gatehouse. She couldn't imagine getting through the next couple of weeks while Gideon was incapacitated. During a quiet lull in the dining room, when there were only two couples lingering over coffee and digestifs, Amelia hurried upstairs to finish unpacking. She had her hand on the doorknob when she heard,

'Ameeeeeel-liaaaaaaaaaa!'

Taking a deep breath, she exhaled slowly then walked along to Gideon's room.

He was looking out the window, his binoculars focused on the area of the grounds just beyond the Stone Manor car park. It was just before nine and the sky was quite dark.

Without taking his eyes away from looking out the window, Gideon said, 'I've switched to night vision now! Everything's got an eerie green colour to it. Can I get another cushion please, these all seem to flatten down quite quickly.'

Amelia trudged along to the linen store and picked up an assortment of plump-looking pillows and returned to Gideon's room, depositing them at his feet.

'I don't suppose you've got a pagany-type ghost that's meant to haunt these grounds, do you?' he said, still not breaking away from his binoculars.

Amelia came up to the window and looked out. 'Not that I'm aware of. There's the headless horseman and a hanged man. Hang on, isn't there meant to be some sort of rogue clergyman too?' Amelia had become quite blasé about all the alleged hauntings that were meant to roam the Stone Manor estate. Although she had never seen anything, there were definitely sections of the long driveway that caused her skin to prickle and made her quicken her pace when she was walking along it, alone, at night.

'Hm, no, the one I saw was definitely more the pagan type. And I think all too corporeal as it kept tripping on the tree roots and undergrowth, almost sprawling the length of themselves at one point,' he said, scanning the grounds. 'Oh, they've gone again. The figure kept going in and out of the treeline, hesitating, as if it wasn't sure where to go.'

'I'm pretty sure ghosts have more of a purpose, like a line of trajectory they repeat over and over again,' Amelia agreed, cupping her hands over the glass and peering out. 'Probably just some folk getting into the spirit of Beltane. Right, I need half an hour to sort through the rest of my case, okay? No more interruptions, please!'

'Okey-dokey, darling,' Gideon said cheerily.

Amelia left him and returned to her room and looked at what else was left to unpack. She took out her hairdryer and straighteners. Although her jaw-length choppy dark-brown hair didn't need too much maintenance, it did have a tendency to stick up at odd angles if she slept awkwardly and despite Jack thinking it cute, it wasn't the sort of look she wanted to go for. She also took out her make-up bag, which bulged due to the years of freebies Sally had passed over to her when she worked as a make-up artist. Inspecting her reflection in the mirror, Amelia quickly reapplied a slick of red lipstick and fluffed up her hair a bit before pulling out a couple of books nestled inside the folds of her pyjamas. Despite the library on the ground floor being full of novels as well as rather dry historical tomes relating to the local area, Amelia couldn't resist spur-of-the-moment purchases whenever she passed a book shop. Alongside a couple of her favourite Agatha Christies, which despite having read before, had never lost their appeal for Amelia, she piled up a couple of other crime- and mystery-fiction paperbacks on the bedside table. She sat on the edge of the bed and turned to the page she'd bookmarked. One quick little chapter wouldn't hurt...

SEVEN

Moira lay in the deep water of her bath, straining to hear the conversation from along the corridor. Swishing her foot around, she watched the water ripple as she heard footsteps receding and doors close. A moment later there was silence and her thoughts turned once again to her internal debate on whether she should check out or stay.

Moira inhaled deeply, the drops of geranium and ylang-ylang essential oils she'd added to the water kicking in with their calming properties. She knew she'd feel strange coming back to Glencarlach, but hadn't quite realised how discomfiting it would be.

Driving her hire car through the village that afternoon, it was apparent not much had changed in the intervening years, since her last fleeting visit, twelve years ago. This status quo was both comforting and disquieting. Returning to her home town was a reminder of her youth, bringing her back to that angry and scared seventeen-year-old who had abandoned Glencarlach with no intention of ever returning. But as the years passed, that blinkered certainty had mellowed.

Curiosity and a desire to return had quietly eroded her shell of determination that had once felt so impenetrable. Back then Moira thought she'd be leaving for good, but of course she now knew nothing was permanent. There were a handful of fleeting return visits for weddings or funerals where she'd spend a night kipping down in a relative's spare room, playing the role of enigmatic Moira, the mysterious relation that left to travel the world and who lived in exciting cities before settling down in France.

But this visit felt different. She couldn't shake that feeling there wouldn't be another visit after this. That this was her final journey; the end of the road.

After driving through the village she'd parked her hire car and walked along Main Street which was decorated for Beltane.

Beltane. Of all the times to come back; the memories resurfacing with that date. But of course it had to be Beltane, her return couldn't have been at any other time. The tarot had told her as much.

Caught up in the slipstream of those walking along Main Street, Moira had followed, turning into the village hall, her curiosity piqued. Then, inside, there were so many faces she recognised that she panicked. Too much too soon. She knew she'd see everyone eventually but she needed to brace herself. Do it on her terms.

She'd stood momentarily at the back, bemused to see Andy McAvoy stand up to speak in some official capacity as a local councillor. She'd thought Andy had looked right at her before dropping his cards, flustered. Had he recognised her? Had her presence caused a shock? She had no idea, but she did remember Andy as being a quiet, nervous teenager. Maybe he'd never changed and that awkwardness had followed him into adulthood and middle age.

Moira had slipped back out a moment later. No one even glanced at her, everyone too interested in the archaeologists trying to justify their intent on digging up another sacred piece of land. Moira sighed.

Maybe she should leave. Maybe Glencarlach had moved on more than she first thought and she was the one not keeping up with the transitions.

She checked her watch and saw it was just after nine o'clock. There was still time to throw everything back into her luggage, check out and find another hotel a few miles away. A place she could be anonymous. Although tempting, she knew she wouldn't do it. And of course, there was the handfasting ceremony and she didn't want to let Hamish and Sally down.

And she also couldn't be bothered to repack her case and get behind the wheel of her car again.

She got out of the bath and wrapped herself in the luxuriously fluffy Stone Manor robe that had been on her bed, along with the complimentary slippers.

Stone Manor was also rather lovely, she conceded as she looked around the room. Despite being disturbed by the annoyingly loud and rather highly strung-sounding man who'd kept yelling for a woman called Amelia, for the first time that day, Moira felt relaxed.

Her eyes happened across the room-service menu and her stomach gave a Pavlovian growl in response. As well as relaxed, she realised she was also ravenous. Luckily she was still within the hours where she could order food.

She picked up the phone and pressed 'o'.

It was picked up after a couple of rings. 'Good evening, Ms Ballantyne, how can I help you?' the cheerful voice enquired from the reception desk.

'Could I order the grilled sea bass in the mussel broth with spring greens and pea shoots, please? And the oatcakes with Mull cheddar to follow.'

'Of course. Is that all?'

She turned the page and looked at the drinks. 'And a bottle of the Pouilly-Fumé, please.' Although Moira would concede that despite its many magnificent cheeses, the French couldn't deliver the equivalent of a tangy, salty Scottish cheddar, she was prepared to die on a hill arguing that France produced the best wine in the world.

'Certainly. We'll get that sent right up to you.'

Moira hung up and sat on the bed, kicking her legs in front of her. That was decided; now she was having wine, she definitely wasn't able to leave.

EIGHT

'*Amelia*!! *Ames!*'

Amelia woke with a start and sat up, her book sliding to the floor with the movement.

There was a frantic knocking on her door as Gideon hissed her name again. She glanced at the clock and saw it read a rather blurred 03:17. She blinked, trying to come to and realised she was still wearing her clothes; she must have fallen asleep whilst reading.

Gideon knocked again.

'Come in,' Amelia called out quietly, realising she hadn't locked the door. What on earth did Gideon want at this hour of the morning?

Gideon threw open the door. '... Body in the library!' he gasped.

She glanced at her pile of books. 'Um... I've got *Evil Under the Sun* and *The Hollow* if you're after an Agatha Christie but I don't have—'

'No! There's a real-life body in the library; *your* library, downstairs. Except it's more a case of being a real *dead* body.'

'What?!'

'Go see for yourself,' Gideon said, but Amelia was already hurrying out of her room, heading for the stairs. In her sleep-muddled head she wondered if she'd got confused and this was one of the murder-mystery weekends they put on throughout the year... but no, she knew there was nothing planned, not for the same weekend as Beltane.

Wee Davey was behind the desk in reception. He looked up in puzzlement as Amelia ran past and round the side of the stairs, passing the dining room, the bar, and billiards room. She continued down the back passageway before coming to a stop outside the oak-panelled doors of the library. The door was open a crack and the light was on inside. She was aware of the mechanical whirr of the lift bringing Gideon down.

Amelia tentatively pushed the door open.

There, lying on the floor was a lifeless body, staring at the ceiling. She looked down at the blood which had pooled around the torso, now turning the rug beneath a shiny dark brown. At first glance Amelia couldn't see where the blood was coming from or how he'd died. There was also something else, just a few inches from the body. Although it was sitting in the blood, Amelia could see it was a tarot card. She dared to go closer. The image of the card looked something like a weird hybrid, bearded man-goat, with two horns. There was a XV at the top and underneath the image, The Devil, was written at the bottom.

Amelia started at the scene in front of her for a few moments. She inched her feet back as the pool of blood was dangerously close to her shoes.

She was aware of Gideon joining her.

'It's the archaeologist, Gus, isn't it?' Gideon said after a moment.

'Yes.' There was no mistaking the piercings.

'There's a lot of blood.'

Amelia nodded. It also looked like he'd been in a fight as there was a graze on his cheek and his lip looked swollen.

'Is that some sort of fetish outfit he's wearing?'

'That's a diving suit, Gideon.'

'Oh. But why on earth is he wearing that here?'

That was a very good question and one that Amelia currently had no answer for. As she stared, Amelia realised it looked as if there was a rip in the front of the suit. Possibly an entry site to whatever had caused the blood and Gus's demise.

She gave an involuntary shiver and realised the French doors were open.

'Did you see anyone? Or hear anything?'

Gideon shook his head as he continued to stare at Gus.

'What made you come down to the library?'

'I couldn't sleep and thought I'd get myself a book. Came down in the lift, opened the library door, put on the light and there he was.'

Amelia glanced back at the open French doors. She hoped whoever had attacked Gus had immediately left Stone Manor by that route.

'We need to phone Constable Williams,' Amelia said as they both slowly backed out the library, closing the door and locking it as they left.

After calling Constable Williams, Amelia sought out Wee Davey to tell him what had happened and check if he'd seen or heard anything suspicious.

The night porter looked shocked.

'No, it's been a quiet night. I heard the lift being used about twenty minutes ago.'

'That was me on my way to the library,' Gideon said.

'And then you ran down the stairs,' Wee Davey said to Amelia. 'But apart from that I wasn't aware of any other guests moving around after I started my shift.

'I'm going to call Toby and double check all the back doors are locked,' Amelia said as she hurried towards the kitchens.

Once satisfied that everything was secured, Amelia returned to the reception area.

'Constable Williams just arrived and is up with Gideon and more officers are on their way,' Wee Davey said.

Amelia took a couple of minutes to brush her teeth and change her clothes before going to the McDermid room.

Gideon was sitting on the sofa when Amelia entered his room. Standing by the window was Constable Ray Williams, looking very serious as he listened to Gideon whilst scribbling into a notebook. But it was on seeing the man a couple of feet away that Amelia's heart sank.

Detective Inspector McGregor.

She'd met him at Christmas when she'd discovered a dead body. Amelia had hoped she'd not have to meet him again. She hadn't taken to his dour, suspicious manner.

Ray cleared his throat and smoothed down his bushy moustache. 'It was fortuitous Detective Inspector McGregor was already in the vicinity.'

'Wasn't it!' McGregor said as he walked over to the table the television sat on and began rifling through everything that was strewn across it. 'I couldn't believe it when I got a call to say a dead body had been discovered and it involved the very same group of people caught up in a previous murder!' He gave Amelia a wintry smile as he picked up a DVD case to read the back of it. '*Carry On Constable*,' he said.

'No, I don't watch *Carry On* films, I far prefer the Ealing comedies like *The Ladykillers* and *Whisky Galore*, you know?'

'Carry on *taking Mr Fey's statement*, Constable Williams,' McGregor said, unamused by Gideon's glib remark.

'Well, I've already told you everything I know. I was in a lot of pain and couldn't sleep and went down to the library to get a book. I opened the door, and there he was!'

McGregor picked up the binoculars and studied the list of birds on the clipboard. 'And you've seen nothing suspicious tonight?'

'Well...' Gideon darted a look at Amelia.

'Go on,' the DI encouraged.

'Well, I suppose it depends on what you consider suspicious. I mean, Glencarlach is an odd little place and what's weird for one person is someone else's normal.' Gideon quailed slightly under McGregor's unwavering gaze. 'Anyway, I was counting owls, watching through night-vision binoculars, and I saw someone acting, well, a little oddly. Hovering around the trees, just beyond the car park.'

'Build? Height?'

'I don't really know. Maybe medium height and build? Well, to be honest, I'm really just guessing as they weren't standing next to a handy height chart as a point of reference. They were possibly a little uncoordinated and unsure.'

'You didn't get any description but think they were uncoordinated.'

'Yes, stumbling a little.'

'Male? Female?'

'No idea, I didn't see their face or form, you see, all of that was completely hidden by the pagany robes they were wearing.'

McGregor's head shot up. 'What?'

'It looked like they were wearing a pagan-type robe. You know, big kind of flowing thing with wide drapey sleeves, with a cowl hood. It reminded me of *Cadfael*, that nineties mystery drama starring Derek Jacobi, based on the novels by...' Gideon trailed off as McGregor's lips thinned.

The Detective Inspector stared at Gideon a moment before saying, in a dangerously low voice, 'Did you not think to mention this unusual fact first?'

'To be honest, I was more concerned about trying to spot a barn owl to question anyone's sartorial choices,' Gideon said huffily.

'And you, Ms Adams,' McGregor said, turning to Amelia. 'Did you see this?'

'No, I didn't,' Amelia said.

At that point Toby came into the room, slightly out of breath from running.

'What the hell's happened? Wee Davey said someone's dead in the library!'

Amelia nodded. 'Gus.'

'What! Oh no... that's awful.' Toby looked around the room, resting his gaze on McGregor. 'Was it... was it a natural death?'

'At first glance, I would say no,' McGregor said. 'SOCO are on their way. I'll need the names of the guests staying and members of staff who have been working today. If you could supply me with a list, Ms Adams?'

'Of course.'

'We'll also need to wake everyone to carry out a search of the premises,' McGregor said before he turned to Gideon once again. 'You are taking some pretty heavy-duty painkillers on account of your accident.' He rattled a box of pills that he picked up beside the television. 'Sometimes these can cause confusion, especially if taken with alcohol. Could this be a possibility?'

'No, it could not!' Gideon snapped. 'My drinking days are behind me. I've not had alcohol for a very long time and I have no inclination or intention to restart that self-destructive behaviour ever again.'

Amelia was horrified at McGregor's insinuations and Ray also looked uncomfortable at his boss's line of questioning.

Although Gideon often referred to his 'drinking days' in a light-hearted manner, Amelia remembered how tortured he'd been with his demons and how his spiralling repression, depression and alcohol dependency had nearly driven him to his death.

Unruffled at Gideon's outburst, McGregor put down the painkillers.

'I know what I saw!' Gideon said.

'Or is it a case of what you *think* you saw?'

'The one thing no one has imagined is the dead body in the Stone Manor library,' Amelia pointed out.

'My DS is on her way to take statements. I'll be in touch,' McGregor said, then left the room.

NINE

'I've got a horrible sensation of déjà vu,' Gideon said as he, Amelia and Toby all watched as scenes of crime officers and police moved about the ground floor of Stone Manor later that same morning.

Amelia watched the proceedings, which also reminded her of when a guest had been murdered just a few months earlier.

'And,' Gideon continued, 'it's going to take more than a spot of Vanish to get rid of that bloodstain. I suppose you can add the library to the long list of interesting crime locations of Stone Manor. There's the piano bar of peril, the stairway of slaughter, the hail of bullets hallway,' he said, subconsciously rubbing his abdomen where he'd been shot a couple of years previously. 'It can definitely become a feature.'

Amelia made a mental note never to let Gideon loose on the marketing for Stone Manor.

She saw Jack bound up the stone stairs, flattening himself against the wall to let a couple detective constables past. Once clear, her fiancé ran in, enveloping Amelia in a hug she badly needed.

'I just woke up and got your message. Gus is dead? That's awful. What happened?'

'That's what we're trying to ascertain, Mr Temple,' DI McGregor said as he opened the door to the drawing room, revealing a visibly upset Isobel sitting in the chair opposite DS Dabrowski who was making notes.

The DI marched down the stairs and headed towards his car.

'Come on, I've made us some breakfast,' Toby said as the others followed him into the kitchen.

'It's obvious. Detective Inspector McGregor is my nemesis.' Amelia made this grim pronouncement as she sat at the table and poured herself a cup of tea. 'Holmes had Moriarty, Clouseau had the Phantom–'

'Doctor Who has the Master,' Jack added as he skewered a sausage.

'Harry Potter and Voldermort,' Gideon said.

'Professor X and Magneto?' Toby suggested.

'Nice!' Gideon said. 'Ooh, Luke Skywalker and Darth Vader!' Gideon added as Toby high-fived him.

'Yes, and McGregor has all their awful qualities rolled into one,' Amelia said.

'Can he be a nemesis if you're both on the same side of the law?' Jack queried as he stirred sugar into his tea.

'He's my own, *personal*, nemesis,' Amelia said.

'If he's threatening to close down the hotel and restaurant until further notice, he's a nemesis to us all,' Toby added miserably.

Wee Davey broke through the silence by lightly tapping on the door, behind him stood Detective Inspector McGregor and Constable Williams.

'I need to get back to base but DS Dabrowski is on hand, as well as Constable Williams,' McGregor said.

'Do you know how long you'll be?' Amelia asked.

'No. We're still working our way through the statements. Obviously the library stays sealed until further notice.'

'We've got a party of twelve booked in for an anniversary dinner tonight,' Toby said.

'We'll let you know when you can trade again.' McGregor stood looking at them all stonily. 'And let me make myself very clear. Do not take matters into your own hands. Leave the detective work to us.' He turned and walked away, pausing to ensure Constable Williams was following.

'He doesn't want to admit you were far better at his job than he was, at Christmas, Amelia!' Gideon said, loudly enough to ensure the two men would have heard as they walked away.

'Can we try and *not* antagonise the cops?' Jack said.

'Come on, Davey, grab some breakfast,' Toby said to their night porter, who'd been hovering by the doorway, listening to their exchange. Amelia handed Davey a plate and he immediately piled it high with the cooked breakfast items.

'Do you think it was one of the protestors who did it?' Davey asked before cramming a large forkful of bacon into his mouth.

'Do you really think that would be a motive?'

'I know feelings were running high after the meeting in the village hall,' Wee Davey said.

'But enough to commit murder?' Toby questioned.

'Maybe it was some pagan Pictish revenge. The dead rising to defend their sacred ground,' Gideon said darkly.

'Or there's another motive entirely and the pagan get-up was just a coincidence. There must be a lot of weird pagan outfits floating about at the moment,' Toby said.

Wee Davey paused shovelling in the food. 'What's this?'

Gideon explained what he'd seen the night before.

'Weird. Maybe it was a coincidence that someone was wearing that, or one of the protestors got a bit waylaid. Or,'

Davey paused, stabbing his fork in the air for dramatic effect, 'it could always be an escaped ghost from the Hunting Lodge!' he said through a mouthful of food.

'What?' the others all said at the same time.

'Aye,' Davey nodded as he squirted ketchup on his plate, 'the Hunting Lodge. It was built in the 1800s and used for weekend shooting parties by the laird at that time, Hector Bain's ancestor. Then, one of their relations lived there, early 1900s, I think, and he was in some kind of weird cult. Walked about in those sorts of pagany robes. Practised the occult. And that's when a lot of bad stuff happened. So, he might have been like, an evil pagan-monk or something. I dunno, Dad'll know more about it than me.'

'Are there people still living in the Hunting Lodge?' Amelia asked.

'Nah. But maybe they left some of their stuff and someone stole it? Or it is an actual murderous ghost pagan-monk.' He said this quite matter of factly.

'Where is this Hunting Lodge?'

'A couple of miles or so out of the village, heading that way,' Wee Davey pointed over his shoulder, 'it's on the coastal side, heading out the village on the back road. There's a fork in the road that either takes you to Gull Point and the outlying farms or you can turn right and go the windy back road to Ullapool that takes forever. The entrance is just before that.'

'What's it like?'

Wee Davey looked up. 'Dunno.'

'You've never been?' Amelia said in surprise.

He shook his head vehemently. 'Not to that place. It's well-haunted. I don't know much about it except bad things happened there. They might still do, if Gus's murder has anything to do with it.'

'You've never been tempted to go and see it?' Amelia said,

slightly incredulously. 'I mean, everyone says the Stone Manor woods and grounds are haunted, and local kids are always daring each other to camp out here. It's like a rite of passage!'

'Aye, but I'd take my chance with the headless horseman or any of the other ghosties out here *any* day of the week over what's meant to haunt the old Hunting Lodge. The weird cult guy hanged himself there from the ceiling of the posh room. Then, a few months back, a guy I used to go to school with went there for a dare. He thought it was nonsense. But he swore he saw a dead body.'

'Oh my God!' Gideon said.

'Nobody believed him though. He's always making stuff up. But he was definitely spooked and hasn't been the same since, I can tell you.'

'Did he report what had happened?'

Davey stopped eating and shook his head solemnly. 'No way was he going to tell anyone else about it. It was the one thing my dad was really strict about. All the parents were, still are. I'd have had my arse skelped if I'd even *thought* of going. As kids we used to scare each other and say, "If you don't give me your playpiece, the ghost of the Hunting Lodge will get you in your sleep!"' He flashed them all a cheeky grin before turning his attention back to his plate, mopping up the end of the ketchup with his last bit of sausage. He patted his stomach then stood up. 'Thanks for breakfast. I need to get going. Dad's opening the beer garden tonight and I've got a ton of fairy lights to string up. See you later!'

Amelia followed Wee Davey through to the reception area to find Isobel pacing the floor, calling someone on her mobile.

'Hi, Isobel,' Amelia said. The archaeologist looked up and gave a distracted smile.

'Are you okay?'

'Not really.' Isobel's eyes were red-rimmed from crying and

she wiped her nose with a soggy-looking balled-up tissue. 'I know Gus could be an antagonistic sod at times, but he was just a wind-up merchant and his heart was in the right place. And good at his job... I just don't understand it. And now I'm doubly worried because I can't get hold of Maja.' Isobel ended the call and pocketed her mobile. 'She's not picking up. But she's probably still with Johno sleeping off a hangover from hell as when I left the Whistling Haggis she'd started on tequila shots.' Isobel nodded towards the bar. 'Tim's on the phone to the students due to arrive next week, telling them not to come. Oh! I'll have to phone the Portaloo people...' She got out her phone again.

'Did the police mention he was wearing a diving suit?'

Isobel nodded. 'He always brought his diving gear with him anytime we were near a coastal location. He especially loved night-time dives. He always said it was a completely different experience seeing everything with a dive light.'

'Did they find the rest of his kit? I didn't see his air tanks or mask.'

Isobel thought for a moment before saying, 'DS Dabrowski didn't mention that.'

'They've not mentioned the cause of death,' Amelia said, remembering the blood. And Amelia couldn't help wondering about the French doors being left open. They opened from the inside. So, had Gus been in the library, opened the doors and let the murderer in? Or had the murderer already been in Stone Manor, murdered Gus, then left? But neither James nor Davey had seen anything or anyone suspicious.

'What will happen with the site now?' Amelia asked.

Isobel shrugged. 'Everything's on hold for now. The police can't rule out the divisiveness of the dig as being a motive. Detective Sergeant Dabrowski asked for all the notes we've had, the ones that were pinned to the tents telling us to go home, but

I threw most of them away. As protest notes go, they were all rather polite and at no point did I ever feel threatened... but even so, I can't put a load of volunteers at risk.'

'What about you?'

'Oh, I have no intention of leaving,' Isobel said with a determined thrust of her chin.

TEN

With Jack back at the Gatehouse, Toby ensconced in the kitchen and what felt like half of Police Scotland milling about, Amelia wanted to get out of Stone Manor for a couple of hours. With nothing else better to do, Amelia was intrigued to check out the Hunting Lodge. Although she didn't fully believe that the building was haunted and that she was likely to bump into a murderous pagan ghost, she didn't entirely relish the thought of turning up to a cursed place without a little moral support.

Gideon jumped at the chance of joining her.

'Are you sure you'll be okay?'

'Of course,' he said, throwing his crutches onto the back seat of the Stone Manor Jeep. 'I'll be absolutely... dandy... poppet.' He pulled himself up and into the passenger seat with some effort. 'I'd rather not spend any more time dwelling on Gus's corpse lying a couple of rooms away. I'm also fed up sitting on that sofa, eating chocolate, and I've had it with counting any more of those infernal birds for the ornithological society!'

Amelia drove them out of the top of the village, careful to avoid the numerous potholes and bumps in the road for Gideon's comfort.

It was a beautiful day. As they left Main Street behind them and continued up the steep incline out of the village, the water below them in the harbour and beyond sparkled in the sunlight. Amelia caught a glimpse of Rory's boat puttering out of the harbour, no doubt packed with people hoping to catch sight of porpoises, dolphins or minke whales, even if it was still a little early in the season.

She tried to ignore Gideon rummaging through the glove compartment.

'What's this?' he asked, pulling out a shiny property schedule. 'This isn't the village estate agent. Have you been cheating on Drew McAvoy?' he asked in mock shock, opening it up.

'I don't see any harm in looking a little further afield,' Amelia said, coming to a stop to allow a farmer to cross the road with his cows, moving his herd from one field to another to take them for milking.

'But these are miles away! You're nearer Inverness!' Gideon said, his head snapping up.

'I simply wanted to see what else was out there.'

'Oh my God! What's this? I didn't realise Montana log-cabin chic had made it so far across the pond!' Gideon said.

Amelia glanced over to look at the photograph of the lovely two-storey wooden chalet with its pointed roof and timber frame. It looked very like the types of houses which were featured on the Christmas 24 film channel that Amelia binged on every winter. All the chalet needed was some snow and Christmas lights strung up around the outside, and Amelia could imagine her and Jack in matching red-and-white Scandinavian onesies in front of a roaring fire enjoying steaming mugs of hot chocolate. Amelia could see past the slight eighties vibe; to her it looked like a cosy romantic chalet.

'No, Amelia, no!' Gideon shook his head. 'And it's in

Aviemore! You can't move to Aviemore! It's almost two hours away. I'd nev... *we'd* never see you! Toby would be devastated! How could you run Stone Manor from almost two hours away? You can't do that to him,' Gideon said in agitation.

'Toby would be fine without me poking my nose in. James is also very good at his job.'

'Toby won't like it, not one bit,' Gideon said as he looked at the photos again. 'All that log cabin ranch-style... what if it encourages you to listen to country music?'

'There's nothing wrong with a bit of country music!'

Gideon practically recoiled from her. 'Oh my God, darling, there is! *So* much wrong with it!'

Amelia reached over and took the schedule from Gideon and stuffed it back into the glove compartment, slamming it shut.

The farmer successfully got the last cow across the road and he swung the gate shut, giving her a wave to thank her for her patience.

She started up the Jeep again, Gideon gazing sulkily out the window as they carried on along the twisting country road.

A mile or so out of the village, Amelia slowed, keeping her eyes peeled as they approached the fork in the road Wee Davey had described. It was a long and circuitous route to get onto the main A-road that linked up with the other villages, despite it leading to the Pictish stones and abbey. It clearly wasn't a top priority for resurfacing either, Amelia thought, wincing as they bounced through a crater-sized pothole.

Gideon pointed out his passenger side window. 'There!'

Right enough, a five-bar gate sat back from the road. It looked as if it led to nowhere but woodland, such was the overgrown and unused look to the dusty old dirt path on the other side. As Amelia slowed down she realised that directly opposite, was a path that led towards the edge of the Stone

Manor estate, which bordered the Bain estate, close to the archaeological site.

Amelia pulled up to the gate and got out of the car.

'Is it locked?' Gideon called out through his open window.

Amelia saw there was only a sliding bolt securing the gate. Anyone could open it. Which is exactly what she did. A faded sign saying 'No Trespassing' hung from the top bar secured by a couple of zip ties.

The bolt was stiff and the gate squeaked, but Amelia was able to push it fully open to allow the Jeep through.

Getting back behind the wheel, Amelia took off the parking brake and slowly trundled down the path. She could see that only a few yards in, the track veered off to the right. Then the left. Then the right again.

Due to the high verges of overgrown bushes and trees lining both sides of the twisty drive, Amelia couldn't see what they were heading towards.

She was slightly taken aback a few moments later when they turned a sharp right and suddenly the path opened up and they found themselves in an exposed area of scrubby grass and gravel. Amelia turned off the engine.

In front of them was a drystone wall, only about two feet high, with a wide entrance with two weathered metal gateposts either side, although the gate was no longer there, having either been removed or possibly rotted away. On the other side, hedges had spread out and upwards, destroying great chunks of the wall with their expanding roots. A few feet back from the entrance gap, two trees had grown and come together to entwine their gnarled branches to make a natural canopy. A few feet ahead of them were a couple of magnificent rhododendron bushes, blooming with lilac flowers.

Then, about two hundred yards beyond those stood the solid stone Hunting Lodge. Amelia got out of the car slowly, taking in the beautiful, lush setting. She felt serenely calm, with only the birdsong and the gentle rustling of the wind through the foliage making a noise.

She was aware of Gideon scrabbling out of the passenger door and grabbing his crutches. After a rather unsteady start, he made his way over to her.

'How can somewhere so beautiful have such a scary history?' he asked.

They walked through the gap in the wall. Nature and time had taken over and none of the full beauty of the area before them was revealed in one go. The further they walked, the more the clearing divulged, and Amelia kept snatching glimpses of colour and shapes through the dense greenery and overgrown shrubs.

'Oh look!' Gideon said as he turned to their right. Amelia followed his gaze.

Under an awning of a cluster of tall trees, sat the ruins of what could have been an outhouse, barn or even a stable block.

'Wow!' Amelia said.

'One thing is clear,' Gideon said, looking up at the ruined building, 'there's no convenient wardrobe inside that thing that's home to a selection of pagan robes, just overgrown weeds and possibly some squirrels and foxes.'

'Let's go check out the Hunting Lodge, unless you want to stay here and rest your leg?'

Gideon snorted. 'I think not!'

They walked over towards the main building, Amelia going first to make sure she picked out a route that was even underfoot for Gideon.

'This is less murderous pagans and more *Children of the Corn*!' Gideon said, swiping one of his crutches against the hip-height weeds that flanked the path.

They were a few feet away when Amelia stopped to look up

at the stone structure. The building was L-shaped, with the main door being nestled on one side of the axis point. To the right of the doorway was a wrought-iron bracket which an old lantern swung from, now devoid of glass. The left-hand side of the building was three storeys high and the ground floor had a bay window. Faded newspaper had been stuck up on the inside of the glass and Amelia couldn't see in. On the other side of the building, the longer part of the L-shape was just two storeys high. On the ground floor there were three large windows, almost full floor-to-ceiling height. Although these were also covered with newspaper, some of it had peeled away, giving Amelia a chance to peer in. Inside was a mess, with a couple of overturned chairs and a glass-fronted bookcase pulled over onto its side, with the books spilling out. On the other was a deep-set fireplace with a tall wooden mantelpiece.

'I wonder when this was built?' Gideon said as they looked up at it.

'I'd hazard about 1886,' Amelia said. Gideon looked at her, eyebrow raised. She held his gaze for another moment before laughing. 'The date's carved into the stone above the door, along with the words *The Hunting Lodge!*'

'Phew! I thought for a moment I'd have to organise an intervention as your obsession with property searches had gone too far! And clearly not everyone is as scared of this place as Wee Davey made out,' Gideon said, nudging one of his crutches against a couple of empty beer cans, half bottle of vodka and a pile of silver tea-light cases.

'Wait here, I'm going to explore round the back,' Amelia said.

'Be careful,' Gideon said from behind her. 'By my bearings, we must be quite near the sea and in my current state I'd be unable to conduct a daring cliff-face rescue!'

'I'll be fine,' Amelia said, following a path around to the

back of the house, aware that she could hear water lapping against rock. What had once been the garden was completely overgrown. She continued to the far end of the grassy area where there were more trees lined up creating another canopy of shade. Exploring further, Amelia discovered more piles of rubble and the foundations of what could have been an even older building, ravaged by time.

Standing at the edge of the property she marvelled at the view of the loch; her eyes were pulled out towards the horizon and the sea beyond. The house was set far enough back from the edge that it wouldn't be seen from the water. Another foot in front of her was an old wire fence which had weathered badly, the posts standing at rakish angles with the wire sagging between them. The view, however, was breathtaking. Down towards her left, she could see Glencarlach harbour and the boats bobbing about. She stood breathing in the air for a moment before Gideon shouted out to check she was okay. She walked back round to join him again.

'Oh my God! I can't believe it!' Amelia exclaimed as she noticed something on the grass by the side of the house.

'Neither can I!' Gideon said, frowning up at the building. 'It's rather dilapidated and I don't trust the woodwork around those windows.'

'No look!' Amelia said with great excitement as she bent down, pulling bits of grass and weeds from a wooden board that had obviously been lying there for a very long time.

With a bit of huffing and puffing she managed to free the section of wood which was also attached to a long post. Lifting it up, she triumphantly showed it to Gideon.

It was a sign that said, *For Sale*.

ELEVEN

'And?' Gideon said, looking quite underwhelmed at Amelia's expectant expression.

'It's for sale!'

'No wonder! No one in their right mind would want to live in a dilapidated haunted Hunting Lodge.'

'But, it's *for sale*. And Jack and I are looking for a house.'

Gideon looked at Amelia as if she were mad. 'But... but... *apart* from hearing rumours of hauntings and that unspeakable things happened here that's caused generations of the locals to stay away, why on earth would you want to live there?'

'I think it has a certain charm.'

'So had Ted Bundy by all accounts! In fact, that place screams *serial killer's lair*!'

'I don't think you're viewing it with an open mind. I'm going to head back to the village to check in with the estate agent to see what he can tell me about it. I'd love to take a proper look inside and not resort to peering through the windows.'

'Don't be surprised if you find rotting corpses in the basement,' Gideon grumbled as he followed Amelia back to the car.

Lily Wu at McAvoy Estate Agents looked at Amelia with a blank expression then repeated slowly, 'The Hunting Lodge?'

Amelia nodded. 'Yes! I found an old for sale sign beside it.'

Lily wrinkled her nose. 'I've worked here for almost two years and haven't heard of any property remotely like that.'

'It would seem nobody talks about it,' Gideon said as he sat on one of the chairs, stretching his bandaged foot out amid much wincing. 'Which I find utterly unfathomable as I've never known such a gossipy place as this village.'

'Quite!' Lily said. Amelia knew Lily had borne the brunt of much speculation when she'd started working in the small estate agent's office. As well as her Chinese heritage setting tongues wagging, the locals also tried to guess if she'd started dating the owner, Drew. She had, but despite trying to keep it quiet, the news flew round the village like wildfire thanks to the gossip network system in place.

Lily went over to a filing cabinet and pulled out the second drawer down and began riffling through the foolscap folders. Amelia held her breath, trying not to get too excited but after a couple of minutes Lily closed the drawer and turned, shaking her head. 'I can't see anything that sounds like the one you've found. Drew only started this place a few years ago so we don't exactly have thousands of properties to sift through. There are more files in the attic space. Wait for Drew to return as he might know something. He's out looking at a farm on the outskirts of the village, something you might be interested in,' Lily added with a hopeful smile. 'We got the call this morning that they're keen to sell.'

Although pleased there was a property to view, Amelia was now desperate to take a look inside the Hunting Lodge.

Realising Amelia wasn't taking the bait of the possible

farmhouse, Lily took a breath. 'Drew won't be long. You're welcome to wait or–'

Drew McAvoy pushed the door open with his shoulder as he held a takeaway cup of coffee in one hand, a briefcase in the other and had a paper bag clamped between his lips. He paused slightly when he saw Amelia and Gideon.

'Amelia's after some information,' Lily said as she got up from behind her desk, taking the coffee and the bag which from what Amelia could ascertain looked very much like it contained two empire biscuits topped with glacé cherries.

Drew's eyebrows shot up. 'About... the dead body?'

Amelia and Gideon exchanged a look. Word had got out.

Lily's eyes widened. 'What dead body?'

'We have our very own body in the library,' Gideon said.

'Who is it?' Lily said.

'The police haven't issued a formal statement,' Amelia said tactfully. She didn't think DI McGregor would be pleased if the spreading of gossip came back to her.

Gideon leaned forward. 'It's Gus, the archaeologist.'

'Fu...ck,' Drew said, sitting.

'It was the tattoos and piercings that gave it away, you could still see them despite the diving suit he was wearing. I was the one who found him.'

'A diving suit?' Lily repeated incredulously. 'But you're quite far from the water!'

'Do you know what happened, how he... you know?' Drew asked.

'There was a lot of blood. And I mean a *lot*!' Gideon said. 'He also had a bruise and a graze on his cheek.'

'Do... do you think he died in your place?' Drew pressed.

Gideon shrugged and looked at Amelia who said, 'We're waiting to hear back from the police, but as Gideon said, there did seem to be a lot of blood so I imagine he was killed there.'

'Definitely murder?'

'Looks like it. Anyway,' Amelia changed the subject, 'I really would like to view the Hunting Lodge.'

'Hunting Lodge?' Drew repeated.

'Yeah, an old abandoned property a couple of miles out of the village,' Lily said. 'But I can't think of one that matches the description.'

'How did you hear about that?' Drew asked. He didn't look very pleased and Amelia wondered if he thought she was taking over his job and going rogue by discovering properties for herself.

'It was mentioned in passing.'

'Wee Davey told us,' Gideon said. 'He said there were all sorts of weird goings on.'

'Weird? What kind of weird?' Drew looked quite disconcerted.

'He didn't go into too much detail,' Gideon said.

'Um, well... I do have something else. I've just been looking at a farm a few miles out of the village. The owners are downsizing, you see. I was going to ring you about it later.' Drew looked a little flustered. He was probably worried Amelia would harangue him on a daily basis.

'Sounds great, but I'd also like to get some information about the Hunting Lodge?' Amelia tried getting back to the point.

'I can't help, as I've never heard of it,' Lily said with a shrug before taking a sip of her coffee. 'Amelia saw a for sale sign there.'

'Oh! You went to see it?' Drew puffed his cheeks out, looking uncomfortable. 'Truth is, I haven't heard that place mentioned in a long time. It's not a place we talk about. There's a lot of folklore and superstition surrounding that area. Growing up here we were all terrified of the place. I still am, if I'm being completely honest!' It wasn't lost on Amelia that he did look a little shaken. Drew's usual sleek and confidently polished persona had definitely slipped and Amelia also couldn't quite believe a grown man could be anxious about what was no doubt an urban legend.

'I've never listed that property.'

'It wasn't one of your boards. The sign didn't have any phone number or name, it was handwritten red lettering saying it was for sale.'

'And it looked as if it had been stuck in the undergrowth for a good few years,' Gideon piped up.

'I'm sorry, but I have no idea who could be selling it.'

'What was the property like?' Lily asked.

'Like a spooky-looking haunted serial killer's lair!' Gideon said. 'The very sort of place where weird things go on.'

Amelia cleared her throat and pulled her mobile phone out of her pocket. 'It's a stone Hunting Lodge, dated 1886. I took a picture of it.' She showed it to Lily.

'Wow!' Lily said. 'Although abandoned it still looks fairly intact. A doer-upper as we say.'

'Would this be on Hector Bain's land?' Amelia suggested.

'Yeah,' Drew said. 'Dad's his estate manager. There's a massive new Hunting Lodge close to Gull Point which Hector's father had built in the mid-eighties. It's where Hector does a lot of fancy corporate entertaining. This one here is probably the original that the new one replaced. Maybe someone thought of selling it in the past but changed their mind. It's not as if Hector needs the money.'

'But it's a shame to have a perfectly good building go to ruin,' Amelia said.

'Who knows? That family has always been eccentric,' Drew said.

Gideon struggled to his feet. 'Righty-ho, let's go, Amelia. Keep us in the loop about the farm, yes?'

'Why don't you let us do a bit of digging?' Lily said helpfully. 'I can ask around. I'm intrigued now and quite fancy checking it out for myself.'

Drew nodded. 'I, um, I suppose I could go and take a look around.'

'Not worried the ghosts might get you?' Lily raised an eyebrow as she opened the paper bag... and removed an empire biscuit, Amelia noted with satisfaction.

'I'd definitely restrict any visit to daylight hours,' Drew said ruefully.

'What about your dad; he might know about it?' Lily said to Drew. 'He grew up here. And if it's on Hector Bain's land, as estate manager, your dad must know something.'

Drew shrugged. 'Possibly.'

'Well, someone will surely know about the house around here,' Lily said. 'I mean, you can't sneeze without someone passing you a tissue in this village.'

TWELVE

Betty arrived at Stone Manor that evening on a wave of chatter, effusive greetings and Chanel No. 5. A firm favourite with the staff when she'd stayed over Christmas, everyone greeted her like a long-lost family member. Amelia went behind the desk to get the key to Betty's room as Toby took the elderly lady's wheelie case and patchwork velvet cloak from her.

Luckily the police and SOCOs had left, taking Gus's body with them.

'Would you like a cup of tea and some shortbread?' Toby asked.

Betty's artfully pencilled-in eyebrows shot up.

'Or I could get you a dry martini, with an olive?'

Leaning in to him, she winked. 'Make it three olives and you've got yourself a deal, young man!' She straightened her hat, also tugging down the front of the bright-auburn wig that had become a little lopsided. 'It's been a long journey.'

'Did you get the ferry or bus over from Skye?' Amelia asked.

'Oh, I wasn't coming from home,' Betty said, with a dismissive wave of her hand. 'I've spent the last few days with some very dear friends in the Italian lakes. We were staying in a beautiful house with a friend of a friend; a lovely man! Quite a well-known actor, in fact. Rather dishy too. He's come a long way from his early television career. Anyway, a few of us old-timers thought we'd take a more scenic route coming home and we high-tailed it into Switzerland and got on the Bernina Express. It was something! And we got to enjoy the views, as the time before we were stowaways and had to think on our feet to evade the guards! Those were the days! Then, when we got to Chur we hitch-hiked to Zurich and it was rather pedestrian from there on in with easyJet flights all the way. No first class to get bumped up to either, unfortunately!'

Amelia handed Betty the room key and the older lady's eyes glittered excitedly.

'Is it the same room as before?'

'The Marsh Room, yes. And let's hope you don't wake up to find any strange men in your room *this* visit.'

'Oh but, Amelia, I'm counting on it!' she said with wide-eyed sincerity as Toby returned with a dry martini, the glass frosted with condensation. He'd balanced a cocktail stick holding the olives on the rim.

'There is something else, Betty. A dead body was found in the library in the early hours of the morning. Gideon came across it.'

Betty let out a wail.

'I completely understand if you'd like us to find you alternative accommodation,' Amelia said.

'Oh no, of course not. I'm just annoyed I didn't get here sooner. I can't believe I've missed the drama.'

Betty downed her martini in one then unskewered each olive with her teeth. After chewing them she placed the empty glass on the tray and dropped the bare stick into the glass.

'That hit the spot. Thank you. Thirsty work, travelling.'

'Would you like me to let Moira know you've arrived?'

Amelia had still not caught sight of Hamish's cousin, but the empty room-service plates regularly left outside the door indicated someone was staying in the Chandler Suite.

'We're meeting in the Whistling Haggis later. Now, when I last spoke to Hamish he said tonight's the night Davey is opening up the beer garden, which means Beltane is almost upon us.' She linked her arm chummily through Amelia's. 'Why don't we head there now, and on the way you can tell me *all* about the murder that dearest Gideon stumbled upon.'

The Whistling Haggis' beer-garden opening was always a moment the locals looked forward to. It heralded Beltane and summer and more importantly to the locals, a special happy hour that extended to closing time.

Wee Davey had done a grand job stringing up the metres of festoon lights, creating a twinkling canopy above their heads. Paper lanterns fell in colourful clusters from overhanging branches and uplighters illuminated the flourishing planters dotted around the perimeter of the seating area. The entire outside area had a lovely ethereal, fairy-grotto feel to it.

When Amelia, Toby and Betty arrived, Gideon, Jack, Sally and Hamish were already sitting round one of the large tables, near an outdoor heater, Amelia was pleased to see. Summer may be ever closer but the nights were still chilly being so far north. Amelia was also relieved to see citronella candles on the tables and a midgie zapper at the far end of the beer garden to rid the area of those infuriating insects so prevalent on the west coast of Scotland.

'Is that a stage erected over there, too?' Toby said, sitting next to Gideon.

'Yes,' Sally said. 'Davey was telling me there are a few local musicians scheduled to play for Beltane. There's even an Arctic Monkeys tribute band for the Saturday night!'

'Ooh, that should be good!' Amelia said, taking a sip of her whisky sour.

'Should it?' Gideon said archly.

'I like the Arctic Monkeys.'

'Exactly. So why would you want their music killed off for you?'

'Don't be such a grump,' Sally said and swiped his arm.

'I wonder if there will be any country music?' Amelia said, looking pointedly at Gideon who rolled his eyes.

'Oh, I hope so,' Betty said. 'I remember one particularly fun lock-in at the Whistling Haggis when Davey and I duetted the Dolly Parton and Kenny Rogers classic, "Islands in the Stream", on karaoke. It wasn't quite as exhilarating as when I sang it with the *real* Kenny at the CMA Festival in Nashville, but it was still a great night,' Betty said with a dreamy expression.

'Oh, Betty, how I've missed you!' Gideon said appreciatively.

As the evening wore on and the drink continued to flow, Amelia went inside for another round and found the bar area to be the quietest she'd ever seen it. Most of the customers were in the beer garden and apart from herself, the only other people in the interior of the Whistling Haggis were Johno and Maja who were wedged into one of the cosy little nooks in the corner.

Johno had his arm around the archaeologist in a comforting way and she was resting her head on his shoulder. They made an attractive couple, Amelia thought. Maja was tall, athletic and tanned, with blonde cropped hair. Tonight she was wearing a strappy vest top which showed off a very colourful and impressive tattoo of lotus flowers on her shoulder. Johno was also very good-looking, despite his rather questionable attire of knee-length orange-and-white polka-dot shorts and neon-green shirt combo. Throughout the summer months, many people, young and old, who never had any inkling to dip as much as a big toe in the sea, found themselves booking water sports courses with Johno. This sudden desire to try paddleboarding, kayaking or snorkelling usually occurred after them passing the SeaShack where Johno stood outside in his wetsuit, unzipped to the waist, showing off his tanned six-pack as he rubbed wax onto his surfboard.

With a large circular scar on his shoulder, which he had neither confirmed nor denied as a shark attack, Johno Davis was the closest thing Glencarlach had to an action hero.

Davey ambled over to Amelia, throwing his dish towel nonchalantly over his shoulder as Johno looked up.

'Isn't it a horrible and shocking thing to have happened!' Johno said to Amelia as he stood and walked up to the bar a little unsteadily. 'Poor Gus. He could be a bit of a... well, sorry, I won't speak ill of the dead but... it's just terrible. And to have it happen in your hotel? Jeezo, man. You must all be totally freaked out.'

Maja came up behind Johno, snaking her arm around his waist. Her normally perfect winged black eyeliner was seriously compromised, with dark-ringed smudges under her eyes from crying.

'Yeah, he was a complete arse at times, but we could have a real laugh together,' Maja said sadly. 'We've known each other for years.'

Johno downed the remains of his whisky and put the empty glass on the bar.

'Amelia's round is on me,' he said, peeling some notes from a roll he took out of the pocket in his shorts.

'There's no need, Johno. I'm getting quite a few drinks,' Amelia protested.

'It's no problem, Amelia,' Johno gave her a lopsided, slightly glassy-eyed smile. 'My ship came in,' he said as he swallowed down a hiccough. 'Quite literally!' he added with a little laugh, then stopped abruptly. 'Sorry.'

Johno put the money on the bar and slid it towards Davey. 'And keep the change, my good man,' he added.

'Thank you!' Amelia called out as he and Maja weaved their way past the empty tables to the door and left.

'Johno's been knocking them back tonight. And spending like there's no tomorrow!' Davey said. 'It's always the same with seasonal workers when the weather's good! He'll not be the same when the weather turns in the autumn.' He gave a little chuckle. 'Now then, same again?'

'Yes, please,' she said as Davey began to pour a pint of Guinness for Hamish. Leaving it to settle he got the red wine for Sally. He glanced up briefly at Amelia.

'You look as if you've got something on your mind, love.'

'You grew up here, didn't you?'

'Aye, I did that.' He put the wine glass on the tray. 'And my father. And my father's father before that.' He went into the fridge and got out two bottles of beer, a bottle of tonic and an orange juice. 'We go back quite a few generations.' He turned to the optics for Betty's gin.

'Wee Davey mentioned an old abandoned Hunting Lodge that some kind of pagan-robed cult lived in that people think is haunted?'

Davey paused, his shoulders tensing momentarily. He put down the glass with gin and then reached up and got down the whisky for Amelia's drink. He stayed silent.

Amelia pressed on. 'I just wondered if you could tell me a bit about it.'

'Why are your wanting to unearth all that nonsense?' he said lightly.

'That's what I'd like to know, too!' a voice spoke from behind them and Davey and Amelia whirled round. A tall, elegantly slim woman stood a few feet behind Amelia. In her early fifties, she had long, thick, slightly wavy hair, that hung loose, past her waist. It was dark brown, apart from one thick silver streak at the front. She was wearing a long, white floaty dress, with a loosely crocheted shawl over her shoulders and, rather incongruously, a pair of hot-pink glittery wellies.

Then the woman smiled, and her already attractive face lit up even more, showing off a slight gap between her two front teeth, before she threw her head back and let out a throaty laugh.

'I see not much has changed around here,' she said, coming forward to the bar in a fragrantly sensual cloud of patchouli, sandalwood and musk. 'Beer gardens for Beltane and the hauntings of the Hunting Lodge that never gets forgotten no matter how hard the locals try.'

'It's good to see you, Moira, you're looking braw,' Davey said, smiling warmly at the woman.

'And you, Davey.' And to Amelia's surprise, Moira pushed herself up onto the bar and leant over to give Davey a kiss on the lips.

Then Moira broke away with another throaty laugh and Davey shook his head.

'Away with you, Moira!' he said with a smile and a twinkle in his eyes. Amelia could see him turning red.

'You know I like to make an entrance. It'll give folk something to talk about!' Moira winked.

Amelia could see very well that Moira and Betty were related.

Hamish came in from the beer garden. 'Moira!' he said in delight as they hugged.

Moira then held him at arm's length, although tall, she was still quite a bit shorter than Hamish. 'What happened to my wee cousin?!'

'I grew!'

'You certainly did.'

'Oh, Amelia, this is Moira,' Hamish said by way of introduction. 'Amelia owns Stone Manor, where you and Betty are staying.'

'Ahh, *Amelia*! Hello. Lovely to meet you,' Moira said as she enveloped Amelia's hand in her own in greeting. 'You have a beautiful hotel and I'm thoroughly enjoying my stay. It's certainly been quite eventful, so far.' Moira's brown almond-shaped eyes glinted warmly with an intensity that fascinated Amelia.

'Come through to the beer garden, I can't wait for you to meet Sally,' Hamish said, as he almost dragged his cousin through behind him.

'And I can't wait to meet the woman who's going to make an honest man of you!' Moira said as she followed.

Amelia turned back to Davey, who watched them leave with quite a soppy smile. He caught Amelia looking at him and he cleared his throat, pulled up his belt buckle and finished off making her whisky sour.

What started as a fun evening soon turned into a raucous one, with Moira and Betty both holding court. Moira called out greetings to quite a few locals with many gravitating towards her to say hello and have a quick chat.

At one point Davey came out with a pint of purplish liquid and placed it in front of Moira.

'Snakebite and black,' he said.

'Ahh, good times!' Moira said, then took a big swallow of the drink. 'Living over in France with all those lovely wines, my palate has become a wee bit more sophisticated with time, Davey, but this is pure nostalgia in a glass. Is Ray about?'

'Working,' Davey said.

'Ah, of course. I imagine there's quite a lot of paperwork involved when dead bodies turn up.'

'Aye, you picked a fine time to check in to Stone Manor.'

'It would seem so. Well, we need to get the old band back together when Ray isn't bogged down with overtime,' Moira said with a wink as Davey retreated inside.

Amelia gave Jack a look and he raised an eyebrow in acknowledgement before taking a swig from his bottle of beer. Amelia knew Ray and Davey were friends from school and she was loving the new dynamic of Moira being added in to this mix and wondered if she'd greet Ray in the same familiar way as she had Davey.

'I was hoping to see Elizabeth tonight. Elizabeth McAvoy, married to Andy. We were such great pals.'

'I doubt you'll see Elizabeth,' Hamish said with a shake of his head. 'There was a bit of a scandal. She ran off with another man about six months ago.'

'What!' Moira looked shocked.

'Aye, her affair caused quite a stir. It was with Paddy Davis. Johno's dad,' Hamish added for clarity to those not born and bred in Glencarlach.

'I can't believe she'd have left Andy and the boys,' Moira said.

'She left a note for them, said she'd be in touch but apart from a card at Christmas there's been nothing. Johno's the same. He got left a note and his dad put the cottage in his name before they went.'

Moira sat back in her chair. 'Wow. We normally write each other a letter and stick it in with the Christmas card but that explains why I didn't hear from her Christmas gone. What about Hector?'

'Never see hide nor hair of him usually, but funnily enough he turned up yesterday,' Hamish said. 'He's only behind the funding of the archaeology dig at the abbey and Pictish site.'

Moira's eyes widened. 'Well, well, well. The lad that was murdered was part of that, wasn't he?'

The others nodded.

'It's all very shocking,' Moira said.

'We're no strangers to murder around here said,' Betty said, leaning into the table.

'I found the body, you know,' Gideon said and then proceeded to give the group a rundown of the whole affair of the previous night and seeing the strange pagan-robed figure loitering in the grounds.

'Have the police found any leads?' Sally asked.

Moira gave a snort of a laugh. 'I doubt McGregor could find his own arse without a torch, map and compass.'

The rest of them gave a murmur of agreement.

'You know McGregor?' Amelia asked.

'Back in the day,' Moira said but didn't elaborate.

Then Gideon leant over the table towards Amelia, giving a little wince of pain. 'Ames darling, I don't suppose you could get me a pack of peanuts and maybe some crisps, I don't think I could manage.' He looked down at his bandaged foot, resting on a stool with a couple of folded up woolly jumpers underneath for extra padding. He seemed to have managed fine earlier in the day when it had suited him to explore an allegedly haunted Hunting Lodge with her, but walking a few feet to the bar was clearly too much of a struggle.

Thinking she could also manage a packet of cheese and onion, Amelia got up and went inside. The place was deserted apart from Rory, who was sitting at the bar, a large whisky in front of him beside his folded denim bucket hat. He talked quietly to Davey, who was nodding along, looking serious.

Rory's head shot up at the interruption. He looked dreadful and as he lifted his whisky to his lips, Amelia could see a slight tremor to his hands. He drained his glass.

'Are you okay, Rory?' Amelia asked.

He gave her a very weak smile. 'I've been better,' he said and nodded thanks at Davey who wordlessly free-poured another generous measure of whisky. 'I just had someone almost throw themselves in front of my car. I had to swerve suddenly and ended up in a ditch. The guys from the local garage can't tow it out until tomorrow, but it looks like it might be a write-off.'

'Are you okay?'

'Air bags gave me a bit of a smack but I'll be fine.'

'What about the other person?' Amelia asked.

'That's the weird thing... I know I didn't hit them because when I was in the ditch I looked in my rear-view mirror and saw them still standing in the middle of the road watching me. But by the time I managed to get out the car they'd gone. I had a bit of search around but it was as if they'd vanished.'

Rory shook his head in disbelief and rasped his hand across the stubble on his chin.

'And that's not the *really* mental bit,' he said, shaking his head. 'The guy... or thing in the road, was like some creepy monk from a medieval horror film and the way he disappeared... I think I'm losing it. I'm starting to wonder if it was real or I imagined it... I sound mad, don't I?'

'Gideon thinks he saw a similar figure in the grounds of Stone Manor last night.' Amelia looked at Davey who had a very grim expression on his face.

'There's something odd about that patch of road and no mistake,' Davey said. 'Only last month Jean Maddox's cousin nearly crashed because of someone in the road.'

'Wearing pagan robes?' Amelia asked.

'No. This was a woman. A woman in white. She had long straggly hair over her face. Jean's cousin swerved and when he'd calmed down he got out but he couldn't see anyone. He'd seen another car's lights, even thought they'd stopped, but couldn't identify the driver. By the time he got out of his car, there was no one. He asked around to see if anyone knew anything but no one else ever came forward, so I'm guessing not.'

'What bit of road is it?'

'The exposed stretch between the village and Gull Point.'

Rory's mobile chirped at him. He read the text message, then typed a brief reply before pocketing his phone, then drained his drink.

'I need to go,' he said, standing up and reaching into his back pocket for his wallet.

Davey shook his head and waved the proffered money away. 'On the house, Rory, you look after yourself tonight.'

'Aye, I will. Thanks, Davey. Night, Amelia.'

'This is surely connected to what Gideon saw!' Amelia said to Davey once Rory left.

'Maybe,' he said reluctantly. 'It's a bad business, anyway.' He forced a smile. 'What can I get you?'

Amelia managed to reel off a selection of snacks she hoped would cover everyone's preferences. 'And a little bit of information about the Hunting Lodge?' she added hopefully.

Davey plonked the snacks down in front of her and then sighed.

'I mean this with kindness, Amelia, but you need to leave this be. Bad things happened at that place and there's always a fear that bad things can easily resurface again.'

'We're a superstitious lot around here,' Moira said as she walked out from the shadowy doorway that led to the garden. Amelia had no idea how long she'd been standing there. 'But maybe it's time to put the superstition connected to that place to rest once and for all.'

'None of us want to open old wounds,' Davey said.

'Maybe letting go of the past might be the only way to properly heal and move forward,' Moira said softly.

Amelia looked between them, wondering what they were talking about.

Davey levelled a look at Moira for a few moments before saying, 'You do what you need to do, you always have. But leave me, and others,' he said, looking pointedly at Amelia, 'out of your plans.'

'I have no *plans*, Davey!' Moira said. 'I'm here for no other reason than to revisit my old home, catch up with folk and be a part of Beltane by worshipping Ostara and do a handfasting ceremony,' she said, annoyance creeping into her voice. 'But maybe it's time... och, I don't know...' She stomped back out to the beer garden.

Davey turned back to Amelia. 'I know you like a mystery, just like your late godmother, but please, believe me when I say the goings on up at that Hunting Lodge weren't just mysterious. They were downright evil. And tragic. And folk won't like you bringing it up again.'

THIRTEEN

Moira stood hidden in the shadows of the graveyard. She looked out, across the road to where DI McGregor sat in his car. The engine was off, but the fascia of his phone lit up the interior, giving off an eerie glow. She'd been observing him for almost twenty minutes. Watching him, watching everyone coming and going from the Whistling Haggis. It was almost midnight. Davey would have called last orders and soon be sending the stragglers home.

Suppressing a yawn, Moira mulled over the events of the evening. She supposed it had gone well. Her arrival had definitely caused a stir, but Davey had seemed pleased to see her. A few familiar faces came over to talk to her. Some were genuine; asking after her, taking an interest in her life, others were clearly just wanting to glean as much information as they could before hot-tailing it to the next stop in the gossip chain. She'd expected as much.

Hamish had turned into a lovely big strapping lad and seemed smitten with Sally. Moira had instantly taken to the bubbly beautician and thought she and Hamish made a lovely couple. And she'd found it quite amusing to put the face to the voice of the man who'd been causing such a fuss the evening before. Gideon still seemed overly dramatic and highly strung, but also came across as very personable with a sharp wit who had quite a cutting opinion about many things. She liked him.

And she liked Amelia. Admired her, even, for setting up Stone Manor and turning it into such a beautiful hotel. More than anything, Moira liked Amelia's spirit. She came across as sympathetic and kind, but there was a clever shrewdness around the eyes which missed nothing.

Dammit, she was starting to take an interest in the people of Glencarlach. She was at risk of being sucked into the village once again.

Moira left the shadows and walked to the front of the church and down the steps to the DI's car. She opened up the passenger door and got in beside him.

He slowly looked up from his phone. 'Moira,' he said evenly with no hint of surprise.

'Murray,' she greeted him in a similar impassive way.

He slid his phone into one of the ledges on the dashboard and continued to watch the door of the Whistling Haggis.

'Keeping well?' he asked, still focused on the outside of the pub. He spoke as if they'd seen each other a couple of weeks ago rather than acknowledge the gap of time between their last encounter. She was determined not to rise to his ambivalence.

'Weather's not doing much for my joints. I forgot how damp it is here. How's life treating you?'

'Not too bad, I suppose.'

She studied his profile for a moment before saying, 'You never do give anything away, do you?' She sat back in her seat, annoyed it had been less than twenty seconds before she got cross with him. He always had managed to push her buttons. And she still didn't know if he meant to or not.

He turned and looked at her, his features just as unyielding as she remembered. His angular face had softened a little over the years but he hadn't changed too much from the intense, serious teenager.

'What do you want me to say, Moira?'

And she didn't have an answer to that.

'You're the one who left. Were you wanting a welcome home banner? Some balloons? A parade?'

'There will be a parade on Saturday.'

Something flashed behind his eyes. 'Why now? Of all the bloody times to come back, why now?' There was a catch of annoyance in his voice. Maybe he wasn't as ambivalent as he liked to make out.

'Of course it had to be now. And it seems I arrived at the right time. Are you going to tell me this isn't a coincidence? A body turns up and someone is seen near the crime scene wearing pagan robes?'

'That witness is hardly reliable.'

'Gideon seems in full possession of his faculties to me. And did you know about the same figure jumping out and causing Elizabeth's lad to crash his car?'

'Ray told me. Not in an official capacity, but he thought I'd want to know.'

'And *do* you want to know?'

Murray sighed.

'Surely you must think something's afoot, what with the pagan robes link?'

'It's Beltane,' he said simply.

'I don't know if you're meaning that as an explanation or an excuse. Either way, it doesn't reassure me.'

He turned and looked at her. 'What do you want me to say? That I think the ghost of Samuel Bain is back, resurrected, to finish the rituals he started a century ago? Or is it your dead brother that's back to finish off whatever it was he was trying to do?'

His words stung. 'I've just been visiting his grave.'

'I go there time to time, myself.'

'Do you ever think about that night?'

'Of course I do,' Murray said, more softly. 'I know you are still in pain. All of us are. We all wish we could go back to Beltane night in 1986 and do something to stop what happened. But we can't, Moira. But know this. All that's happening now has nothing to do with Cameron.'

There was a beat of silence, broken by a rowdy group leaving the Whistling Haggis. Moira saw Big Davey step out to watch them go before turning back inside, closing the door and switching off the outdoor coaching light that illuminated the entrance.

'Do you know I'm staying in Stone Manor?' Moira asked. Moira had wondered if McGregor would be taking her statement, but instead, she'd been questioned by DS Dabrowski. And when Moira said she'd been sound asleep all night after turning her light off at half past eleven, Moira noticed the way the DS's eyes had slid to the almost empty bottle of Pouilly-Fumé. Sound asleep? Half passed out? It amounted to the same; Moira had not heard or seen anything. She wondered if the DS had reported this snippet of information back to Murray. Well, what if she had? With Moira's increasing bouts of insomnia and wakening from crazed dreams, quite often the only way Moira could guarantee sleep was when she'd drunk a few glasses of wine.

But Murray said nothing, he just continued to stare out the windscreen, watching the group walk home.

'You, Murray McGregor are just as unmoving and taciturn now as you were back in the day,' Moira said hotly. She went to get out of the car but McGregor initiated the central locking, prohibiting her exit.

'And *you* are still every bit as infuriating,' he said conversationally as he checked his mirrors, signalled, and pulled out of his car space.

'What are you doing?'

'Driving you back to Stone Manor. You just told me that's where you're staying. There seems to be a murderer on the loose and I'd rather no one was out, unchaperoned.'

They drove up the illuminated driveway in silence and he pulled to a stop at the fountain before the steps leading up to the Stone Manor entrance.

She sat in silence, waiting until he released the central locking system.

Without a goodbye or a glance in his direction, Moira got out of the car, slammed the door then stomped up the steps and into the hotel.

In her room the nagging anxiety that had been plaguing her recently ramped up a notch and she felt restless and light-headed. Bending over, Moira breathed deeply until the dizziness passed. Could history be repeating itself? What if the thing that had obsessed her brother was back to haunt others?

Moira believed that the veil thinned between worlds at times like Beltane and Samhain. Had something evil slipped through? Was this why she'd been getting the dreams about her brother and the messages through the tarot?

She quickly shut her mind to that possibility. No good would come from allowing herself to spiral.

Maybe Davey was right; the past should be left there and no one should dig it back up.

Moira pulled the curtain shut to keep the draught and the darkness out.

A darkness which was creeping in both literally and figuratively.

FOURTEEN

Main Street was busy the next morning. People lingered by the harbour area, clustered in little groups, ignoring the chilly wind blowing in off the water as they discussed the police presence that had appeared overnight. News of the dead body was now widespread and a patrol car was stationed at each end of Main Street with DCs making enquiries door to door.

Many of the shop owners were standing out front, observing the goings on. Seagulls cawed and swooped, no doubt hoping the bystanders would have scraps of rolls and other breakfast fare going spare to throw their way.

Amelia almost bumped into Rory as he was coming out of the café with a couple of takeaway coffees.

'Morning, how are you?' Amelia asked.

Rory tried to stifle a yawn. 'I'm okay, still a bit freaked out, but it's a case of business as usual. No duvet days in my line of work, especially as I'm sold out for today's tours.'

From his bleary eyes and greyish pallor, it didn't look as if Rory had managed to get much sleep.

Amelia watched as two officers crossed Main Street and walked into Johno's diving and surf shop, the SeaShack.

Rory nodded in their direction. 'The police are keen to question Johno because of the diving suit and it hasn't helped that he had a bit of an argument with Gus in front of half the village. Mind you, if you suspect everyone that had beef with Gus, the police will have a long list. I'd better take this along to him.' Rory lifted up one of the coffees. 'He evidently sank quite a few last night and feels rough as. Hopefully this'll help,' he added before striding towards the SeaShack.

Amelia watched him go, seeing Lily poke her head out of the estate agents as Rory passed. She looked along Main Street, then darted back inside again.

Amelia walked along the pavement, thinking there was no harm checking in with Drew and Lily to see if they'd unearthed any information about the Hunting Lodge.

The door to the estate agency wasn't closed properly and a gentle push from Amelia opened it. Clearly, Drew and Lily hadn't heard her as they were both standing at the rear of the office, deep in conversation. One that seemed quite heated.

'I wish you'd let me know you'd gone out!' Drew said, stabbing a couple of buttons on the photocopier.

'I didn't think I had to! It was just a walk! And you were asleep.'

'But when I woke it was late and you weren't there!' He plucked some sheets from the copier.

'It wasn't *that* late! And anyway, you go out and stay out till all hours! Am I not meant to have a life or do you just want me waiting at home for you for whenever you roll in?'

'But after what happened to the archaeologist—'

'You know when I get these bouts of insomnia, walking helps.'

'Maybe you should go see the doctor for sleeping tablets instead of going wandering.'

'And walk about the next morning like a zombie?' Lily exclaimed. 'I don't think so!'

'They don't make you like that. Dad takes them and he's fine!'

'I don't know how! The ones he has are strong enough to knock out an elephant! Anyway, hasn't the GP refused to prescribe your dad any more because he was going through too many? So, *obviously* they're highly addictive and I don't want to be taking stuff like that!'

'All I'm saying is to go an–' Drew looked up from the photocopier. 'Amelia!'

'Oh hi, Amelia!' Lily said, looking a little flustered.

'Hi, sorry, is this a bad time?'

'No! Not at all!' Drew said, stapling some sheets together and walking over to drop them onto his desk. 'How can I help?' he said, giving her a professional smile, that belied his agitated state moments before. For someone who stayed out drinking until all hours, Drew looked very well and had a glow about him. The weather had been brighter over the last few days and Amelia wondered if he was one of those lucky folk who tanned with even the tiniest amount of sunshine.

'I wondered if you'd had any luck finding out about the Hunting Lodge?'

'Not yet, I've been a bit busy. Considering where it is, I think it's best left alone.' Drew ran a hand over his eyes, and added, 'Folk shouldn't be wandering about up there.'

That seemed to be the general consensus.

'I've got the schedule for the farm that's coming on the market,' Drew said, changing the subject as he held up a glossy-looking folder with his business brand stamped on the front. 'I don't have the photos yet, but I've got the description along with the room sizes and floor plan. I mentioned you were keen to see it. They're happy for you to view it before it goes on the open mar...' He was distracted by a police officer walking past, their radio crackling into life.

Lily, eating a fruit scone, went over to the window and looked out and up the street, the direction the officer was walking.

'Do they know the cause of death yet?' she asked.

'Not that they've told me,' Amelia said.

Lily looked back at Drew and Amelia as she continued to eat her scone.

Drew cleared his throat. 'So, Amelia, the owners of the farm said you're welcome to go out there at twelve today. Can I let them know you'll be there?'

'Yes, that would be great, thanks.'

Leaving Drew and Lily, Amelia continued to walk along Main Street. She passed SeaShack and could see the police were still talking to Johno. Rory was standing near the front of the shop, idling beside a display of board shorts and swimming gear, watching the exchange with his friend and sipping from his takeaway coffee cup. He made eye contact with Amelia through the window and smiled and nodded at her in acknowledgement. As she headed towards where she'd parked the Jeep she felt a little prickle on the back of her neck as if someone was watching her. Instinctively she turned. McGregor was sitting in his car, staring at her out the windscreen. Giving him a little smile that wasn't reciprocated, Amelia turned and continued on, a little unsettled by his grim and watchful expression.

FIFTEEN

'Hey, you!' Jack said, getting into the passenger seat of the hotel Jeep moments after Amelia pulled up outside the Gatehouse just before midday. He reached over and gave her a kiss.

'How's it going?' she asked as Jack buckled up.

'I think I'm on my last edit. So far, I haven't discovered any major plot holes so that's good.'

'I'm available to proofread it if you want,' Gideon piped up from the back seat and Amelia tried not to laugh as Jack jumped in surprise at his presence.

'Gideon was at a bit of a loose end and I thought it would be nice if he joined us to give another point of view,' Amelia explained to Jack, not adding that Toby had practically begged her to take Gideon away as he was going mad from Gideon's incessant demands and interfering; the final straw being that morning when the bandaged-up actor had suggested revamping the menu for the Beltane feast, now just two days away.

'Great!' Jack said. 'The more the merrier.' And Amelia couldn't for the life of her tell if he was being sarcastic or not as she drove off.

'Here's the schedule,' Gideon said as he thrust the papers at

Jack. 'And don't ask me what those rather dubious orangey-brown smudges are at the top!'

'It's probably just icing from a fudge doughnut!' Amelia said, having observed that Lily appeared quite a fan of the café's baked offerings. 'Or a smear of ink from the printer.'

'Well, I think it screams unprofessionalism,' Gideon said sniffily.

The farmhouse was situated up a very badly potholed track a few miles from the village.

Amelia came to a stop outside, mentally going through her house checklist. It didn't exactly have the kerb appeal she was looking for.

'Jesus, it's bleak!' Gideon said as they looked up at the ramshackle house through the windscreen.

'Is it meant to be sloping down so dramatically at the right?' Jack said.

'The lean-to at the other side is a bit too lean-to as well,' Amelia said with a sinking heart, tilting her head slightly in an effort to make the property look a little better. 'The schedule does say it's in need of modernisation.'

'Looks like it needs a ruddy great wrecking ball,' Gideon said.

'It may be amazing on the inside,' Jack said.

Gideon tutted. 'You and your all-American cheerleading positivity,' he moaned as they got out of the car.

The interior was no more promising than the exterior. Pokey-sized rooms in a confusing, labyrinthine layout made Amelia feel quite claustrophobic as they walked around. The most promising room was a relatively new extension with large patio doors, but it had been built directly in front of a massive cowshed which obliterated any sort of view.

The three of them returned to the Jeep. They sat in silence for a moment or two.

'It's not the nicest of days to view a property. It's very overcast,' Amelia said as the windscreen became distorted by a light shower.

'Lifting that house and transplanting it in the middle of sun-drenched Ayia Napa would not make it any more appealing,' Gideon said with a snort of derision.

'And it needs a lot of work,' Amelia said, not even sure where she would start with the 'modernisation'.

'As I already said, it needs a ruddy great wrecking ball!' Gideon repeated.

'I don't think it's for us, Ames. The best we could do would be to buy it for the land, knock it down and start again,' Jack suggested.

'But I don't even like the setting. I didn't get a good feeling.'

'Oh God, not more "feelings" about properties,' Gideon said, 'you're becoming as superstitious as the locals!'

'Oh yes, the notorious Hunting Lodge. I need to check it out,' Jack said with a smile as Amelia started the engine and pulled away from the farmhouse.

Gideon leant forward, poking his head between the front seats. 'Who's up for a mini road trip? Let's go look at it now!'

'I was not expecting this!' Jack said a few minutes later when they'd left the Jeep by the crumbling old wall and entered the Hunting Lodge grounds. The clouds had dispersed letting the sun make an appearance.

Gideon swept his crutches over the weeds and undergrowth next to the derelict stable block. 'Someone's been here since we were,' he remarked. 'The empties and tea lights have been removed.'

'That's odd. For a place that no one ever goes to,' Jack said as he walked over to the Hunting Lodge.

'Isn't it lovely?' Amelia said, standing next to Jack.

'*Lovely?*' Gideon repeated in horror.

'It does have a certain fairy-tale charm to it,' Jack agreed, looking up at the house and nodding appreciatively.

'Clearly, we've had very different upbringings!' Gideon said. 'Fairy tale? It's straight from a horror movie!'

'Come see the back,' Amelia said as she walked round the side of the building, feeling bolder now it was her second visit but she came to a sudden stop when she met a large garden spike embedded in the path with a dead squirrel skewered on the top.

'Oh God! That's disgusting! Why would someone do that!' Gideon exclaimed.

'Someone doesn't want people like us around here,' Amelia said, giving the dead animal a wide berth as she passed it. 'Which seems to be the entire population of Glencarlach!'

At the back of the property there was a plain, solid wood door, on which someone had painted a large blue symbol, which had faded and weathered with time.

Gideon took a step back and squinted at it. 'What is it?'

'It looks like crossed spears,' Amelia said. The arrowhead tips pointed upwards.

'Is it phallic?' Gideon said, doubtfully. 'Maybe it used to be an orgy house back in the day. That would explain any moaning and groaning heard, mistakenly thought to be ghosts!'

Jack squinted at the symbols. 'They're definitely spears.'

'A potential battleground?' Gideon suggested. 'Do you still want to go in?'

Amelia gave the door a push but wasn't surprised to find it was locked.

'Looks like our hunt stops here unless either of you know how to pick a lock?' Amelia joked.

'Obviously!' Gideon said, following her gaze to the lock.

'No! We can't!' Amelia said. 'That would be breaking and entering.'

'Surely your amateur detective senses are *tingling* at the thought of going inside... what mysteries can you uncover?' Gideon said. 'You were the one who was desperate to see the place!'

Amelia touched the door. Gideon had a point.

'But I can see you're scared, given the...' Gideon gesticulated in the direction of the squirrel.

'The only reason someone puts up a warning like that is to keep folk out, it would be good to know why,' Amelia reasoned aloud. She turned and looked at Gideon suspiciously. 'But you hate this place, why are you so keen we see inside?'

Jack folded his arms and leant against the door. 'It's a double bluff. Gideon's hoping you realise how hideous it is and then forget all about it!'

'Amateur psychologist!' Gideon said through a weary sigh. 'They don't cover issues like this in *Escape to the Country*! Have you got your Swiss Army knife on you?'

Amelia handed it to him.

'Hold these,' he said, thrusting his crutches at Jack before hopping up to the door and, leaning against the stone for balance, selecting two of the longest and thinnest army-knife accessories and beginning to wiggle them into the cylinder lock.

'Do you know what you're doing?' Amelia asked.

'Darling, I've had to break in to plenty of locked cocktail cabinets in my time, and once a pair of police regulation handcuffs after a rather debauched weekend house party.'

There was a satisfying click and Gideon turned the door handle and it opened. 'Taa-daa!'

'This is probably trespassing,' Jack said.

'I'll just tell Hector Bain I'm after a cup of sugar!' Amelia said.

'Wait!' Gideon cupped his hand over his ear. 'Is that a cry for help I hear, from some murdered zombie pagan monk? Isn't that what they say in police dramas to justify entering a building?' He pushed the door open fully. 'Having said that, I'd still rather not go in first in case it's been booby-trapped by a gruesome ghoul of Glencarlach.'

Amelia led the way. The door opened into a narrow hallway which had rather rickety shelves down one of the walls. Two doors led from the little room.

She picked the one in front.

The handle was stiff but the door opened, albeit with a very squeaky hinge. A small, narrow passageway led from the door. It was dark and a cool dampness settled on Amelia's skin like a delicate veil. Unwilling to buy into the haunted rumours, Amelia did, however, feel a little disquieted as they silently made their way along the narrow little hallway. There were a couple of smaller rooms off this passageway, before another door led them out into a much wider, less pokey part of the house.

'We've probably come from the old servants' entrance,' Jack said, his voice sounding incredibly loud in the bare, echoey hallway.

'Yes, this does seem quite a bit grander,' Gideon agreed.

They came to a dog-leg staircase with an intricately carved banister and Gideon inhaled sharply. Positioned up the wall were a dozen or so mounted stags' heads.

'This is giving me the creeps,' Gideon said.

'I suppose it is a Hunting Lodge,' Amelia reasoned.

Gideon shook his head sadly. 'Why would anyone want to shoot those beautiful animals for sport?'

Amelia got a little closer, feeling sad as she looked at the glassy eyes of what had once been a stunning red deer.

'That one's massive,' Jack said, pointing out one to Amelia.

She counted the points on its antlers. 'That's a Monarch. Any red deer with twelve points, six per antler, is known as a Royal Stag, fourteen points is an Imperial stag and anything more than that is a Monarch. I read it in one of the books in the Stone Manor library.'

Amelia tested her weight on the bottom step. There was an ominous creak and she decided not to climb any higher, not trusting the old, bare wood. Staying at the bottom of the stairs, Amelia peered up. On the half landing there was a tall and narrow stained-glass window and in the left-hand corner was a plinth with a golden eagle taxidermy atop; the beautiful animal's impressive wingspan outstretched. More mounted animal heads continued up the stairs to the first floor.

'Can we move on?' Gideon said in a rather reverential hushed tone. 'I don't like the way that one's looking at me.'

Still on the ground floor, Amelia pushed open the door next to the stairs and opened up the bay-windowed lounge. It was bright and filled with light despite the newspapers being stuck up at the window. On the side opposite the stairs was a rather outdated toilet.

'This is like a museum piece!' Gideon said as he pointed to the toilet cistern positioned halfway up the wall with a chain flush hanging from it.

'No electric showers here,' Amelia agreed as she looked into a yellowing wash-hand basin with a large crack running along the grimy bottom. 'Although I don't think *this* is antique,' Amelia added as she picked up the four-pack of Asda loo roll that sat beside the toilet.

'Oh my God! Do you think someone's living here?' Gideon said, his eyes widening as he looked over his shoulder in a panic as if he expected a disgruntled owner to jump out from behind the door.

'I wouldn't have thought so,' Jack said, 'but maybe it's best we don't hang about too long.'

'I want to have a quick look through the other rooms on this floor,' Amelia said.

They walked past the front doorway, where little slivers of sunlight filtered through the gaps in the boards over the entranceway. Amelia opened the double-panelled doors which led into a huge room. Despite the unwashed windows, Amelia was startled at how bright the room was from the sunlight flooding in through the three tall windows at the front. Amelia loved the original features; a set of old wooden shutters were folded back from the window and there was ornate cornicing running around the tops of the walls. In the centre was an elaborate ceiling rose, where chunks of the plaster had come away. Amelia thought back to what Wee Davey had told her about the demise of Samuel Bain. Had he really hanged himself and would it have been in this room? There was a faded Persian-style rug in the centre of the room with pieces of broken furniture lying, scattered around. A grand fireplace with an imposing wooden mantelpiece took up a large proportion of one wall and was thick with a combination of melted wax, dust and mouse droppings.

Gideon wrinkled his nose in disgust when he saw this.

'Is that some original art?' he commented as he nodded over to the other side of the room where *Love is the law, love under will*, had been daubed in black paint over a faded floral wallpaper that had half peeled away. Beside this message were strange-looking signs and symbols of triangles.

'There's something else written here,' Jack said, bending down beside the mantelpiece. *'Let the magician, robed and armed as he may deem fit, turn his face towards Boleskine.'*

'These days, when people mention magicians, they're usually talking about Harry Potter or David Blaine, but this seems a tad more sinister,' Gideon said, limping up behind Jack to look at the inscription. 'Robed, just like the figure I saw before Gus died.'

Amelia bent down by the broken glass-fronted cabinet and picked up one of the books that was on the floor. It was old, musty and leather-bound. '*The book of the sacred magic of Abramelin the mage,*' she read from the spine. She gently turned the browned, fragile pages. '*First published in 1897.*'

'I hope it was the first *and* the last publication!' Gideon said disdainfully.

'There's a whole selection of grimoires here!' Amelia said, looking through the other books.

'They certainly make for grim reading!' Gideon said, looking down at them. 'There's *The sacred magic of Abramelin the mage, translated from French.*' He bent to rifle through them. '*The Key of Solomon,* and, with the catchy title, we have *The Tarot, its occult significance, and methods of play.* I may give that one a go for my bedtime reading!'

'There was a tarot card next to Gus's body,' Amelia said as she looked along the other spines which were all variations of the same theme of occult books.

'And that's not at all sinister!' Gideon said.

'I googled the meaning. It seems there's a whole load of interpretations but one is The Devil can be a representation of a person's darker side.'

'Do you think Gus had a darker side?' Jack asked.

'It doesn't get much darker than being murdered,' Gideon said.

'Look at this,' Jack said as he lifted a piece of loose wallpaper.

Underneath, scored into the plaster was an inscription:

The Watchful Wiccan. Love and protection forever. McDrehm.

'Watchful Wiccan?' Gideon repeated sceptically. 'Sounds like a prog rock band. And is McDrehm a surname?'

'If it is I don't know of anyone around here called that.'

Leaving the graffiti, Amelia went through another set of double wooden-panelled doors which led to a similar-sized room which was completely bare and gloomier, due to the windows being situated at the side where the light was blocked by overgrown bushes. Through another door was the kitchen.

'What's all this?' Jack said as he went over to a farmhouse-style table on which there was a mug, a newspaper and ashtray overflowing with stubbed out cigarettes.

Amelia went over and saw that amongst the ends of roll-ups and normal-looking stubs there were a couple of black filters. 'They look odd, don't they? Black cigarettes.'

'Weren't coloured cocktail cigarettes popular in the eighties?' Jack said.

'Very *Dynasty!*' Gideon said as he continued to walk around the kitchen, opening cupboard doors to look inside and banging them shut on discovering them empty. 'Black cigarettes were all the rage over in Amsterdam when I was there shooting that spy thriller last year. Called Black Devils or something like that. God, even the tobacco is giving off a sinister vibe in this place! I don't know about you two but I'm feeling a little bit like Goldilocks having stumbled into this lived-in house and the jury's definitely undecided if the bears are friendly.'

Gideon opened a cupboard where Amelia saw a jar of supermarket own brand instant coffee, bag of sugar and a couple of unopened packets of biscuits. On closer inspection, Amelia realised they must have been bought recently as they were all well within their use-by dates.

Amelia looked at the newspaper on the table. 'This is dated two days ago.'

'The night Gus died,' Gideon said hollowly. 'Without wanting to sound overly dramatic, I'm getting a bad feeling.'

'You were the one that suggested we come here on a mini road trip then facilitated the break-in!' Amelia pointed out.

'That's when I thought it was completely uninhabited and didn't know about the trophy heads up the stairs. We should have turned back as soon as we found that squirrel kebab!'

Ignoring Gideon, Amelia moved around the rest of the kitchen. There was a teaspoon in the sink, and apart from a portable camping stove, a little stainless-steel kettle and a torch, there was nothing else on the kitchen worktop. On opening up the cupboards and drawers, Amelia found them to be empty too, certainly not containing a pagan robe. She opened up the last cupboard where there was an almost finished bottle of something. She pulled it out.

Gosling's dark rum.

'This is the same brand of rum that Gus got from Davey,' she said, holding it up to Jack.

'Yeah, I recognise the label. You think Gus was here?'

'Possibly. We are nearer the water, but it's a sheer drop off a very high cliff to get to it,' Gideon said.

'Do you want to let McGregor know about the rum?' Jack asked.

Amelia didn't think he'd approve of her breaking and entering and meddling in a murder he was in charge of investigating. 'I'll ask Davey to see how many bottles he sells or gets through before I mention anything.'

With all the cupboards explored, Amelia opened another panelled door and found herself back in the little square hall where they'd started their explorations.

Retracing her steps into the grand room with the overturned

bookcase, Amelia stood looking at the graffiti for a moment. She got out her phone and took photos of the room, all the writing and the symbols. They left, going out the way they'd come in. Amelia paused briefly and rapped her knuckles against the wall beside the kitchen.

'I hope to hell you don't get an answering knock,' Gideon said with a look of horror.

'Just checking to see if it's a supporting wall or not.' It sounded hollow and Amelia could imagine knocking a door through from the kitchen and using it as a utility room.

'Can we quit the Kirstie Allsopp routine and hurry up! I don't want to meet whoever's living here,' Gideon whispered.

'I don't think someone's been staying here permanently, it feels too temporary,' Amelia said.

Jack nodded thoughtfully. 'But why would someone be hanging about here and using it as some dilapidated man cave?'

Gideon sniffed disdainfully. 'You'd expect at least a dartboard if that was the case. Was someone waiting here?'

'A romantic assignation?' Amelia guessed.

'It wouldn't get my motor running!' Jack said.

'Kids?' Gideon suggested. 'Actually, scrub that, there aren't any cans of Monster, massive bottles of cider or disposable vapes.'

Amelia looked around again. 'The stubs in the ashtray would point at adults. As would the coffee and newspaper. The empty beer bottles at the ruined stable would suggest that's where teenagers would be more likely to congregate.'

'Maybe whoever owns this place checks in from time to time.'

'Like some creepy housekeeper. It's still not a very comforting thought!' Gideon said.

Amelia turned to Jack. 'I wonder how many bedrooms there are? One for us, a spare and a study for you would be perfect.'

'Oh dear God! Stop!' Gideon said. 'Before we start discussing Farrow and Ball paint colours, can we *please* leave as I'm starting to get very creeped out at the thought of whoever sat at that table smoking those cigarettes and drinking that coffee coming back! Especially if they were responsible for killing Gus.'

There was a loud thud.

Gideon clutched Jack's arm. 'What the *hell* was that!'

They stood frozen.

A moment later there was a slightly muffled thump.

'I am out of here,' Gideon said, covering a fair amount of ground in a short space of time on his crutches, Amelia and Jack close behind.

'It could have been a tree branch knocking against a window,' Amelia reasoned when they got to the Jeep. She looked back at the Hunting Lodge.

'That may be so, but I think we outstayed our welcome,' Gideon said.

Starting the engine, Amelia was now more resolute than ever to find out who'd been using the abandoned Hunting Lodge as a den and why.

And how much a property like that would go for in the current market.

SIXTEEN

Driving back into Glencarlach, Amelia saw a police car was still parked at the end of Main Street. Despite the lack of anything newsworthy to look at, many villagers were still milling about and, with the sun now shining, the harbour wall was full of people sitting enjoying a coffee and filled roll from the café for lunch.

'Can you let me out here?' Jack said. 'I'm going to grab a coffee and walk back to the Gatehouse before I hide away with my computer and manuscript.'

Amelia stopped, level with SeaShack, and Jack got out. Before she could drive off, she was aware of Rory waving her down. She pulled in behind Johno's old battered Fiat.

Johno was leaning against the doorway of his shop, looking serious and biting the skin on the side of his thumbnail.

'I was about to come and see you.' Rory brandished a bundle of the newly printed leaflets advertising his cruises. 'As promised.'

'Thanks.'

'Right, I'm heading over to the boat, got a bit of a tidy up to do before this afternoon's wildlife cruise.'

'Okay. See you in the Whistling Haggis later,' Johno said. 'I'll definitely need a hair of the dog to perk me up again.'

Rory paused for a second. 'Actually, tonight's a bit tricky.'

'But we always go for a drink on a Thursday.' Johno scratched his blond head. 'Wait, it is Thursday, isn't it?'

'Yeah, sorry, but something's sort of come up,' Rory said with an apologetic smile.

'No worries, we'll have all weekend to catch up.'

'I saw the police were in, questioning you,' Amelia said.

Johno scuffed the toe of his flip-flop against the loose gravel and gave Amelia a wan smile. 'Not great with a hangover from hell. I don't think I was much help, though.'

'Were they questioning you about Gus?' Gideon asked.

'A bit. They asked me a load of questions about diving equipment. I don't know if they think every diver must automatically know other divers.'

'I did think it was strange for him to be wearing a wetsuit so far from the water,' Amelia said.

'It was a dry suit,' Johno said. 'I mean, from the photos they showed me, it was definitely a dry suit he was wearing.'

'What's the difference?' Amelia asked.

'Clue's in the name. Wetsuits rely on having a layer of water in between you and the suit to keep you warm. So, when you wear them, you get wet. Dry suits are totally sealed and keep you warm from a layer of air. Depending on what the dry suit is made of dictates what you can wear underneath, if you need extra insulation or whatever. If you have a high-quality Neoprene like the one Gus was wearing you'd only need lightweight clothes under it.'

'Right. So, when would you use a dry suit rather than a wetsuit?'

'It's all down to water temperature. Normally, you can get

away with a six- or seven-millimetre wetsuit in summer here if you're surfing or paddleboarding.' He looked up at the sky. 'But despite the sunshine, the water's still very cold in the spring, this far north. A dry suit allows for a longer time in cold water so he's clearly used to being in these waters, or areas with similar temperatures, probably for scuba-diving. You don't use dry suits for surfing as they're too bulky to move around gracefully in.'

'Ah.' Amelia let this sink in. 'Did the police find his scuba gear?'

'They didn't say. They weren't exactly forthcoming. They asked to see my recent sales for that kind of gear, which isn't much. Asked about any folk who'd taken an interest in diving. I mean, I supply a few locals and I sometimes order specific items in for them, but I don't keep that kind of stock on site as it's bulky and I don't have the room in the SeaShack. It's more the touristy stuff I sell from now throughout the summer. Thing is, I couldn't supply a handy printout list of my customers. I'm not the best at admin; contacts tend to be on scraps of paper and in here.' He tapped the side of his head. 'They're setting up an incident room in the church and asked me to drop by with the information ASAP. I would have agreed to anything to get them to leave. I mean, them just being there makes you feel guilty, right?' He gave a bit of a shaky laugh.

'Especially if it's that McGregor,' Gideon said heatedly.

Johno gave them a rueful smile. 'Trouble is, as well as not being up on admin, I'm not great at tidying either. I don't even know where to begin. All this extra hassle because Gus was found with a dry suit on.' Johno sighed and pushed himself off the doorway and took the couple of steps to his car and opened the boot. Taking out a small bottle of Irn Bru, he unscrewed the top and drank thirstily from it.

Rory clapped his friend on the shoulder. 'Man, you *are*

suffering today!' He glanced into the boot and gave a chuckle as he pulled out a couple of bottles of champagne. 'You won the lottery, mate?'

Johno snatched them back in annoyance and returned them to the boot, rolling them up in a tartan picnic blanket before wedging them next to a bag.

Rory gave a chuckle. 'Oh aye! Have you got another romantic cave excursion planned? Is Maja still the lucky lady or have you moved on to one of those lassies camping up at the top field?'

'Fuck off,' Johno said light-heartedly, with more of a trace of his old humour. He slammed the boot shut. 'Right, I'll see you later. I'm going to get myself a bacon roll.' He flipped over the sign on SeaShack which said *back in five minutes*, locked the door then headed down Main Street.

'Romantic cave excursion?' Gideon asked Rory once Johno was out of earshot.

'Aye, he discovered a hidden cave not too long ago. He rows out to it in his dinghy and takes a bottle, some oysters, bit of candlelight under the stars. It seems to be a very successful seduction technique by all accounts. And the bastard won't tell me where it is!' Rory added, then laughed. Giving them a small salute-type farewell, he turned and half-jogged across the road, towards his boat.

'Was it just me who noticed Johno seemed to take the police questioning badly?' Gideon said a few moments later.

'That's what I was thinking,' Amelia agreed, squinting into the sun, watching Johno's retreating figure; shoulders hunched, head down, a beacon of bright in his Day-Glo-green shorts and pink Hawaiian shirt.

Maybe Johno was supersensitive and hated the thought of someone dying near the village, Amelia thought. Or maybe he was stressed at having to sift through his disorganised lack of filing system.

Or maybe he knew more than he was letting on.

SEVENTEEN

Leaving Gideon to browse the grocery shop for chocolate, Amelia crossed the road and went into the Whistling Haggis. There was no one waiting to be served and Amelia went straight up to the bar where Big Davey was flicking through the local paper.

'Hello Amelia, don't often see you in at this time.'

'I wanted to ask you about a dark rum; Gosling's?'

'Oh yes.' He turned and looked at the shelf behind him. 'Ah, we did have it, but I gave the bottle away. To Gus, as it happens.'

'Yeah, I saw that, I'd never seen that rum before. Is it popular?'

'Not really. We only had it in because of an old fellow who liked it, but he passed and that bottle just sat there gathering dust until the other night.'

'Does Jean sell it, or anyone else around here?'

'No, that was always a moaning point for the old guy. But he refused to buy anything from Jean's shop anyway as he said her prices were too high. Here was the only place he could get it for miles, he used to tell me.'

So, it looked like that bottle of dark rum was the one that

Gus had taken from the Whistling Haggis. Amelia wondered how it had ended up in the Hunting Lodge.

'Speaking of Gus, I don't suppose you've heard any more about what happened?'

'No, I haven't,' Davey looked up, over Amelia's head and gave a slight nod, 'but here's someone that may be able to shine a bit more light on the matter.'

Amelia turned to see Ray walk in, clearly off duty as he was wearing jeans and a T-shirt. He got up to the bar and asked Davey for a pint.

'How's it going?' Davey asked. 'Amelia was wondering if there's any more information about the case?'

'Any information that's come to light is being kept within the CID unit. They're going to set up an incident room in the church. I hung about to glean what I could and luckily that DS is a bit more forthcoming.' Ray looked around to make sure no one was listening in before carrying on in a low voice. 'She told me it was a stab wound to the chest that caused the fatality. But no sign of the murder weapon. Gus had also suffered a heavy blow to the back of the head. There was a bit of bruising and grazing around the face and knuckles to indicate he'd probably been in a punch-up earlier in the evening. They found his scuba tanks and what-not by the excavation site. I know there's been a bit of toing and froing with units in Glasgow and the Met. *And* Europol. And there's talk of a joint teams investigation, but I don't know why. Cross-border cooperation was a lot easier a few years ago. But if McGregor has any *real* insights he's certainly not sharing them with me.'

'He never was a sharer; the selfish wee shite never let us play with his fancy football when we were bairns, remember?' Davey said.

Ray gave a snort of a laugh but said nothing.

'You know the detective inspector?' Amelia said, amazed this had never come to light before.

'Aye, we all grew up here, went to the same school.'

'I had no idea!' She remembered Moira had said she knew of him from way back, but Amelia hadn't realised they'd *all* grown up together.

'Aye,' Ray said. 'We all bumped along together in school holidays. Just a couple of years between us all.'

'It's slim pickings for friends growing up in the back of beyond in the seventies,' Davey said with a wink to show Ray he was teasing. 'There was a few of us that all hung out as teenagers. A tight wee group of pals we were. Back then.'

There was a wistfulness in Davey's voice that made Amelia press a little more.

'So, who all was in your group of friends, when you were teenagers?' Amelia asked.

'Us two,' Ray said, 'Murray, Moira, Hector, Elizabeth—'

'Andy's wife, the one who left him?'

'Aye, that's her. Someone's clearly been gossiping!' Ray gave a little chuckle.

'And Cameron,' Davey said with quite an air of solemnity.

'Tragic.' Ray shook his head. 'Cameron was Moira's brother. He died.'

'I'm so sorry.'

'It was a long time ago,' Davey said. 'Cameron's death was the catalyst to us all drifting away. Well, some of us stayed.' Davey patted the wooden bar top with fondness.

'McGregor doesn't live here in Glencarlach now, though, does he?' Amelia said, sure that she'd have known if he did.

Davey shook his head. 'Nah, McGregor finished school and went to police college. And then he was off to London, Manchester, Glasgow... His parents moved to the east coast a couple of years after he left. And now he's in

Inverness, eyeing up the detective chief inspector's job, isn't he?'

'Aye, so he can interfere even more, no doubt,' Ray said under his breath before taking a deep swallow of his pint. He wiped the back of his hand across his bushy moustache to remove any beer froth.

'What did everyone else do?'

'Moira hung around for a year or so, a shell really. She was broken. Then she left to go travelling, and that was her. Hector went to some boarding school.'

'A military one,' Ray said with a raised eyebrow.

'So it was! Then he moved to London. And Elizabeth, she went away for a few months, remember?'

'Yeah, looking after a sick relative. She was away that whole summer. She was back briefly before going to college, but she couldn't stick the course and dropped out. When she returned she hooked up with Andy McAvoy and they got married and had Drew and Rory.'

'What about Andy McAvoy, Elizabeth's ex? He grew up here too, didn't he? Was he part of your group of friends?' She thought they would have been around the same age.

'No, he didn't hang around with us. He was a quiet lad. We probably scared the living daylights out of him what with all our nonsense. We pulled some crazy stunts, didn't we?' Ray said with a melancholic smile.

'Even McGregor?' Amelia said, rather disbelieving.

'I know McGregor can appear a po-faced bastard, but he's all right,' Davey said.

'You don't have to work for him!' Ray moaned into his pint glass before taking another swig. 'I suppose off duty he's fine,' he conceded.

'Now, Amelia, can I get another type of dark rum for you?'

'You know, I think I should really be getting back, but

thanks, Davey. Maybe another time... Oh, one other thing,' Amelia said to Ray. 'I couldn't help but notice there was a tarot card by Gus. It was quite soaked in blood. Do you think it was his, from a pack or do you think it was left there post mortem?'

Ray and Davey exchanged a glance. Ray cleared his throat.

'That I don't know, Amelia.'

'The card was The Devil, do you think that's significant at all?'

'As I say, I've not been privy to much information, but if it's the tarot you want to know about, Moira's the woman to ask,' Ray said.

'Okay, thanks.'

Amelia left as the two men continued reminiscing about their teenage years and headed to her next stop.

On entering the outdoors shop, Amelia was met with Runrig blasting loudly over the speakers as she almost tripped over a display of citronella tea lights and hats with netting attached to keep midgies away.

'Hello, Amelia!' Christine McGuthrie called out as she walked past carrying a bundle of rain ponchos, plonking them down on an open camping chair beside the carousel of sunglasses and sunhats. She took a step back to look at the display.

'Don't you just love the vagaries of a Scottish spring? Keeps us on our toes!' She put on her glasses, which were hanging round her neck on a gold chain. 'Now what can I get you?'

'I'm looking for some of the large three-wick citronella candles and some of the torch-type ones you stick in the ground?'

'Oh yes, midgie season is upon us! That citronella chases them away, right enough. I have a feeling I've only got those diddly wee tea lights but I'll go check my stock levels.'

Amelia glanced around the well-stocked shop. She'd

practically haunted the place when she'd first arrived in Glencarlach. Definitely a 'softy Southerner', Amelia had arrived in the village wholly unprepared for the cold temperatures and biting winds. Her wardrobe had consisted of cute little vintage numbers, a variety of kitten and high heels and only one very thin coat and a couple of chiffony-like scarves. Before long, Amelia was bulk-buying fleeces, storm-proof outerwear, walking boots, wellies and waterproof trousers. Although she'd never adorn the front pages of *Vogue* in her new get-up, she was considerably more comfortable, dry and warm; and even sported a selection of coordinating beanie hats and thermal gloves.

'How's business?' Amelia asked.

'Can't complain. It's good being an all-seasons kind of shop. Maggie in the gift shop was having a moan the other day that she's hit the quiet spell between Easter and the summer. There are only so many scented candles and slate cheeseboards the inhabitants of the village get through in a year. Although, I don't know why she's worried as she cleans up between Hallowe'en and Christmas!' She gave a laugh which turned into a bit of a cackle.

The door opened and Moira walked in. She was wearing a dark purple velvet smock-type dress which reached her ankles and her crocheted shawl was tied round her waist. Her long hair hung down over one shoulder in a loose plait and from her neck dangled a necklace of rose quartz, left natural and unpolished.

Christine popped her glasses on top of her head and gave Hamish's relative a cheery smile. 'Moira! I heard you were back!'

'You heard right. You're looking well, Christine.'

'And you haven't changed a jot since you were last here. Still living in France?'

'I am, yes.'

'What else are you up to?' Christine asked.

'This and that. I studied aromatherapy, also became a herbalist and trained as a reiki practitioner. I make my own natural beauty remedies, too.'

'And I hear you're doing Sally and Hamish's handfasting ceremony tomorrow night,' Christine said.

'Yes, I'm also a humanist celebrant.'

'So many strings to your bow! Lovely!' Christine said. 'The ceremony will hopefully take people's minds off this awful murder business. It's all very sad. I hope it doesn't spoil anyone's Beltane.'

'We're a hardy lot around here. I think we'll be fine,' Moira said.

Christine looked a little flustered. 'I didn't mean to be glib, after...'

Moira laid her hand over Christine's and smiled warmly at her. 'You're not being glib, Christine. But we are a hardy lot, despite what we've all faced over the years.'

The two women exchanged a look.

'Now, Christine, do you have any of those pressure-point wristbands to help with seasickness? I don't think the handfasting ceremony will be quite as lovely if I'm green and hanging over the side of the boat,' Moira said.

Christine gave another cackle as she went over to a wicker basket and came back with a small box.

'Lovely, thank you,' Moira said, handing over the money and dropping her purchase into one of the massive pockets in her dress.

'Amelia, I've only one of the three wickers and none of the torch ones. I'll put in an order and let you know as soon as they're here, is that okay?' Christine said a few moments later after checking in the back storeroom.

'That would be great, thanks.'

Amelia and Moira left the shop together.

Out on the street, the sun was still blazing.

'Moira, Ray mentioned you know about tarot?' Amelia said as they slowly walked along Main Street.

'I do. Fancy a reading?'

'It's not so much that I want a reading, but could you tell me the significance of a specific tarot card? Number XV, the–'

'The Devil.'

'I read that it can signify the darker side of someone's nature. Is there anything else?'

Moira nodded slowly. 'That's one very sweeping meaning. Cards are normally read in a layout, with other cards, and the interpretation comes from all of them being read together, in a sort of overview. A single card can then be picked if someone wants to go a little deeper into a meaning. Broadly speaking, The Devil means temptation and enslavement. It can involve greed of sex, food, drugs... At first glance it looks scary but, as with all the tarot, its interpretation can be taken many ways, depending on the other cards beside it. Why the interest?'

'Just something about the occult came up.'

Moira gave Amelia a curious look before saying, 'You know occult actually means hidden knowledge. There's a sensationalism that many associate with the occult, under the misapprehension that it's evil. I'll not lie, there are some that do branch away from the secret knowledge and go down a darker path and get involved with Satanism and dark arts, but that's very much the exception rather than the rule. Tarot can help offer gentle guidance.' Moira smiled. 'What are your plans now?'

Amelia looked over at the church. 'I need to pop in and see DI McGregor about something. Ray said he's setting up an incident room in the church.' Amelia knew he probably wouldn't like it if she kept the information on the bottle of rum to herself; she'd been well warned. Although how she was going to tell him without implicating herself into the breaking and entering, she had no idea!

'I'm heading that way myself,' Moira said as they crossed the road together.

The front doors to the vestry were closed and locked.

Amelia knew there was a side door that led to the little hall the parish meetings were held in and she walked around the corner. It too was locked.

Moira had headed away from the building and was crouched down by a grave which was covered with freshly placed flowers.

Moira glanced up and with a smile, beckoned Amelia over.

As Amelia approached, she read the inscription on the gravestone.

Cameron Ballantyne, 1st May 1968 – 1st May 1986.
Beloved son, devoted brother, cherished friend.

Born and died on Beltane. He'd only been eighteen.

Moira bent down to gently move one of the bunches of flowers a little and Amelia could read the Gaelic at the bottom of the headstone:

Gun robh suaimhneas sìorraidh agad.

'I thought I'd come and visit my big brother. Not that he's there.'

Amelia must have looked confused as Moira explained. 'His body was never found, but we put up a memorial stone anyway. It gave my parents a place to visit, which helped them a little, I suppose.'

They stood looking at the grave for a few moments as a breeze ruffled the petals of a bunch of golden chrysanthemums.

'The flowers are beautiful.'

'They are and that's fitting. Cammy was beautiful, inside and out.' Moira's eyes looked shiny for a moment and she cleared her throat. 'It's odd coming back after so long. I was quite anxious about how I'd feel, if I'm being honest. Especially around this time. Cammy loved Beltane because it was his birthday too. When he was a wee boy, he thought all the parades and festivities were for him because he was special.' She laughed. 'He wasn't even two years older than me and I would trail around after him in the holidays. He was always too good-natured to tell me to get lost.'

'You were lucky,' Amelia said with a smile.

'I was. He was one of those people that everyone loved. I know Ray and Davey and Elizabeth put flowers on his grave every year to mark the day. These are from Ray and Davey,' she pointed to the chrysanthemums, 'and this big one's from Elizabeth,' Moira said softly. 'It's quite magnificent, but then again, she is a trained florist.'

As well as being a stunning arrangement, Amelia thought the bouquet was also quite revealing. As Sally's maid of honour and having Stone Manor as a wedding venue, Amelia had spent quite a few hours poring over romantic flower arrangements and knew there was a lot of meaning revealed with flowers. Tulips signified love. Yellow tulips were for friendship bouquets, but the ones here were red and purple; romantic love. The bright, heavy-headed sunflowers, as well as adding a burst of colour conveyed loyalty and hope. The pretty delicate red flowers with the dark, purplish-black centres were anemones, which, if Amelia remembered correctly symbolised death and forsaken love. But most interesting of all were the tall snapdragons. Amelia would have to double-check but she was quite sure those represented discretion at a secret being kept. Elizabeth, being a florist, would surely know that.

Amelia bent down and looked at the card. It read:

Gone, but never forgotten, E, xxx

'This florist is just a few miles away,' Amelia pointed out. 'Maybe Elizabeth and Paddy haven't gone far.'

Moira peered at the card. 'That's Elizabeth's shop. Maybe she is only a few miles down the road. I'm going to give it a call as I'd really like to see her.' She sniffed and wiped away a tear.

'I'm so sorry you lost your brother so young,' Amelia said. She couldn't bear to think of anything happening to Toby. That kind of loss was unimaginable. 'Can I ask what happened to Cameron?'

'Drowned.' Moira said matter of factly before elaborating. 'Accidental death was what the death certificate said. Death by misadventure someone else said and I remember thinking that made it seem less... tragic somehow. It was his birthday and we'd all been celebrating. We'd got some vodka and cider and a bit of hash. It all got a bit hazy for me, looking back. There was a drunken argument, and I'd had far too much to drink and was sick. Elizabeth hadn't been well and wasn't drinking so she looked after me and drove me home. She'd just got her licence you see and a car, this rusted old orange Ford Fiesta, it was her pride and joy! Cammy had said he was going to celebrate all night but the others couldn't keep up with him and one by one went home.

'Anyway, the police got a call from a dog walker very late that night to say he'd seen a young lad that matched Cameron's description who was stumbling about the cliff path. He looked drunk and was shouting things and... well, when the police got to the spot they found some of his belongings and a bottle of vodka and they concluded he'd slipped and gone over. The weather had been wild that night with the wind and rain and the ground was slippy. Search parties and a lifeboat were sent out but his body was never found. He's somewhere in the bottom of the loch out there. Or more probably, was carried out to the North Atlantic.'

'I'm so sorry.'

'A few less-kind folk around here said it was suicide, but he would never have done that.' Moira sniffed and wiped a tear away. 'Oh, for goodness' sake! Look at me!' She tried to laugh away her emotion.

Amelia handed her a tissue from a pack in her bag and Moira gave her a smile of thanks. She wiped her eyes and blew her nose.

'I'm sorry if I've upset you.'

'Don't be. It's this place. At this time. There's too many around here don't want to talk about it. Our culture tends to shy away from death. We like celebrating life and renewal, like at Beltane, but we often lower our heads and pretend the other bookend of our existence isn't real. Maybe leaving this place has given me some perspective. I want to talk about Cammy. Yes, it makes me sad, but it keeps him alive in here.' Moira tapped her head. 'And in here.' She placed both hands across her heart.

EIGHTEEN

Returning to Stone Manor with Gideon, Amelia pulled into the car park and saw a mud-splattered SUV in one of the spaces.

'Maybe you have a new guest checking in,' Gideon suggested as they got out and went into the hotel.

But rather than a new arrival, Amelia found Hector Bain and Andy McAvoy sitting in the bar with Isobel, Tim and Maja.

'Gawds! You don't think he knows we broke into his old Hunting Lodge, do you?'

Amelia peered closer. 'No, it looks like they're having a meeting about the excavation site.'

'Thank goodness!' he said before limping into the kitchens to seek out Toby.

Amelia hung around in reception for the next hour or so, sifting through invoices and catching up with James.

The meeting in the bar broke up.

'Amelia Adams, isn't it!' Hector Bain boomed when he saw her, marching over. He was wearing tartan trews with a black Metallica T-shirt and a pair of sky-blue classic-clog Crocs on his feet. 'Lovely to meet you at last. Hector Bain.' He shook her hand enthusiastically, as if he was powering a water-pump handle.

'Fantastic place. I remember old Dorothea. Wonderful woman,' Hector said, referring to Amelia's beloved godmother, who she'd affectionately referred to as Dotty.

'I always thought my old man had a bit of a pash on her,' Hector continued, 'once brought her a brace of pheasants, still warm, in an attempt to woo her. She was far too sensible to give him the time of day. Kept the pheasants, though.' He laughed loudly, all the time looking round at his surroundings, his eyes drawn to the glass cupola above his head. 'Marvellous.'

'Do you remember the old girl, Andy?' Hector shouted over his shoulder.

Andy McAvoy had come out of the bar and was hovering a little bit behind Hector.

'Yes, yes, I do... She had a great spark about her.' Andy nodded as he spoke. 'Everyone wondered what would... happen to this place... but you've done a great job... you really have... yes.' Andy spoke softly, in little breathless rushes and Amelia wondered if it was a technique he'd honed over the years while trying to get a sentence out in the presence of Hector.

'Hector!'

Both Hector and Amelia turned towards the entrance to see Moira coming in.

'My God! Moira! What a sight for sore eyes you are!' Hector bounded over to her, engulfing her in a bone-crushing hug. 'You must still be doing your witchy incantations as you haven't aged a bit! Cast a spell for me next time, yes? I'm getting the dratted Bain jowls.' He slapped the bottom of his face with the back of his hand then guffawed. 'Now, what in heavens are you doing here?' he asked.

'I thought it was time I visited Glencarlach.'

'Are you staying in this wonderful hotel?'

'I am.'

'Well, we simply have to get together. All the old gang! Let's book a table here, eh? You, me, Davey, Ray, Murray. Obviously not Lizzie, though. Heard she ran off with–' He stopped then winced slightly and mouthed 'oops' as Andy looked down at his boots.

Hector turned back to Amelia.

'A table! Tonight. Eight o'clock, for five. No, make it six, you'll join me as my guest, Ms Adams.'

'I don't want to intrude on your group of friends,' Amelia said.

'Nonsense, you're coming.'

Moira laughed. 'Shouldn't we check everyone else is free first?'

Hector waved his hand dismissively. 'Of course they'll be free. Can't pass up an opportunity like this.'

Amelia had the distinct impression Hector Bain was used to getting his way.

'Andy, you'll be free to drop me off, won't you?' Without waiting for an answer, Hector turned back to Amelia.

'Wine!' he exclaimed, a finger in the air. 'We'll need *lots* of wine. Claret, if poss. That'll need a decent decant. Best open it now. And no expense spared as I'll pick up the tab!'

'Of course! Shall I get you the wine list?'

'No, I'll leave it in your capable hands, my dear. Moira! Do the honours and round them all up? Three-line whip, yes?'

He turned and winked at Amelia. 'I'd best get home and spruce myself up a bit. Hector then marched towards the door, bellowing, '*Andy*, with me.'

Moira stood grinning as they left, Andy giving them a little smile and a wave as he closed the door behind them. 'Hector hasn't changed a bit. Still a whirlwind.'

Isobel, Tim and Maja came out of the bar. Isobel's face had

two bright-red splotches at the top of her cheeks. She looked quite flustered.

'Is everything okay?' Amelia asked her.

'Yes, I think so,' Isobel said as she balanced a pile of books and folders on her hip. 'I was worried he'd want to pull the funding, but he's happy to go ahead. In fact he's given us more money to get additional helpers in, and he definitely wants to go ahead with the cultural centre.'

'You've just been Hector'd,' Moira said kindly. 'He can be quite a force of nature.'

Amelia could well imagine the old group of friends getting up to crazy stunts if Hector was in charge.

Hector had been right; everyone made it to dinner that night.

It was rather strange for Amelia to have DI McGregor in the hotel and not have him questioning her. He still looked cheerless and had an air of suspicion, but Amelia was starting to think that was just his natural demeanour.

Hector was by far the loudest of them all. He also made sure to keep everyone topped up on the red wine he'd insisted on.

'I suffer from cenosilicaphobia!' he joked to Amelia as he refilled his glass to the top. 'Fear of an empty glass of drink,' he said, then laughed.

Amelia only had one small glass of wine that she managed to keep out the way of Hector's generous top-ups.

McGregor said from the start he was on soft drinks only, in case he was called away. On hearing this, Ray also said he'd only have a couple of glasses, clearly being careful with McGregor present.

Davey and Moira had no hesitation having their glasses

regularly topped up though, and along with Hector, they got very merry throughout the meal.

The food had been a great success with Hector managing to persuade Toby to sit with them over dessert. After many thwarted attempts to leave, Amelia's brother finally managed to sneak back to the kitchen when the group left the table to go into the drawing room where the fire was crackling invitingly in the hearth.

Hector moved towards one of the wingback chairs but before he sat he raised his glass. 'I know I don't come back very often, but I'm so glad we're able to meet up. Or most of us. A toast.' He raised his glass. 'To the Watchful Wiccan.' He smiled then took a drink.

And realisation dawned on Amelia. The Watchful Wiccan wasn't someone with the surname McDrehm, it was the first letter of the forenames of a group of friends. Moira, Cameron, Davey, Ray, Elizabeth, Hector and Murray. She felt silly for not realising it earlier; it was hardly the Enigma code.

'I haven't heard that for a long time,' Ray said.

'All that feels a lifetime ago,' Moira added, gazing into the fire. 'I haven't thought about the Hunting Lodge in a long time. Do any of you ever go there?'

'No,' Davey said firmly and the others shook their heads.

Moira looked up at Amelia. 'I know you were asking about the Hunting Lodge and you mentioned the occult earlier today. We used the Hunting Lodge as a kind of den. We found a whole load of books and got a bit carried away with our Watchful Wiccan group. But looking back we were far more Enid Blyton than Illuminati! The Hunting Lodge has quite a history attached to it, a very dark one, thanks to Hector's ancestor Samuel Bain. He took it to extremes and went down a dark path. And then we all stumbled in with the naivety of youth, fooling around with things that were maybe best left alone.'

'I just wanted to get drunk and listen to music,' Ray said with a little chuckle.

'Do you think it really was cursed?' Moira asked, glancing around the group. No one answered.

'I do remember Cameron started to take it all a bit more seriously,' Davey said.

'He became quite fixated on some of the old books.' Moira looked uneasy. 'I didn't like it. It was the only thing Cameron and I ever really argued about. I didn't like him messing about with all that.'

'I don't think he properly believed in it though,' Hector said.

'Cameron brought you into it, Hector, didn't he?' Moira continued. 'It was like your own mini secret society within our secret society. And then Lizzie got involved. What was it the three of you did, Hector?'

'It was all just silly stuff, really, wasn't it?' Ray said. 'While the rest of us drank cheap cider and smoked roll-ups, you sat and read those books left by Samuel Bain. You would read parts aloud. I never understood half of it!'

Hector swirled the drink around in his glass, staring into the liquid. 'We played around with the incantations, but it all seemed a bit of a laugh. Cameron did get fixated on this resurrection and reanimation nonsense, but it was all a bit too Stephen King's *Pet Sematary* for me. I didn't really have the patience for it. Too much like hard work. It was Cameron who got the three of us those pagan robes and insisted we wear them. He'd seen a photo of Samuel Bain wearing something similar and thought it would add authenticity to what we were doing.' He paused for a moment before saying in a quiet voice, 'I thought it was nonsense back then, but do any of you think you know, that maybe sometimes those spells and what-not might have worked?' He looked up at them. 'Do you think some things *can* come back? From the dead I mean. God, I must be getting pissed.' He gave a half-hearted rendition of his usual loud guffaw.

Moira leant forward in her chair. 'What makes you say that?'

There was silence. The fire popped and crackled as everyone waited for Hector to continue.

'That night. When that young chap was murdered. I saw something.'

'If you saw something you should have informed the police,' McGregor said.

'Damn it, Murray, if I went on record with this, I'd be carted off to the funny farm. Anyway, it wasn't Gus I saw. It was something else. Some*one* else. I was with Andy. We were talking by the door before he left. And we saw... something.'

'What?'

'Oh, Goddammit. I saw a bloody pagan-robed figure, didn't I? In the exact get-up Cammy, Lizzie and I wore. When Cameron tried to channel Samuel bloody Bain and all that went before him.'

Hector's hands shook a little and he rested the brandy goblet on his knee to steady the tremor.

'He was standing midway along the drive, staring at the house. I was freaked, I tell you. I was all for going and getting my shotgun but Andy stopped me, talked sense into me. And by the time I looked back, the figure had gone. Vanished.'

That was the exact same thing that had happened to Rory, Amelia thought.

'And what do you think this means?' Moira asked.

'How the blast should I know?'

'Someone's dressing up in the pagan robes to freak you out. Or...' Davey trailed away.

'Samuel Bain's back from the dead? Or Cameron?' Hector said scathingly. 'Oh don't worry, my thoughts turned to that for a fleeting second. Of those three robes, I know mine's in the attic. I even checked to make sure. Lizzie is off canoodling somewhere with Paddy Davis so I very much doubt she'd be bothered to come back to scare poor old Hector for a joke. That just leaves...'

'His body was never found,' Moira said hollowly.

'It cannot be Cameron,' Davey said firmly. 'Where could he have been all these years, eh? Holed up in a bedsit in Inverness?'

'Or maybe he took a note out of your book and high-tailed it to France, Moira,' McGregor said.

Amelia picked up a note of bitterness in his voice and it wasn't lost on Moira, who drew him a dagger of a look.

'We all know Cammy talked about leaving,' Ray said. 'Remember the days leading up to... it all? He was acting like he had some big secret thing planned.'

'If he'd told anyone about it, it would have been you, Moira,' Murray said.

'Well, he didn't,' she snapped.

'Let's face it, there aren't many places you can just run off to these days,' Ray said.

Amelia couldn't help think of the Hunting Lodge and the fact there had been someone at least visiting the place. Could Cameron be the one smoking the cigarettes and buying Asda toilet roll? The idea was very far-fetched and she didn't want to suggest it to the group; emotions were clearly still very raw over Moira's brother.

But what if it was Elizabeth? Maybe she hadn't gone far. Was she popping back from time to time to stay at the Hunting Lodge? But why would she not want to get in touch with her sons... or maybe she had? What if Rory and Drew knew where their mother was staying?

But why would Elizabeth want to dress up in the pagan

robes and terrify her old friend and son? And what would the benefit be to murdering Gus, the archaeologist...?

Amelia felt she couldn't say anything. And it wasn't that she was averting the course of justice, or trying to hide anything. She just thought it was best to get proof before wading in clumsily with any theory.

'I know it won't be Cameron,' Moira said firmly. 'No matter how much I wish it was. And that's the torture. Because he was never found, there will always be that glimmer of hope.'

There was a lengthy silence, with everyone at a loss for what to talk about.

'Isobel told me you're giving more funding for the excavation site,' Amelia said to Hector, trying to fill the conversation void.

'I am.' Hector bobbed his head enthusiastically. 'In for a penny, in for a pound!'

'How did that all come about?' Moira asked.

'Isobel approached me. She got hold of my work address in London and asked to meet me. She'd been doing a talk at the national museum just along the road. Nervous little thing, you know. I had to really draw it out of her, that she wanted access to my land. I suppose those academics are used to jumping through hoops for peanuts and she was floored when I offered a ton of money. The cultural centre idea was mine.'

'I'm all for it. It'll be good for the local economy,' Davey said.

'To be honest, I'm quite ambivalent,' Ray said. 'As long as it doesn't cause problems in the area, I don't see anything wrong with it.'

'But it has caused problems,' McGregor said.

'A lot of the protestors are the usual suspects that like jumping on any cause,' Davey said. 'You know what it's like around here.'

'I'm torn,' Moira said. 'I like the thought of finding out more about the history but at the same time, wonder if things are best left be.'

'Is it painful, sitting on that fence?' Hector said, then laughed.

'What about you, Amelia?'

'I can see why the environmentalists are concerned but it was good listening to the points the archaeologists made. I think it's a good thing.'

'I don't know what Cameron would have made of it, to be honest,' Moira said.

'What about Elizabeth?' Amelia asked.

'She could very well have been one of the ones up at the tents with a placard,' Davey said. 'She loves a local cause.'

Hector nodded before adding, 'And although Andy has to stay neutral because of him being a local councillor, I don't think he's keen. He's high up in the wildlife committee after all.'

Moira reached over to put her glass on a table and nearly missed. 'Urgh.' She shook her head. 'My head's spinning. I blame you, Hector. You were always the one to lead us all astray. I've drunk too much and I need my bed. Goodnight.'

She stood and made her way slowly and carefully to the door, where she stopped and turned back to the group. 'Seeing as we're all here, I'm going to hold you all to doing our usual Beltane practice. In memory of Cammy.'

'No, Moira!' Davey shouted.

'What?' Ray said, aghast.

Hector gave a roar of laughter while McGregor said nothing.

'I'll be in touch,' she said with a secretive little smile before closing the door.

'Come on, I'll give you all a lift home,' McGregor said, standing.

'Thanks, but I think a walk in the fresh air will do me some good,' Davey said.

Ray looked at his watch. 'I'll take that lift, thanks. Mrs Williams will be wondering where I've got to. We always have an Ovaltine and a fig roll before bed.'

Hector stood and stretched. 'I'm fine, I'll call Andy.'

'Why don't you give him the night off?' McGregor said.

Hector looked surprised. 'He likes to keep busy. So he doesn't dwell on Lizzie, you know.'

'I'm sure he has a life outside working as your estate manager and being at your beck and call whenever you're home.'

Hector looked as if he'd never even considered this. 'I don't think he does. He doesn't seem to do anything else other than meet with the wildlife group. He's quite the workaholic. Poor man was in shock when Lizzie left him. He asked for a couple of days' compassionate leave. I said to take longer but he was adamant he didn't want to. And that was all he has ever said on the matter. I was back a couple of weeks later and he was just the same as he always was, you wouldn't have known he'd had the world ripped out from under him. The man obviously threw himself back into his work and I realised he likes keeping busy. And anyway, I need him to drive me as I have a small issue of doing it myself...'

'What? You've got a driving ban? Hector!' McGregor said with more than an air of disapproval.

'Idiot,' Davey said.

Hector blustered for a moment before saying. 'All right then, I'll take you up on your offer of–'

The door to the drawing room burst open and a visibly agitated Moira came in.

'Don't tell me this isn't a sign!' she said. She held up a brightly coloured card. 'It was on my bed.'

'What's that?' Hector squinted. 'I don't have my specs.'

Amelia could see it was a tarot card.

'The Page of Cups,' Ray read.

'Cammy always saw himself as this. He picked this card as his significator. It was his joke. He'd sign off notes to me as that. Amelia, you were asking about The Devil tarot today, why?'

'It was lying next to Gus's body.'

Moira reeled back slightly.

'Have you got your tarot cards with you?' McGregor asked.

'Of course.'

'Is this from your pack?'

'I don't know. I think so, maybe. I can go and check but it's the same ones I use and it looks as worn.'

McGregor took a breath. 'Cameron's been on your mind. If it represents him, could you have taken it out, unintentionally and–'

Moira looked furious. 'Do *not* patronise me, Murray! And did I write this unintentionally too?' She thrust a piece of paper at McGregor. 'And *unintentionally* weigh them both down with a sprig of hawthorn?' She stared him down with a belligerent thrust of her chin.

The DI looked at the note a moment before reading it aloud. '"Death is not the end. I will return".'

NINETEEN

While McGregor had a rational explanation for the tarot card being on Moira's bed, no one had any plausible ideas on how the note and hawthorn could have gotten there.

'It is not Cameron doing this. Nor is it his ghost,' McGregor said firmly.

'But you heard Hector. Cameron got right into all the occult stuff, started looking at resurrections!' Ray said. 'What if he summoned something?'

'You're all more drunk than I thought,' McGregor said in disbelief. 'Do you hear yourselves?'

Amelia decided to speak up. 'You all say how lovely Cameron was. Do any of you think he was the type of person to be vindictive like this or scare someone when he was alive?'

Everyone unanimously agreed he wasn't.

'And he wouldn't want to try and kill a young archaeologist either,' Davey added. 'Even if he did want to protect the Pictish site.'

'It wasn't Cameron who was wearing the pagan robes and freaking out Hector,' McGregor said. 'Nor was it he who jumped out and scared Rory McAvoy into driving nose first into a ditch. And it *wasn't* Cameron who killed Gus. It was a very real person that committed murder.'

He ran his hand through his hair, looking troubled, before saying resignedly, 'Gus, the victim, was known to us. And it isn't in relation to pagan antics. We're currently liaising with police abroad and that's all I'm saying on the matter and none of the information I've told you leaves this room.' He looked around at everyone and settled his gaze on Amelia.

'What we need to look at is why someone wants us to *think* Cameron is back and floating about in pagan robes,' McGregor continued. 'And to work out who left these in your room, Moira. Amelia? Who's staying here?'

'The other archaeologists.'

'Isobel, Tim and Maja.' He nodded. 'And?'

'Betty.'

'Betty would *not* be behind this,' Moira said.

'And just Gideon and myself.'

McGregor strode to the door and opened it. Isobel, who was on the other side jumped back and gave a little start of surprise.

She looked at everyone, her face reddening. 'Sorry, I didn't mean to eavesdrop. I wasn't sure if this was a private party or other guests.' She held a couple of books up. 'I thought I'd read for a bit before bed.'

'Have you been here, in Stone Manor, all evening?' McGregor asked.

'No. I've been at the Whistling Haggis. I just got back. With Tim and Maja. They've gone up to their rooms,' she said, her eyes wide.

'Aye,' Davey said. 'I do remember they booked a table for tonight.'

'Have you seen anyone else around the hotel?' McGregor asked again.

Isobel shook her head. She looked from him to Hector to Davey, then Ray and seemed unable to speak.

'Come on, leave the poor lass alone,' Moira said. 'I think we all need to sober up and get some sleep.'

McGregor looked as if he was going to say something else but then thought better of it and the little party left to go home, with Moira going back upstairs again, promising to lock her door, after rejecting McGregor's offer to search her room.

'Were they talking about someone in pagan robes?' Isobel asked when it was just her and Amelia.

'Yes, Gideon saw someone in our grounds wearing them a few hours before Gus was found. Hector Bain also saw someone wearing them outside his house that same night.'

'Oh, I see.' Isobel looked worried. 'Do they know who it is?'

'No.'

'Do they want the person in the robes to hand themselves in?'

'Well, he didn't say, but it would probably be useful to their enquiry.'

'Right. Um, the police allowed me back into Gus's room, they're finished going through it. Someone will be coming to collect his personal belongings.'

'We can store his luggage until then.'

'Thank you. Thing is... I don't suppose you've come across his notebook anywhere? It has a bright-yellow glossy cover.'

'No, sorry, I haven't seen it.'

Isobel looked disappointed.

'Is it important?'

'It's not the end of the world if I don't get it but it would be useful to have. Gus always kept a really thorough record of his findings and breakdown of the day's work as well as his thoughts and random intuitions. It wasn't at the site, so I assumed it would be in his room, but it wasn't.'

'I'll keep an eye out for it.'

'Thanks. It's a little frustrating as he was really excited by this potential second phase but he didn't want to share anything further with Tim or I until he had done a bit more research. We saw him head off with a metal detector at times. It's not really an official tool for archaeologists, more just for amateurs, but Gus still used it. He liked taking it random places to see what he could find. I'm sure he would have noted it in his book though.'

'Could he have told Maja?'

'Ah, no. He never really took her seriously or valued her opinions. Oh, I mean, they got on well enough,' Isobel added hurriedly. 'They even had a bit of a thing at one point. But no, Gus was very ambitious. And not just in archaeology. He liked to go off and do his own thing. I had to remind him on more than one occasion that we were part of a team.'

She gave a sad little shrug then looked down at the books she held.

'This was in Gus's room, but it's from your library.' Isobel handed Amelia a large book on the history of the area. 'I haven't been able to face going back... there.'

'I understand, don't worry, I'll return it.'

'Thank you. Right, I think I'll actually just go up to bed, after all. I need to be up early tomorrow to send some emails, then get up to the site.'

They said goodnight and Amelia walked round to the library then paused a moment at the door. Isobel wasn't the only one a little reticent to enter. The police tape had gone and Amelia knew fine well there was no body... but she still braced herself before entering.

Amelia's eyes were drawn to the spot where Gus had lain. There nothing to indicate the tragedy as a professional cleaning team had been in and worked wonders at removing the bloodstain and all traces of the SOCOs' presence. Despite all that, Amelia still hurried past the spot.

Before returning the book to the shelf, Amelia noticed pages had been bookmarked. She turned to the first of the little neon Post-it notes.

Gus had highlighted chapters on the abbey. Another sticky note marked information on the Pictish stones. Amelia also found a receipt from the village grocery store nestled in the centre of those pages. It was for a selection of confectionary, beer, bread and tinned food. There was writing on the back and she turned it over. It was a handwritten list of dates, starting from the end of March. The first four had been scored through. The fifth date listed was Tuesday just past. The day of, or just before Gus had been killed. The next date on the list was for Monday, 2nd May.

She put the list in her pocket and removed the bright little markers. There was a third bright-pink Post-it. This chapter was about the whisky distilleries in the area. Maybe Gus had been hoping to visit a local one.

Always interested in whisky, Amelia skim-read the article. Published nearly forty years previously, it needed updating as at least one distillery mentioned had been mothballed since publication, whilst another had been recently set up.

There was also an interesting little aside; an abbreviated history about the excise board that was set up in 1707 as part of the Treaty of Union which was seen as a way that the English could interfere with Scottish matters by taking extra tax on whisky production. Amelia read that, as a result, hundreds of illicit stills went into production. These whiskies were of far greater quality than anything made under the eyes of the excisemen and very much in demand, with even George IV preferring non-licenced Glenlivet. Officers of the excise board were employed but had a difficult time policing the hostile members of the public. Amelia could quite see that! She continued to read that these officers were often kidnapped and held hostage so they couldn't testify against illicit distillers. Those officers that weren't too scrupulous were happy to take bribes to turn a blind eye. This went on until 1823 when the Excise Act came into being. This new act cut duty and made the export market to England more attractive. The number of licenced distilleries rose, production of whisky trebled and illicit distilleries went into decline.

Amelia smiled. Her late godmother also loved whisky and had often remarked she could taste the history in every drop.

Under the passage was a small black-and-white photo of an area of coast, and a description underneath, *the rugged coastline of north-west Scotland hides many inlets which proved ideal for smuggling illicit whisky to waiting boats.*

Amelia had been in Glencarlach long enough to get to know many of the residents whose families went back generations and she could well imagine a few being embroiled in illicit whisky smuggling.

She closed the book and was putting it back in the gap on the shelf when she noticed a slim booklet on the Bain estate.

Taking the little book with her, Amelia headed to her tiny office. Settling down she opened up her laptop. But instead of working, she fired up a search engine and typed in *Samuel Bain...*

———

'Wow! Your office seems to have changed into CSI Glencarlach!' Gideon said a couple of hours later when he poked his head round the door.

Amelia looked up. She'd pinned up the receipt with the list of dates and then gone to town with a pack of sticky notes and most of the wall was covered in bright little squares which she'd scribbled questions she still had no answers for. She'd also stuck a selection of pins into the plaster, with strands of coloured wool connecting events and people as well; so many it resembled a map of the London Underground.

Looking at it made nothing any more definite and frustratingly seemed to create more questions.

'I've been doing a little bit of research about the Hunting Lodge,' Amelia said. 'Remember that quote about Boleskine that was written on the wall? It's to do with a man called Aleister Crowley. He was part of the Hermetic Order of the Golden Dawn which was founded in 1888, before going on and forming the religion Thelema in the early 1900s.'

'That sounds very hippyish.'

'It was actually esoteric and based on occult spiritual philosophy.' She clicked on a Wikipedia tab on the computer and a selection of symbols popped up. 'Recognise these?' They were the same symbols that had been drawn on the Hunting Lodge wall.

'I do! So, this Crowley owned the Hunting Lodge?'

'No, he bought Boleskine House on the banks of Loch Ness. It was built on the grounds of a church and a cemetery which dated back to the tenth century. But it turns out Hector's ancestor Samuel Bain was obsessed with Crowley.

She turned to a page of the Bain estate booklet and showed Gideon an old photograph. 'This is Samuel Bain.'

'Well, he'd certainly cut a dash around these parts!'

Hector's ancestor was wearing an ankle-length fur coat over silk harem pants displaying a bare chest. Although the photograph was old and grainy, he was clearly standing outside the Hunting Lodge.

Gideon peered at the photo. 'What's that on his head?'

'Looks like a turban or towel or something.'

'He looks quite fierce.'

'Possibly high on opium or some other drug; I'm pretty sure that's a hookah in his hands.' Amelia handed Gideon her magnifying glass and he studied the image in closer detail.

'Anyway, Aleister Crowley over in Boleskine planned to do the Abramelin ritual. It was a six-month rite that was meant to bring forth his guardian angel after first summoning the twelve kings and dukes of hell.'

Gideon pulled a face of revulsion.

'Evidently, he didn't complete it, but neither did he catch and send back the spirits he'd already released and it's alleged that they remain, to this day, haunting Boleskine House and its grounds, leading locals to believe the entire area is cursed.'

'Crikey! You think Samuel Bain tried it too? Here in Glencarlach?'

'Possibly. And I think that same ritual, or something similar was tried again in the late eighties by the group that called themselves the Watchful Wiccan.'

'That was written on the wall too!'

'Yup, and it was a group that included Moira, Davey, Ray, McGregor and Hector.'

'What do you think would happen if someone successfully completed this Abracadabra Melon ritual?' Gideon asked, looking quite unsettled at the notion.

'I'm guessing nothing good.'

TWENTY

Moira paced her hotel bedroom, fluctuating between being incensed with anger and tingling with fear.

The tarot card and note left on her bed had freaked her out as had the hawthorn. As well as symbolising hope, faith and beauty, the plant was also said to offer a gateway into the faerie realm.

She didn't fancy entering any such realm and she sure as hell didn't want anything slipping from it, into her world.

And then Amelia said a tarot card had been left beside Gus.

Did this mean Moira was a target? Or a suspect?

If someone was trying to get inside her head and make her think she was going mad, they were well on their way to making it a success.

As soon as she'd come back up to her room Moira had looked through her pack. With great relief she saw the Page of Cups was still there. McGregor had removed the one left in her room alongside the note, to keep as evidence. Evidence of what, she had no idea. She also checked to make sure The Devil card was still in her pack. It was.

Placing the cards back in their silk cover, she fleetingly

wondered about doing a quick reading for herself but she had no real inclination to turn to them for assistance. She didn't want to look at the illustrations and to decipher the meanings within. Not when she knew whoever had left the cards had the same images to look at. Did they think there was a link between them because of this? She reminded herself that the pack she used was universally popular, but she didn't feel very reassured.

Cameron had used the same design.

No!

She balled up her fists and pressed them into her eye sockets, trying not to remember their argument.

Cammy had tried to convince her of the deeper-realm magic, citing Samuel Bain's old books as evidence. He wanted her to read them and understand.

He'd told her he'd show her and then she'd believe him.

Was this him exacting his promise?

Moira climbed into bed, pulling the duvet up, over her head.

Surely the amount of wine she'd consumed would ensure she'd sleep a dreamless sleep. She closed her eyes, hoping Cammy didn't visit her tonight. Neither did she want the recurring tangible visions of the suffocatingly cold damp earth, the silver dagger glinting in the moonlight, nor the woman in white standing in the road with her hair over her face.

She especially didn't want to see the woman in white.

TWENTY-ONE

It turned out the eve of the eve of Beltane was an unofficial holiday for Glencarlach.

Amelia was not surprised to see the Whistling Haggis crammed with locals when she and Jack rolled up on the Friday evening. Having sent off his novel to his publisher, Jack was in a jubilant mood and suggested heading to the pub for drinks. Amelia had caught Jack up with her recent findings on the walk from the Gatehouse.

'Even if it had been used for occultism, are you telling me someone actually summoned demons?' Jack scoffed as they waited at the bar to be served. 'It's a load of nonsense. Dukes and kings from hell? Seriously?'

'I agree. But clearly the same thing that attracted Samuel Bain to that world held the same fascination for a bunch of teenagers decades later.'

'I know there was a resurrection of that kind of thing in the eighties and nineties; *Satanic panic*. Over in the States parents were seriously concerned about these kinds of antics. They thought Devil worship was linked to heavy metal music and role-playing games and America's youth was doomed and on the brink of unleashing hell. Maybe it was less so over here, but get a small community like Glencarlach, which is already steeped in history with a few spooky ghost stories attached, and I can imagine it wouldn't take much to start the superstitious stuff again. And maybe people here are so conditioned into fearing the Hunting Lodge, that rather than question anything, they clam up and don't talk about it, which perpetuates the superstition and fear surrounding it.'

'Moira said she and Cameron disagreed on his dabbling in the darker stuff. She also said they all argued the night Cameron died, but she didn't go into specifics so I don't know if it was about that or something else.'

'I doubt anyone would want to talk about it. Imagine if the last memory you have of someone is having an argument over who gets the last beer, or over a girl?'

Amelia agreed.

Their conversation was interrupted by a commotion at one of the tables as someone shouted out. The bar went quiet as all attention turned to Isobel who had jumped to her feet. She was sitting at a table with Tim, Maja, Drew and Johno.

Drew was sitting with his arms raised, looking indignant. 'I only touched your knee, for God's sake. You don't need to make such a fuss.'

'Don't, it's... disgusting,' Isobel said, looking distressed.

'Oh my God, overreacting much?' Drew protested.

Tim stood up, towering over Drew. 'Maybe she didn't want her knee to be touched,' he said in a low voice.

'Come on! I was just flirting, there's no need to freak out,' Drew protested as he stood up. 'Fine, I'll go somewhere else.'

'Oh dear, I hope Lily doesn't find out Drew's been trying it on with someone else,' Jack said as they watched Drew take his pint and move over to a table of his friends, glancing back at Isobel in annoyance.

Especially if it caused another row between the couple, Amelia thought.

As the evening wore on, the Whistling Haggis became quieter and Jack and Amelia managed to get a table by the fire.

'I think it's time we spoke to the one person bound to know about the Hunting Lodge,' Amelia said, giving Jack a nudge.

She gestured over to the bar at Hamish's grandad, Archie McDonald, who was sitting in his usual spot; third bar stool in from the left. He was chatting to Wee Davey who was working behind the bar.

'Why don't I go buy him a drink, it might loosen his tongue,' Jack said.

Amelia watched as he went and ordered some drinks with Wee Davey whilst exchanging a few words with Archie before the older man slowly got down off his bar stool and made his way over to Amelia, carrying his pint and a double whisky as Jack followed.

'Thank you for the drink. Jack asked if I'd come join you,' Archie said, sitting at their table.

Amelia was very fond of Archie. Many decades before, he'd had an affair with Amelia's late godmother, Dotty. It was only on unravelling the mysteries of Stone Manor and unearthing hidden letters did Amelia realise how much the weather-beaten farmer had meant to her godmother.

'You don't mind if we talk, do you?' she asked him.

'Not at all. I hear you were asking about the Hunting Lodge a couple of nights ago.'

'How did you know?'

The old man raised an eyebrow. 'Word gets around. I like to keep my ear to the ground.' He tapped a finger against the side of his nose then let out a hearty laugh. 'Ach, I ken nothin' of the sort. Moira told me you've been asking in here. And Davey got in a bit of a tizz.'

'It seems no one wants to talk about that place.'

'Aye, well there's nothing like a bit of Devil-worshipping, suspicious deaths, and suicide to make folk clam up.'

'There really *was* Devil-worshipping?'

'Or Satanism, if you prefer to call it that.'

'And Samuel Bain did commit suicide there?' Amelia asked.

'Why don't you let me tell you the story and I'll come to that in due course.'

'You're not going to warn me off asking questions?'

Archie gave a little chuckle. 'I can imagine the good that would do! You may not be a blood relation to Dotty, but you are as near as damn it the same person,' he said with a wink. 'I could never tell her what to do either.'

Amelia smiled in gratitude. 'So, what can you tell me?'

'Oh, I can tell you many things, but what you care to listen to is what's important,' he said rather cryptically before pausing to take another swallow of his pint. 'Ah, I sometimes think it's only stories and nostalgia that hold me together now.' He set his glass down. 'Right, more pertinently, what is it you want to ask?'

'Why are so many people frightened of the place? I read about Samuel Bain but it all sounds a bit far-fetched to still be scared so long after he was there. And I don't want to question Moira and the others too much.'

Archie sat back slightly. 'It's still a raw subject for them. Let me give you a wee back story on the place. Back in the day, that bit of land the Hunting Lodge was on was part of the old Brown estate. Now, at the point my story begins, about 1740-ish, or thereabouts, the Browns had farmed the land for generations, probably from when the abbey was newly built and smelt of fresh paint,' he said, then chuckled. 'Anyways,' Archie continued, 'let me set the scene for you both. My family, the McDonalds, and the Browns had had history for decades. Thick as thieves one minute, cursing each other the next. Even in the times of so-called friendship, we McDonalds slept with one eye open because the Browns could turn on a sixpence and stab us in the back if the wind as much as changed direction. Frenemies, you young ones would say nowadays.'

A log shifted on the fire and Archie leant in closer to the table, inviting Amelia and Jack to do the same.

'I want you to picture the scene. As I said, it was 1740-ish. Or thereabouts.' He swept his hand dramatically across the table, looking out at an imaginary horizon. 'It was a snell night. The wind howled, the sea squalled and only the brave or the foolish ventured out. But there was a card game to be played. Possibly at this very table–'

'But the Whistling Haggis has only been here since 1795,' Jack pointed out.

Archie gave an exasperated sigh, clearly annoyed at the interruption to his storytelling. 'Maybe the pub before this one was situated in this very spot a half century or so before.'

'Okay. Sorry,' Jack said, taking a sip of whisky.

'Where was I, ah yes, the card game. Now, old Duncan Brown and my ancestor, Shuggie McDonald, were both the competitive sort. Stubborn men, neither liked to back down and as the night wore on and the storm gathered and battered at the shutters, the card games inside became as tempestuous as the weather. Many of the other men dropped out and went home but as neither the Browns nor the McDonalds were quitters, the games continued, with the stakes getting high. The air was thick with the peat fire and the men thick with ale and whisky. And neither the spirits they were drinking nor the gambling were exactly legal at that moment but it was no night for excisemen or the like to be checking up and so the drink was consumed as they continued to play the Curse of Scotland–'

'The what?' Amelia and Jack said in unison.

'Poker was still a few decades away from being invented,

you see. Roulette was popular too but it was cards that ole Shuggie liked. Especially playing the Curse of Scotland or Pope Joan as it's sometimes known. It's when the nine of diamonds is the cursed card no one wants. Anyway, what they were playing is of no relevance, it's what happened next that's the crucial part to my story, if you'll be gracious enough to let me finish.'

'Sorry, Archie,' Jack said.

'Aye, so Duncan Brown thought his luck was in but he'd lost all his money so he bet the only thing he had left, well, apart from his wife, but no one would have wanted to have won that sour-faced ole witch; Duncan bet three acres of land. Now my ancestor, Shuggie, he played his hand with a flourish, so it's said, and Duncan lost. Always a sore loser, Duncan tipped over the table in a rage and marched out. Many feared he'd top himself in the storm rather than pay his debts. But the Devil always looks after his own and Duncan survived the night and had to keep his word as there was a room full of witnesses; drunk they may have been, but they remembered. Shuggie was so delighted with his cards and the thought of getting one over on ole Duncan that he never thought to discuss the finer points o' the bet. Right enough, Duncan signed over three acres, but not the lovely fertile grassy land that Shuggie expected. Oh no. Duncan handed over the three acres the abbey and the Pictish site fell on. The rest of it was a scrag-end of land, not fit for grazing and too close to the cliff face, where many a sheep had fallen to their death if a strong wind picked up. Oh, the air was blue then, let me tell you, but technically, Duncan had kept to his word.'

'So, if it was your ancestor, how does the land belong to Hector Bain?' Amelia said.

'I've still got a bit of my story to be going on with. Now, although this land seemed to be just a bit of remote and unusable craggy rock with an ancient graveyard attached, old Shuggie wasnae daft and built a wee cottage up there, nothing more than a but 'n' ben.' He paused and looked at Jack. 'That's a wee hoose of two rooms, aye?'

Jack nodded that he followed.

'Ole Shuggie managed to make a fine little earner from it too. In such a remote spot that no one ventured out to, he stored a load of illicit whisky, that got smuggled off down a hidden path to a secret cove where it was picked up by small boats and taken south. Aye?'

'Aye. I mean yes,' Amelia said.

'So, as I said, the Browns and McDonalds were linked through generations and Duncan and Shuggie each had their own vices, which cost them dearly in the end. With ole Duncan's fondness for cards, he managed to gamble away most of his land. Lost his livelihood and then no one wanted to marry into the family, bunch o' scoundrels and sheep rustlers the lot of them. The line died out in the 1920s and rumours were rife that half of them were inbred by the end.

'Poor Shuggie, his problems stemmed from too much bevvy.' Archie mimed a drinking motion. 'Drunk most of the time, he drank away the lucrative profits from the smuggling and ended up having to sell on most of his land to keep the bailiffs away. Fortunately, he had two other brothers who weren't as fond o' the drink. They worked hard and carried on the McDonald name. With no family of his own Shuggie had no heirs to pass his land on to and he ended up selling everything he owned. Most of it to his canny brothers. He kept that piece of land for his smuggling as long as he could though. But sell it, he had to. Not to his brothers, mind. They didn't want anything to do with illegal shenanigans.'

'So he sold it to the Bain family.'

'That he did. And word is when he sold it, he spat on the ground and said it was cursed. I think the curse was more his weakness for the booze, but well, it makes for a good story.'

'And it was the Bain family who built the Hunting Lodge?'

'A century or so later, yes. And very quickly moved the family black sheep, Samuel Bain, into it, to keep him well away from the rest of the clan who stayed in Gull Point. And that's when the bad things started.' Archie gave Amelia and Jack a shrewd look. 'I ken you think we're backwater bumpkins and scared of folklore, but you see, it's not just a bit of superstitious mumbo-jumbo that's connected with that place. When Samuel Bain moved into the house, things changed. The place up there became evil and that very evil has clung to the brick and mortar ever since. It's hard to erase a legacy like that.'

'So there really *was* Devil-worshipping going on?' Amelia said, looking at Jack. 'Way back to the 1900s.'

Archie nodded.

'And was it Samuel Bain who committed suicide?'

'Aye, he wasnae right upstairs.' Archie tapped his temple. 'He was evidently a fine-looking man, clearly had money; a good catch by all accounts. He married a local lass but she ran off not long after the ink was dry on the wedding register. She told stories of him doing these strange rituals, trying to summon the Devil. He'd wander about in pagan robes, spouting all sorts of weird things. Friends of Bain visited from time to time to help him out with these practices. As a result, folk stayed away and being on his own for long periods of time, Samuel went stranger and more reclusive, eventually even his family had nothing to do with him. He couldn't keep any staff. They left after mere days of working for him. And it didn't look good when a stable boy was found, drained of blood it was said. That's when the rumours of the poor lad being a human sacrifice started.'

'Surely he'd be arrested.'

'The Bain family covered it up with money.' Archie raised a sceptical eyebrow.

'It has been said that when the wind blew right, his chanting and drumming could be heard down in the village. Locals spoke of seeing a beast with glowing red eyes on their land and next morning some of their livestock would be missing. Some of the heads of the animals were stuck on spikes around the boundary of the Hunting Lodge's property and bloodied symbols smeared on trees and the front of the lodge. If people hadn't been scared away before, they were now.'

Archie paused to take another swallow of his pint. Amelia looked at Jack. Animals on spikes! Just like the squirrel they'd discovered.

Archie shook his head as he continued with his story. 'Most around here believed Samuel Bain could put the evil eye on people. Anything bad happening was laid at his door. Milk turning sour, a fever going around the village, a poor crop yield, it was Samuel Bain to blame, said the village folk. After a particularly brutal winter, the men of the village went up to banish the demons. They made sure Samuel Bain was inside the house and the villagers stood around the Hunting Lodge while the minister read from the Bible. A short while later, Samuel walked up behind them, bold as you like. He told them bricks and mortar couldn't contain him, that he was magic and could shapeshift anywhere. The men all fled, terrified he was the Devil and would be able to appear in their homes and kill them in their beds.

'A month or so later, a smaller, braver group went up to see him. I don't know what they planned to do but I'm guessing it wasn't for a cosy chat. And that's when they saw him, from the big front windows; hanging from the ceiling. Been dead a few days. That was in 1905. They found a note that said he'd put a curse on the house and the land and although his flesh was dead, his spirit would continue to haunt the area and he'd return one day to get his revenge.'

Amelia shivered as she thought of the note left on Moira's bed. *Death is not the end. I will return.*

'The group, just to be sure, set fire to the stables. Oh, don't worry, there were no horses in it. They were about to burn the Hunting Lodge down when someone from the big house, one of Bain's staff, shooed them away. I do wonder if it wouldn't maybe have been a good thing if that house had gone up too.'

'What happened then?' Amelia asked.

'I don't think anyone lived there again, not properly. Someone thought to sell it but there were no buyers. In the early eighties some yank was over, chasing his family's British ancestors, you know the way Americans do. Anything older than fifty years is history to them.' Archie paused and glanced at Jack. 'No offence.'

Jack raised his hands to show none was taken.

'But he ended up pulling out of the sale, said he had a bad feeling about the place. And then it sat, empty, until Moira and Cameron and Hector and all the others decided to use it as a den. Smoking and drinking obviously, but then they started with the old occult nonsense too. Thought they were wide. Hector and Cammy even ran around with the same pagan robes Samuel Bain did. They were all just daft kids. And then, after Cameron died, Hector's dad got angry. Told them they should never have meddled in the occult. He paid a lot for his son's name to be taken out of any kind of link in the papers and sent Hector off to military school.'

Wee Davey came over at that point. 'That's me closing,' he said as he gathered up the empty glasses from the table.

'This is what you do on a night off from Stone Manor?' Amelia said, standing up and putting on her jacket.

'No rest for the wicked. I like it and it gives Dad a bit of time off,' Wee Davey said, taking the empties to the bar.

Archie stood up, popping his cap on his head. 'Does that answer some of your questions?'

'It does. Thank you, Archie.'

The three of them left, calling out a goodnight to Wee Davey who was wiping down the bar.

Archie made his way along Main Street as, arm in arm, Amelia and Jack walked along the lane and onto the Stone Manor driveway in companionable silence as Amelia mulled over everything Archie had said. She wasn't just dwelling on Samuel Bain. Amelia was thinking about Shuggie's house that was built within the grounds of what became the Hunting Lodge. She also thought of the information on whisky that Gus had been reading. What if the archaeologist hadn't been planning on visiting a distillery, but was interested in finding an old smuggling route? It could explain his presence in the Hunting Lodge and why he had scuba gear with him.

Amelia stopped walking. 'What are you thinking?'

Jack also stopped walking and turned to face her. 'I think that now I've sent off my book there's no reason to be staying in different places anymore. I'm sure Gideon could cope one night if you stayed in our Gatehouse.'

Amelia stood on her tiptoes and kissed Jack.

'I think that's a great idea. And what do you think about what Archie was saying?'

'That he should write a book on the history of this place? Or have his own television show? Come on, let's get inside, it's almost midnight, or should I say the witching hour!' He gave a deep booming, horror movie-like laugh.

'Oh don't!' Amelia playfully slapped his arm, but then she paused, cocking her head to the side.

'What is it?' Jack asked.

'Probably my imagination playing tricks on me, making me think I can hear things!'

They stood and listened. For a moment all Amelia could hear was the wind rushing through the leaves. But then, the wind died down momentarily and there was a faint drum beat to be heard.

'Okay, I hear something too,' Jack agreed.

Amelia looked longingly at the Gatehouse, where fleecy pyjamas and their bed awaited them.

'At least we're too far from the Hunting Lodge for it to be the ghost of Samuel Bain. Come on, let's go check it out.'

They crossed the drive and jumped down the verge towards the dense trees and followed the noise.

After a couple of minutes Amelia stopped and slightly turned to the right. 'Look, over there, is that a light?'

Jack peered through the trees. 'Looks like it. Possibly a fire? Maybe people out camping?'

They headed towards the noise of the drum. As the trees thinned slightly and they got nearer a clearing they could see a fire blazing and smell the wood smoke.

'Is that people dancing?' Amelia whispered as they got as close as they dared, crouching behind a large fallen tree trunk to remain hidden.

'And singing!' Jack agreed. Five figures stood around the fire, three with their backs to Amelia and Jack, one was hitting a large drum. There was a lot of laughter. A woman stood on the other side of the fire, facing the other figures, her long hair flying about her head in a frenzied fashion as she began to whirl round, her dark dress swirling like a spinning top at her knees.

'That's Moira!' Amelia whispered, as the woman momentarily stopped dancing to take a swig from what looked like a bottle of whisky. She staggered a little, then bent over, laughing a deep husky laugh. It was definitely Moira.

'Who is she with?' Jack said quietly. The other figures looked as if they were wearing long tunic-style tabards held with rope around their waists. Amelia guessed by their build they were men.

At that moment, one of the men broke away and walked around the fire to stand next to Moira, and Amelia let out an involuntary gasp. Whoever it was had the most hideous face.

Then Amelia realised it was a Green Man mask, seconds before the owner pushed it up to sit on the top of their head, to take a swig from the bottle that Moira passed to him.

Detective Inspector McGregor.

TWENTY-TWO

'Were they naked?'

Amelia nearly choked on her coffee. 'What?'

Gideon leant forward and repeated his question. 'Were they naked? You tell me that Moira and McGregor, and probably Davey, Ray and Hector, were dancing around the fire at midnight and I'm imagining naked pagan goings on! I'm not being weird!' He looked to Toby for backup.

'They were fully clothed. Seeing them dancing around like that was weird enough,' Jack said, clearly quite discomfited at Gideon's suggestion.

The four of them were in the Stone Manor kitchen while Amelia regaled Gideon and her brother with what she and Jack had gleaned from Archie the night before and then seen going on in the woods.

Having left Ben to take over the Stone Manor breakfasts, Toby plonked down a plate with a selection of pastries between them.

'It was quite funny,' Jack conceded, selecting a pain au chocolate.

'Made me see DI McGregor in a whole new light. He seems almost human!' Amelia added.

Gideon gave a shudder. 'Seeing them cavorting naked would have probably sent me over the edge.' He dipped the corner of a croissant in his espresso and ate it, chewing thoughtfully before saying, 'But what if it isn't a bunch of middle-aged folk reliving their youth? What if all this is more sinister? With all this talk about Satanism, what if we've found ourselves in a real-life *Wicker Man* situation?'

'Oh God,' Toby said quietly with a groan and lowered his head onto his folded arms on the table. 'We haven't.'

'But there was a policeman in that film, wasn't there?' Gideon continued.

'Yes. Although the policeman character that Edward Woodward played in the original film ended up being the sacrifice,' Jack pointed out.

'And last night it looked like McGregor was more the sacrificee!' Gideon said excitedly.

'Whoa!' Toby looked up. 'No one here has been sacrificed inside a large burning effigy!'

'That we know of!' Gideon said shrilly. 'What if Gus was the original victim? And maybe it was discovered that he didn't fit the criteria of sacrifice. Didn't they have to come willingly? Be a virgin? Obviously something didn't meet the conditions!'

Gideon dunked more of his croissant into his espresso, so fiercely the dark coffee spurted out onto the table.

'And here's us trusting DI McGregor, when really, he's going to turn and murder us all!' Gideon narrowed his eyes. 'And if we carry on along the *Wicker Man* line of thinking, is the whole of Glencarlach involved?'

'I'm finding it difficult enough to process pagan fire rituals and Wiccan magic in the Hunting Lodge without adding a horde of murderous occult villagers into the mix,' Jack said gloomily. 'And didn't the locals get upset with that Samuel Bain person because he *was* dabbling in the occult?'

'Maybe he started a trend. His own little group of acolytes.' Gideon brandished his half-eaten croissant at Jack. 'Maybe it's to do with him cursing everyone and promising to come back. Maybe every year he returns and drags another into his hell army?'

'*Maybe* we all need to take a little step back from flinging these fanciful theories about?' Toby suggested.

Gideon shook his head. 'If the local police force can't be trusted, it's down to Amelia to work out what's happening.'

Amelia was about to protest that that was quite a responsibility when he added, 'You're the crime-fiction fan. What is it Hercule Poirot always says about working it all out?'

'I need to use my little grey cells?'

'Yes! I'm not going to feel safe until the murderer is found and arrested.'

'Maybe we shouldn't be in that much of a hurry to find a permanent house around here,' Jack said.

'Quite!' Gideon said, his nostrils flaring slightly as he got more worked up. 'If you're moving away, Toby and I are coming with you! As the relative newcomers we're at risk. Is Jean Maddox hiding a nefarious streak and plans on poisoning us with some contaminated Pot Noodles? Is Big Davey going to lock us in his cellar? Oh God, and because of my injury, I'm an easy target as I can't run away if they start chasing me through the streets with pitchforks!' Gideon started hyperventilating.

Toby put out a hand to rest it reassuringly on Gideon's arm. 'No one is going to chase us or lock us in a cellar. And I don't recall ever seeing a pitchfork anywhere around here.'

'All that fire stuff we saw last night is a bit weird, but let's face it, Glencarlach is kinda quaint,' Jack said. 'Pagan Beltane rituals seem strange to us, but it's just something perfectly innocent and usual for here.'

'I'll remind you of that when we're bound and gagged and feeling the flames tickling our feet,' Gideon said.

'Do you think Betty is also involved?' Amelia said, winking at Toby.

'If she is,' Gideon said grimly, 'you can bet she'll have a sweet little anecdote about a time she had afternoon tea with Charles Manson where they dropped some LSD before going on a Satan-inspired killing spree.'

With Toby using the hotel Jeep to ferry the bulk of the food over to the trestle tables set up at the harbour wall, Amelia took the golf cart, loading it up with the last of the supplies her brother needed.

'I'm so glad I can now properly enjoy Beltane,' Jack said as he settled into the front with Amelia.

'You might not be saying that when you find out Toby may accidentally trigger an orgy!' Gideon said from the back seat.

'What!' Jack looked aghast.

Amelia rolled her eyes at Gideon's over-dramatics. 'Toby did some thorough research about Beltane, wanting to keep true to the rituals. Because Beltane's about celebrating life and fertility a lot of the traditional foods are aphrodisiacs, like almonds, asparagus, figs and oysters. There's also a beef and goat stew, although I'm not sure if that would be considered an aphrodisiac.'

'Maybe in years gone by cows would have been seen as attractive companionship if the men got desperate in these isolated rural areas!' Gideon said. 'I told Toby that no one will be bothered what they're eating after enough booze and he could shove down some cocktail sausages and a large bag of kettle chips and everyone would be happy!' he continued as Amelia pulled up at the end of the lane at the side of the Whistling Haggis.

'Woah, Gideon, what happened to your bandages?' Jack said as Gideon got out of the golf cart, tentatively lowering his injured leg to take his weight as he stood.

Gideon glanced down at his Levi's. 'The time had come to dump the stretchy sportswear for my five-tens. There are only so many consecutive days a man can wear an expandable waistband before he lets himself go entirely, and it's a slippery slope from joggers to stained T-shirts and watching reruns of *Cash in the Attic*.' He took a deep breath. 'I now have to rely on nothing more than the kindness of strangers to help me about the village.'

Gideon had talked Amelia into taking him back to his cottage to pick up emergency fashion essentials when the actor caught wind there might be local press at the Beltane parade. Amelia had to rifle through a mind-boggling array of shirts inside the triple-doored antique monstrosity of a wardrobe in the upstairs bedroom while Gideon waited downstairs, calling out additional requests for his Tom Ford aftershave, Sisley face mask, lip balm, hair wax, brow shaper, hand cream and Clarins self-tan lotion, due to him feeling a little pasty. After a couple of hours of primping, Gideon cut quite a dash in his skinny fit jeans and Cavalli shirt as he led the way on his crutches.

Main Street was packed with people lining the streets waiting for the parade and floats to go past and they joined a part of the crowd, three-people deep.

'I'll be back in a minute, Toby needs these paper plates and napkins,' Amelia said, taking the box from Jack, before she squeezed through the throng of people and headed towards the food stalls.

She found Toby and Ben setting out the last of the food. Toby glanced up from adjusting the portable gas burner stove on which large urns of stew bubbled.

'Great! I think we're going to need those extra plates, it's mobbed. Can you stick them back there?' Toby gestured to the seven-foot-tall screen which ran the length of their prominent corner position. 'And can you grab me some more of the blinis? I've marked the boxes. Be careful, it's a bit of a mess.'

Amelia picked her way past the plastic tubs of sauces and ingredients and went behind the screens. Toby wasn't wrong; precariously angled cardboard boxes were piled high next to areas of last-minute prep and Amelia almost tripped over the mobile catering generator which kept the refrigerated storage units running. Luckily, more screens concealed the carnage from anyone walking past. Still holding the plates and napkins, Amelia studied the writing on the boxes, trying to decipher the almost illegible scribblings in a bid to find the blinis.

She moved on to the next column of crates, wondering if she dared reorganise her brother's haphazard storage system. She gave a little start as she continued along the boxes and realised she was not alone. Nestled between a pillar of boxes and the screen were two people kissing passionately.

Amelia instantly recognised Rory, with his denim bucket hat.

She turned to leave the couple in privacy but accidentally nudged one of the boxes which began to keel over. Amelia had to drop the paper plates to grab hold and steady the column of boxes to avoid them falling down.

The disturbance put a halt to Rory's amorous ventures. He turned around and Amelia couldn't help but register surprise when she saw the object of his affection; Lily Wu, his brother Drew's fiancé!

Amelia managed to find her way back to Jack and Gideon moments before a large cheer went up as the first float appeared.

'Oh my, how bucolic!' Gideon remarked when they saw the trailer loaded with hay bales, being pulled by a tractor. It was the local primary school's entry and was decorated with flowers and garlands. It trundled slowly past with little children waving at their families in the crowd. Next up was the Glencarlach knitting and crochet society who'd very artistically recreated a 3D version of the main street of the village in various types of yarn that they held up for everyone to look at as they passed by. Float after float passed by with some very weird and wonderful themes – Amelia couldn't think how the film society's display of *Smokey and the Bandit* had anything to do with Beltane but the group, comprising of mostly middle-aged men, had taken a huge amount of care and attention to detail with their costumes and a particularly fine 1977 Pontiac Trans Am replica made from boxes.

'Oh dear God!' Gideon exclaimed under his breath as the wildlife society float came into view. Everyone taking part was dressed as an animal, which were very obviously homemade, most of them furry. All sported face paint.

'What is Christine McGuthrie dressed as?' Jack asked as the owner of the outdoors shop bent over to shake a long flat tail at the people in the crowd.

'I think she's a beaver,' Amelia said, reading the sign she and grocery store owner, Jean Maddox, held up between them which said *Protect Our Beavers*.

'The jokes write themselves,' Gideon muttered wide-eyed with incredulity as they applauded.

Andy McAvoy, dressed as a badger, waved at people in the crowd. His face paint was running under the heat of the midday sun and Amelia thought he must have been sweltering in his furry costume. He caught Amelia's eye and gave her a smile of recognition and a friendly wave as the float slowly trundled past.

Next up was the ornithological society float which had clearly tried to compete with the wildlife float and everyone on it had made hats with beaks attached.

'There's something more than a little sinister about them,' Jack commented as a cross-eyed crow flapped its cardboard and marabou-stork wings.

Towards the end of the parade was the trailer with the Beltane Queen. Stone Manor's waitress, Ruth, looked beautiful in a long flowing gown, her hair adorned with a flower garland. The chair which she was sitting on had been decorated to resemble a floral version of the one from *Game of Thrones*.

'Can everyone else see the massive great rabbit or have I been working too much?' Jack said as he looked beyond the Beltane Queen float.

Amelia went up on her tiptoes to see over the heads of the people in front. Right enough, sitting on the last float was a woman with the head and shoulders of a rabbit made out of papier-mâché.

'It's a hare, not a rabbit,' a voice said from behind and Amelia turned to see Moira. 'The hare represents the Celtic goddess Ostara, or Eostre as she's also known,' she explained. 'Let's follow everyone.'

As the last float passed, the crowd joined on the end of the parade, heading towards the far end of Main Street, which had been closed off to vehicles other than those in the parade. When the tractor pulling Ostara's float stopped, a couple of people scrambled aboard to help the woman down. She then began to dance around the maypole and under an archway of branches that bystanders held up.

'They're birch,' Moira explained to Amelia, Jack and Gideon. 'Birch is considered a feminine tree and is associated with love and fertility. Traditionally, lovers give each other wreaths made from it.'

'Ah, is that why Sally was looking for some?' Amelia said.

Moira smiled and nodded. 'Along with some hawthorn which is what the maypole is adorned with. It represents sex and fertility and opening up the faerie realm. You'll see it on the front of many of the houses along with some rowan.'

'More sex?' Gideon asked.

Moira shook her head. 'Rowan's for healing, and protection from the evil eye and angry faerie folk who wake up during hibernation.'

'Hmm, I hate being woken from a good sleep too!' Gideon remarked.

Their chatter was broken by an electric guitar chord being struck as a local Celtic rock band took to the hay bales beside the maypole and started to tune their instruments. A regular act at the Whistling Haggis, the band had a loyal following.

'I'm starving,' Jack announced.

'Luckily, we know a chef,' Amelia said as they wandered over to one of the long trestle tables laid out with a selection of delicious-looking food.

The seafood stall was opposite SeaShack and Amelia saw Maja alternating from peering into Johno's shop window and banging on the door. Maja turned to scan the crowd, looking far from happy before making a beeline for the beer tent.

Amelia returned her attention to the food and had her plate piled high with fresh oysters when her elbow collided with someone and her plate dipped dangerously.

'Oh, I'm sorry!' Isobel said, grabbing it before any of the precious cargo fell onto the ground. 'I wasn't looking where I was going,' she added, repositioning a big black duffel bag on her shoulder and she carried on through the crowd, squeezing past Johno who stood with a faraway look on his face.

'Someone's been looking for you,' Amelia said teasingly as she liberally shook a bottle of TABASCO over the oysters glistening in their half-shell beds.

Johno whipped round to Amelia with a worried expression. 'Who?'

'Maja.'

Johno looked relieved then cast a worried glance at his watch. 'Damn, I was meant to meet her. Have you seen Rory?' he said, looking around him in agitation. 'I really need to speak to him.'

'I saw him earlier,' Amelia said evasively. After Amelia stumbled upon their tryst, Lily had flushed scarlet and hurried away. Rory had looked at Amelia with a helpless expression for a moment before running after Lily. Then Amelia noticed they'd been canoodling right beside the blinis.

'Have you tried his boat?' Amelia suggested.

Johno shook his head. 'It's berthed. He's only got Sally's handfasting ceremony booked in for today.'

'That's not until nine.'

Johno swore under his breath.

'Have you tried calling?'

He nodded. 'He's not picking up.' He bit the skin on the side of his thumb as he scanned the crowds. He turned back to Amelia. 'I'll call again and leave a message, and then I'll wait for him by the boat. If you see him can you let him know that's where I'll be?'

'Of course.'

Giving Amelia's shoulder a squeeze in thanks, Johno walked off.

The band played the first chord of their opening number and Amelia pushed through the crowd as she didn't want to miss their set. A few feet away she saw Johno stop next to the wildlife society float where Christine was standing above him, collecting the animal costumes. Johno was talking into his phone animatedly. He finished his call and looked up at Andy McAvoy. They had a moment's conversation and Amelia saw Andy shrug and point towards his son's boat. Johno waved in thanks then glanced back at his phone as he walked away, melting into the crowd, until Amelia could no longer see any flashes of his yellow shirt with the neon-green palm-trees print.

TWENTY-THREE

As afternoon settled into evening, the vendors selling arts and crafts packed up. Kids running around with floral headdresses and horned oak-leaf masks were corralled home for dinner and bed. The food stallholders began winding in the striped canopies and folding up the tables as they ran out of food. Much of the crowd dispersed, leaving Main Street far less busy. People leaving certainly didn't dampen the spirits of those that remained though, as the Glencarlach residents moved on towards the Whistling Haggis, spilling over into the temporary beer tent where the Arctic Monkey's tribute act, the Baltic Baboons, played their music set.

The setting sun signalled the final part of the Beltane ceremony; the lighting of the bonfire. Everyone congregated around the large pillar of wood and sticks and a path cleared to allow Ruth, the Beltane Queen, to walk forward with a glowing torch and touch it against the bottom of the bonfire. Within a couple of minutes, the flames ignited to a chorus of 'oohs' and a smattering of applause from the crowd.

Jack stood behind Amelia, his arms wrapped around her,

chin resting on her head as they watched the flames get higher and lick the sky.

'It's been an amazing day,' Jack murmured into her hair.

Amelia squeezed his arms back in agreement as the orange glow lit up the faces of the onlookers.

The day had been pretty perfect, and the cherry on the cake would be Sally and Hamish's handfasting ceremony. Aware of a movement beside her, she looked up to see Moira beckoning her.

It was time.

They snaked their way through the crowd, Amelia tapping Toby on the shoulder as she passed him to let him know they were heading to Rory's boat.

The little procession made its way down to the *Amber Dram*, which was glowing with an abundance of twinkling lights.

Rory helped everyone over the gangway and directed them to a little trestle table laid out with glasses and bottles of Prosecco, beer, and cartons of orange juice.

With everyone aboard, Rory started the boat and they slowly puttered out onto the water.

It was a magical scene, Amelia thought, watching Glencarlach getting smaller and the beacon of the Beltane fire blazing strong on the Main Street.

Rory waited until they were quite far out into the water before he cut the engine and the boat bobbed gently up and down as they waited for Moira to begin.

Sally and Hamish stood at the bow of the boat and Amelia thought Sally had never looked more beautiful. Her long auburn hair shone and was loosely caught up at the sides and held in a garland of spring flowers and what looked like twigs, but Amelia guessed was probably the very symbolic birch and hawthorn branches. Hamish was also beaming with happiness as he gazed into Sally's eyes.

Moira, standing on the other side of the couple, facing all the guests, held her hands up in the air and a hush fell. Amelia noticed she was wearing the anti-sea-sickness pressure bands.

'We are gathered here, this Walpurgisnacht, to herald in the summer, to feel the earth energy.' Moira paused and looked out at the water with a raised eyebrow. 'You know what I mean,' she added with a smile, 'and most importantly, we come together to celebrate the love of Hamish and Sally in their decision to follow the tradition of a handfasting ceremony. They would now like to say a few words.'

Hamish cleared his throat, he looked slightly embarrassed as he glanced round at his family and friends, before turning back to Sally and he began to speak.

'From the moment I saw you, I fell in love with you, Sally. You are the kindest, warmest and most loving person I have ever met. You make me laugh every day and even on the darkest days you bring sunshine to my life. You are also the undefeated champion of Scrabble, but although I regularly lose to a triple-word score, I feel I have won at life, as long as you are at my side. You are my future.'

Amelia could feel tears well in her eyes as she looked on. Jack squeezed her hand.

Sally, brushing her finger under her eyes, smiled up at Hamish.

'When I came to Glencarlach,' she said, her voice cracking a little with emotion, 'I thought I was only here for a couple of weeks while I helped my best friend renovate a house and worked out what I wanted to do with my life. And from the first night we met, I did know what I wanted from life: you. I felt I'd come home. You give me happiness, and peace, and a strength of belonging. I love everything about you, Hamish, especially the fact you take your Scrabble defeat with good grace.' She winked. 'A year and a day will be the start of our journey together as I'm excited at the thought of sharing my life with you.'

Moira smiled down at them as she brought out a long length of red ribbon and began to entwine it around their clasped hands.

'We honour life and love,' Moira said as she passed the ribbon round three times in a figure of eight, 'and for a year and a day, you are bound.'

Sally and Hamish looked adoringly at each other as a cheer went up on the boat and Betty let off a very loud whistle through her fingers.

'They don't have to be tied up for that entire time, do they?' Gideon asked Amelia quietly as he leant towards her.

Amelia smiled and shook her head as Moira slipped off the ribbon in one swift move. Another cheer went up.

Rory, still clapping, went to the back of the boat as Hamish's dad started singing the Robert Burns love song, 'A Red, Red Rose', his strong, lilting voice carrying the beautiful folk song over the still water. Rory caught Amelia's eye and motioned her to follow him.

She caught up with him by the controls.

'That was lovely, wasn't it,' she said although she doubted Rory wanted to talk to her about the details of the handfasting ceremony.

Rory smiled a little distractedly. 'Yes, it was. Thing is, Amelia, about earlier...' He trailed off, clearly unsure what to say.

'It's not what it looked like?' Amelia raised an eyebrow.

Rory gave a half laugh. 'No, I think it was probably exactly what it looked like. We're... she's... We didn't set out. I mean, we never...'

Amelia rested a hand on his arm, hoping to end his

embarrassed stammering. 'If you're worried I'm going to tell anyone about you and Lily, don't. I haven't said a word and I don't intend to.'

Rory looked relieved. 'Thank you. Lily wants to end it with Drew. She's desperately unhappy. It's finding the right time. And because he's my brother, I feel so guilty.'

'I can imagine. But don't worry. Drew won't hear anything from me. Did you manage to catch up with Johno, he was looking for you earlier?' Amelia asked.

'Yeah, Dad said. I had a ton of missed calls from him. He left a message, a really weird one, even for him. He sounded upset, told me he was going to wait on the boat, but when I got here, there was no sign of him. Typical!' Rory rolled his eyes.

'Did he say why he needed to see you?' Amelia asked.

'No, but he sounded stressed out, which isn't like him. I was worried. I kind of still am, to be honest.'

'Have you still got the message?' Amelia asked.

Rory got out his phone. 'See if you understand what he's on about. It didn't help that the band started up as he was talking. It's a really bad line,' he said as he pressed play.

Johno's voice crackled onto the voicemail. He sounded agitated. *'Rory, I need to see... I found...'* There was a squeal of feedback from the band in the background. *'...your mum... wears and I don't know what to do!... ust have drop... It's bad... all this shit's happened... stuck with... and... something really stupid... n't thinking... And I want to sort... how... I need to speak to you!... pronto! You... what to do. I'm... your boat. I'll meet you there.'* The call ended.

Amelia looked at the phone, as if waiting for more clarity. 'And you've no idea what he was talking about? Or where he could be?'

'Haven't a clue, but it's probably a storm in a teacup. He's my best mate, but he's shockingly bad at being reliable. He'll have freaked out over something trivial, after smoking too much hash no doubt, then left that message, gone for a drink, which would turn into half a dozen, hooked up with Maja and forgotten why he's upset.'

'Ah, I saw her looking for him earlier, too.'

'I rest my case.' Rory smiled, the whites of his teeth flashing in the lights from around the deck. 'He'll roll up tomorrow with a stinking hangover all shagged out with a sheepish apology!'

Amelia conceded Rory did have a very valid point.

Rory switched the engine back on and slapped the side of the ship's wheel. 'Come on, let's go rejoin the celebration.' They got back to the other guests as Hamish's dad was on the last couple of lines of the song.

'...and I will love thee still, my dear, till a' the seas gang dry...'

There was a moment's silence then everyone applauded and a couple of the guests dabbed at their eyes.

'Perfect timing, Captain,' Betty said as she sauntered over, waving her empty glass at him. 'I think some of us are in need of a refill.' She gestured to the table where all the Prosecco bottles were lying empty.

Rory chuckled as he went over to the bench seating that ran around the inside perimeter of the boat. 'Luckily, I stocked up,' he said as he lifted the seating up. He started reaching in but then stopped, letting out a cry as he stared into the storage space.

Beside him, Betty gave a little gasp and the glass slipped from her hand, smashing on the deck.

Amelia came round beside Rory and looked, but instead of there being extra bottles of Prosecco, Johno lay squashed into the storage space, his blond hair matted with blood, and his lifeless eyes staring up at the stars.

And beside him, a tarot card depicting The Fool along with a Green Man mask made of ivy and oak moss.

TWENTY-FOUR

After Moira got back to Stone Manor, she sat on the bed and unscrewed the cap of one of the little bottles of whiskies from the mini bar. Without bothering to pour it into a glass, she drank it all in one go, barely registering the burning sensation in her throat. She sat like that for another twenty minutes before she picked up the hotel phone and called.

He answered on the third ring.

'I'm a bit busy at the moment.'

'I need to see you,' she said, annoyed to hear how shaky her voice sounded.

There was a pause.

'Okay.'

'The abbey ruins. Half an hour.' She hung up before he could protest.

She got there with fifteen minutes to spare. She hurried past the gazebos and the empty archaeology site. It was a cold night and she wished she'd brought her hat and gloves but she couldn't turn back in case she missed him.

She held her breath as a car came along the back road, its headlights arcing up as it came over the brow of the hill, then sweeping round as it pulled into the lay-by. He was early too. She hurried towards it, slipping into the passenger seat.

Thankfully he had the heater on.

'This looks bad, doesn't it?'

Murray's face was grim as ever. 'Well, it doesn't look good.'

'I checked my tarot and I've got all of them.'

'That's something. What about the Green Man mask?'

'I don't know. It looks like the ones I made for us the other night. I can't remember what we did with them. I'm pretty sure I left mine.'

'They'll check for DNA.'

'So it'll be a lottery as to which one of us it belonged to.'

'Davey took his home.'

'Anyone could have gone to the site after we were there and picked one up–'

'Maybe more than one mask.'

'Oh God, you think there might be...' Moira didn't finish her thought.

'I'm aware how this looks. I come back and a matter of hours later there's a murder in the place I'm staying and there are links to Cammy and the tarot and everything... and all the past is coming back.' She could feel her heart starting up its fast tattoo beat.

'I know.' Murray reached out and held her hand. 'Jesus, you're freezing.' He put the heater up high and gave her a pair of gloves from the glove compartment.

'You actually keep gloves in the glove compartment.'

'I do. I'm a man that takes things literally.'

Moira rested her head against the back of the car seat, staring at the magic-tree air freshener hanging from the rear-view mirror. 'When did things get so messy?' she asked, not really expecting an answer.

'Things might get a whole lot messier for me depending on what is found on the Green Man mask next to Johno Davis.'

'I have a feeling it was my mask.'

'Is there a reason you feel this?'

Moira picked up the suspicious tone and turned to look levelly at him. 'Do you really think I'm behind any of this?'

'No. But I'm not the one you need to convince.'

'I've just got a *feeling*. I've had a dread in my stomach for weeks, like something's coming. I'm just not sure...'

'Moira, listen to me. This isn't Cameron. He is not back from the dead, or from being missing. Understand?'

'But, do you remember that last night, when we argued?'

'Everyone had been drinking.'

'I know, but...'

'Cameron loved you. He loved everyone. He was a sensitive soul and felt things passionately. He didn't mean the things he said.'

'That's all very well for you to say, but I've been the one living with it for the past thirty-odd years.'

'He told Hector to fuck off too, remember?'

'We told Hector to fuck off all the time. What with his weird ideas. It was water off a duck's back to him.' Moira gave a little laugh despite herself.

'I'm going to get to the bottom of this. As long as I'm allowed to stay on the case.'

She looked at him in alarm. 'Why wouldn't you?'

'Well, there might be a tricky conversation to be had if it's my DNA found on the mask. And don't get me started on conflicts of interest.'

Moira hadn't thought of that.

'I'm going to go. Thanks for meeting me, but I don't want to put your career at any more risk.'

'Why did you call me?'

'I don't know. I just wanted to talk... and you were always a good listener.'

Murray looked at her for a long moment.

'Does this mean you've stopped being angry with me?'

'What do you mean?' Moira bluffed.

He gave a little laugh. 'I'm not being paranoid. Since you've been back I've picked up vibes from you. Angry vibes.'

'I suppose. I felt angry at everyone for a time.'

They sat for a moment, the blast of the heater the only sound.

Moira checked her watch. 'I'd best go. You'll be up to your eyes in it, I'm guessing.'

'Let me drive you back?'

'Thank you, but no, I want to walk.'

He started to protest, but Moira slipped out of the car and went round the front of it, breaking the beam of the headlights. She retraced her steps, past the archaeology site, not caring to dwell on how sinister the ruined arches of the abbey looked in relief against the moonlit sky.

TWENTY-FIVE

'I can't believe it. It's awful. Truly awful.'

Amelia nodded in agreement. It was the fourth or fifth time one of the group had uttered something similar as they sat around the table in the Stone Manor kitchen the next morning.

'He seemed a lovely young man,' Betty said, taking out a hip flask and topping up her tea with whisky. She offered it around but everyone else declined. She added another splash before putting the flask back into the pocket of the Fair Isle cardigan she was wearing. Betty had eschewed the formal dining room for breakfast, preferring to sit with the others in the kitchen, although no one seemed to have had an appetite for food and the rounds of toast sat going cold. There was, however, an unspoken need for everyone to stay together. And to drink numerous cups of tea.

'Do you think Rory will be okay?' Gideon asked.

Amelia thought back to the previous night and the split-second pause after Johno was discovered, before Rory dropped to his knees, shouting Johno's name, trying to shake him awake, not believing his best friend was dead. Jack and Hamish had to gently pull him away, realising they'd need to leave the crime scene intact.

'I hope so,' Toby said as he put his finished mug of tea down on the table.

'I feel for Hamish and Sally,' Betty added, shaking her head.

Amelia's heart had gone out to the couple at the speed such a happy occasion had turned into one of horror. She remembered Sally looking down at the body, her face frozen in shock as the red ribbon from the ceremony slithered from her grasp, blowing out to sea on the wind.

Rory had managed to compose himself enough to radio the incident ashore.

Then, so much happened so quickly. Everyone was talking at once. Someone was crying. The wind had picked up, causing the boat to rock dramatically. A guest was sick over the side of the boat and Amelia could see Moira taking deep breaths as she pressed hard on her anti-sickness wristbands. Another, older man, began talking loudly about the tragedy being a portent of doom for the handfasted couple until other relatives took him away to hush him up. There was even a flash of light as one ghoulish guest took a photograph of the body, which caused Rory to fly into a rage, threatening to throw the phone overboard if the photo wasn't deleted immediately.

Then the police arrived.

And the noise stopped as everyone sat in silence, waiting to disembark.

Names and statements were given and the scenes of crime officers arrived.

Then, what seemed like hours later, they'd been told they could leave, under the watchful scowl of Detective Inspector McGregor.

A clatter of a teaspoon dropping onto a saucer broke Amelia out of her reverie.

Betty stood up. 'Thank you for breakfast. I'm going to pop up to check on Moira and then we're going to see Hamish and Sally.' She left, leaving Amelia, her brother, Gideon and Jack.

'I wonder how Sally is,' Gideon said.

'She's okay,' Amelia said. She'd called her best friend first thing this morning. Although still distressed and shaken at the previous night's events, Sally hadn't taken heed of the superstitious relative and wasn't buying into the gossip about bad omens and curses or panicking about her future with Hamish being doomed.

'Why would anyone want to kill Johno?' Gideon asked no one in particular. 'I don't understand.'

'It could have had something to do with the message he left Rory,' Amelia said quietly as she looked up from staring at the now lukewarm tea in her mug.

'What message?' the others asked in unison.

'Earlier on I bumped into Johno at the seafood stall. He was looking for Rory, said he needed to speak to him urgently. Then, when we were on Rory's boat, I asked if Johno had gotten in touch and Rory played me the message Johno had left for him. You couldn't hear it properly but he mentioned finding something about Rory's mum and he didn't know what to do. Then he said he'd done something stupid and needed to speak to Rory.'

'That's weird. What did Rory say about it?'

Amelia shook her head. 'Nothing. He had no clue what Johno was talking about. He thought he was being weird or drunk, but then...'

'Clearly it could have been something to warrant his head being caved in,' Gideon said.

'Do the police know about this?' Toby asked.

Amelia nodded. 'I mentioned it in my statement and I saw Rory handing his phone to Detective Inspector McGregor.'

'Maybe he can get to the bottom of it,' Toby said.

'Maybe,' Amelia agreed.

Jack laid his hand over Amelia's. 'Come on, why don't we go and get some fresh air?'

Amelia and Jack ended up walking for miles over Stone Manor's grounds. Cherry blossom floated from the trees like confetti, creating a pink carpet on which they walked. They circled back through the woods, pointing out the new buds on the flowers and the trees sprouting young leaves. The cycle of renewal seemed particularly poignant for Amelia after the suddenness of life-loving Johno's death. They followed a path through the trees which brought them out halfway along the Stone Manor driveway. Without discussing where they were going, Amelia and Jack passed by the Gatehouse and continued on to Glencarlach.

The village was busy. With a ramped-up police presence.

Beltane flags still flapped against the lampposts and a few garlands remained on doors, but all other signs of the festivities had been removed.

Police stood at the entrance to the harbour and a large area had been cordoned off around the *Amber Dram*. A tent had been erected which obscured most of Rory's boat.

A local news anchor was talking to the camera with the harbour behind her, getting ready to fill the country in on the tragedy at the next bulletin.

Rory stood on the other side of Main Street, a lonely figure at the harbour wall, eyes fixed on the area around his boat. He clutched a takeaway coffee but made no effort to drink from it. Amelia and Jack crossed over to him.

He turned and gave them a distracted nod.

'We're so sorry...' Amelia said, but trailed off, not having a clear idea of what else to add.

Rory nodded again, his face like an emotionless slab of granite.

Today, there was no sign of sunshine. The sky hung low and was uniform grey with a brutal wind blowing in off the sea. Amelia pulled her jacket closer around her body for warmth.

They stood in silence for a few moments more until Rory said, 'I keep thinking... if I'd got to the boat sooner, would this have happened? If I'd even been half an hour earlier, would he be alive? I could maybe have saved him, or stopped it, or scared whoever did it away.' He narrowed his eyes against the wind. 'He was clearly worried about something. Why didn't he go to the police?'

To Amelia's ears, on the message he'd left Rory, Johno hadn't just sounded worried, he'd also sounded scared.

'I wasn't there for him.' Rory's voice broke slightly and he cleared his throat, wiping his hand across his eyes. 'We always had each other's backs, but I wasn't there.'

Amelia watched as DI McGregor walked down from the church and ducked under the police tape, his raincoat flapping in the wind as he strode purposefully past the boats, towards officers at the end of the dock where they spoke for a moment. But then, instead of boarding the *Amber Dram*, McGregor went into Rory's little harbour-master's shed.

Rory raised his head, frowning as he looked on. Two minutes later McGregor walked out and handed a clear evidence bag to one of the uniforms.

'What's that he's got?' Rory said, brows furrowed.

'It looks like a bag or a jacket,' Jack said.

'That's odd, I don't keep anything like that in there as there's a leaky roof, and there's no point when my boat's right there.'

They watched as McGregor spoke with another couple of

uniforms. He then took out his mobile and called someone, looking up at where Amelia, Jack and Rory stood while he talked. McGregor finished his call and pocketed his phone, still watching them.

'I've got a bad feeling about this,' Rory said softly under his breath as they watched McGregor make his way towards them, striding past the news team, shooing them away as the anchor shouted a question that got carried off on the wind.

'Rory McAvoy, I think we need to have another talk. This time at the station,' DI McGregor said as he stopped in front of them.

'Am I under arrest?' Rory said stonily.

McGregor looked at him for a long moment before saying, 'No. At this moment I'd simply like your help with our ongoing enquiries. But let's see how the day unfolds, shall we?'

Rory's jaw clenched slightly as the wind whipped his dark hair around his head. He said nothing but handed Jack his coffee then leant in and hugged Amelia, who was slightly taken aback by his action.

But Rory wasn't looking for comfort. 'If you see Lily, tell her not to worry, I won't say anything,' he whispered in her ear.

Amelia nodded that she understood and Rory broke away and walked slowly to the waiting police car, head held high, ignoring the people who'd come out of their shops to stare.

TWENTY-SIX

Sally opened the door to the farmhouse, smiling a little when she saw it was Amelia and Jack standing there.

Amelia gave her best friend a hug. 'How are you?' she asked once they broke apart.

'I'm okay,' Sally said, closing the door and leading them into the cosy, cluttered kitchen. 'Although I still can't believe what's happened.'

Hamish was at the sink washing dishes and shouted out a hello when he saw they had guests.

Sally got some mugs out from the cupboard and switched on the kettle to boil. 'One of Hamish's aunts popped in with the rather flimsy excuse of dropping off a vase she thought we might like.' Sally raised her eyebrows sceptically. 'Clearly wanting to gossip, she said she'd seen Rory being arrested and taken away in a police car. Could that be true?'

'No,' Amelia said, going to sit down but finding a large pile of magazines and letters piled up on the chair.

'Oh, sorry, I'll move them,' Sally said as she grabbed the pile and added it to the top of another tower of stationery at the end of the table. 'Coffee?' she added, waggling a jar invitingly at Amelia and Jack.

'Yes please,' Jack said.

'Thanks,' Amelia said. 'We were there when McGregor came over and asked if Rory could go with him to answer more questions.'

Hamish peeled off his yellow rubber gloves, dropping them over the edge of the sink, and came to sit opposite Amelia and Jack. 'So, no handcuffs or reading of rights then?'

'And he didn't try and do a runner?' Sally said, bringing over the coffees and plonking a packet of chocolate digestives between them.

Amelia shook her head. She felt bad for Rory; that the village gossips were in full swing and clearly unconcerned about truth getting in the way of a juicy story.

'McGregor didn't look happy, but then, he never does. It seemed he'd discovered something in the harbour-master's shed that he then put in an evidence bag,' Amelia said.

Sally gave Amelia a questioning look.

'I don't know what it was, it was something dark and bulky like a bag or a jacket. Rory had no idea what it could be either.'

'I really can't imagine Rory having anything to do with Johno's death,' Sally said sadly. 'They were such good friends and his reaction when he found his body... he was completely traumatised. And also, why would he hide Johno in his *own* boat, beside the Prosecco, where he was *bound* to be found.'

'Unless that was a double bluff, so that people wouldn't think he'd do anything so stupid.'

Sally looked shocked, her biscuit poised halfway to her lips. '*You* don't seriously think he had anything to do with it though?'

'I wouldn't have thought so,' Amelia said. 'I'm wondering aloud a possible line the police could take.'

'Johno was in the salon the other day. He had one of my

early-bird appointments on Friday morning,' Sally said, giving Amelia a sad smile. 'Those sun-bleached tips on his surfer mop sometimes needed a helping hand. As did his all-year tan.'

'How did he seem?'

'It was all rather odd.' Sally paused then sighed. 'Or maybe I'm reading something into nothing and letting what happened to Johno influence my memory.'

'Tell us.'

'Well, I thought Johno had forgotten about the appointment. He was due in at half seven, it was always early in the morning. Sometimes, if Main Street was busy as he was leaving, he'd go out the back door of the salon and sneak along the lane to the SeaShack so nobody saw him. I think it would have ruined his street cred if it was discovered he liked a bit of a bleach and blow dry. Anyway, it was getting nearer to eight and I thought I'd best go along and check, you know what he's like; so forgetful and laid-back. Anyway, I knocked on the door of SeaShack and it took him ages to come to the door and when he did, he peered out from behind the blind he had pulled down. He seemed relieved when he saw it was me and remembered his hair appointment. He came out and as he opened the door I could see inside and oh my, the shop was in a complete state. He saw me staring and made a comment about stocktaking and how it was easier to count everything if it was spread out on the floor. To be honest, I'm surprised he'd even think to do a stock count!'

It seemed quite out of character to Amelia also.

'How was he during his appointment?' Amelia asked.

'A bit subdued to be honest. We talked about Gideon discovering the body and the pagan figure Gideon and Rory saw. I mean, nothing unusual there as everyone in the village is talking about that. And then I mentioned the creepy past of the Hunting Lodge you were telling me about. He asked if I knew anyone who went there. And I was totally honest and said that until you told me about it, I never knew the place existed.'

Hamish reached for a biscuit as Sally continued.

'And then I said something glib about it being haunted and Johno laughed at that, but not a humorous laugh, more a cynical one and said something like it wasn't ghosts that scared him and then he said something odd, along the lines of the hauntings being convenient.'

'He said that, *convenient?*'

Sally nodded.

'There is definitely something up with that place, though,' Hamish said as he brushed biscuit crumbs from the front of his woolly jumper. 'Obviously as a lad growing up here, I heard the rumours of ghosts and restless spirits and was warned never to go there. But whenever I asked my parents why not, something came over them. They clammed up, wouldn't say a word and told me if I asked again I'd get a clout around the ears. I didn't like to push it.'

'Do you think that the mess in Johno's shop could have been caused by it being turned over?' Amelia asked. 'Or could it have been from him making a mess while looking for the paperwork the police had asked for?'

Sally thought a moment. 'All the shorts were lying on the floor. Unless Johno had a very odd filing system, I would say it looked like SeaShack had been broken into and ransacked.'

'I told the police what I'd seen. It was DS Dabrowski I spoke to. I'm quite glad it was her and not McGregor; he seems a bit forbidding!'

'Everything about this feels a bit forbidding,' Amelia said and they all lapsed back into silence.

TWENTY-SEVEN

'What are you up to now?' Gideon asked Amelia later that afternoon when he saw her take the keys to the Jeep off the hook by the storage rooms.

'I need some supplies, I'm going to head out to that retail unit a few miles away.'

'Can I come? It's dead around here.'

Amelia stared at him for his poor choice of words, but he was completely oblivious and, using his crutches to open the back door, pushed past her and hobbled towards the car park.

As she closed the back door, Amelia noticed a twiggy wreath had been nailed to it.

Gideon turned to see her looking at it.

'I'm surprised you've found the time to decorate.'

'I didn't do this.'

Gideon looked surprised. 'I wonder who did.'

They were barely out the village when Amelia saw someone sitting on the low wall by the road sign that stated careful drivers were welcome. Seeing the light-blonde cropped hair and a flash of floral tattoos on the woman's shoulder, Amelia slowed down and pulled into a passing place a few yards further along the road.

'What are we doing?' Gideon asked.

'Can you please stay in the car for a minute? There's someone I need to have a quick word with.'

Gideon turned to look out the rear window, wincing as he twisted his injured ankle.

Amelia got out of the car and hurried over to the woman who watched her approach.

'Hi, Maja,' Amelia said, 'I wondered if I could speak to you for a moment?'

'Of course, Amelia.' Maja's icy-blue eyes studied her.

'I wanted to see how you are, after... you know.'

Maja sighed. 'I'm sad. At first I thought he was being a shit, standing me up. British men can be like that, one minute so keen, the next, not. You know?'

Amelia nodded. She knew.

'And then I heard what happened and I thought, what the fuck!' Maja said incredulously, eyes widening in shock.

Maja stretched her long, tanned legs out in front of her and took off her dinky little backpack, unzipped it and brought out what looked very much like a joint. She lit it and yes, Amelia caught a whiff of the sweet, herbal tobacco; definitely a joint.

Maja took a couple of drags then offered it to Amelia.

'No thanks,' Amelia said as she sat down beside her.

Maja sighed, lost in thought as she took another draw.

'I saw you looking for Johno at Beltane,' Amelia said.

'Ja,' Maja nodded, 'he told me to meet him at his SeaShack shop. But he didn't show. I thought he wanted to make it up to me after the last couple of days. But, if he was dead, no wonder he wasn't there.'

'What happened on the previous days?'

Maja snorted, smoke coming out her nostrils. 'No idea. One minute we were good, next, it seemed he'd lost interest!' She made an expressive 'pfft' noise and waved her hand dismissively in the air.

'Would you be able to tell me what happened? About your time with Johno?'

Maja looked at her suspiciously, moving the joint behind her back slightly. 'You ask a lot of questions. Do you work with the police?'

'No! Johno was a friend and I want to know what happened.'

Maja still looked a little uncertain. 'I've been asked so many questions. First about Gus, then Johno. I don't like police.'

'Neither do I,' Amelia said, thinking of the dour DI McGregor.

Maja held out the joint again to Amelia. This time, Amelia accepted it and took a draw. Clearly, this action melted away any doubt in Maja's mind about Amelia's connection to the police and she settled back into recounting her story.

'So, me and Johno, we'd been flirting since I got here. He sold me some flip-flops and some of this.' She waved the joint at Amelia and smiled. 'He said he'd show me the local area. Obviously a line, but he was good-looking and had a fit body so I said yes. We got on. We met up a lot after that.'

'Where did you go when you met up?'

'Mainly the Whistling Haggis or his place. Or walks. He was very into his fresh air and sports. One time he said he had somewhere cool to show me. We got into his little boat, his dinghy, and we went out to a secret cave. He said no one knew about it. I'm not stupid. I knew I was not the first woman he'd taken there. You couldn't see the entrance from the water, it looked like rock, but when we got close there was a little cave and he put candles there and it was romantic. We had some vodka. And sex. Then we smoked some pot and went further into the cave. There was a tunnel, very narrow and steep and we followed it up and came out at a big house. It was creepy.'

'Did you go in?'

'No.' She pulled a face. 'It looked deserted. There was a pagan symbol painted on the back door. Crossed spears which means someone had wanted to protect the house. I didn't like it so we went back to the cave and had more sex. It was nice.' She shrugged.

'When was that?'

'March? Not long after I got here.'

'What about the last few days? Did you see Johno much?'

'Oh yes. I saw him nearly every night. For the sex and drugs and rock and roll.' She took another draw of the joint. 'Although the rock music he played was awful. I like Rammstein and Slipknot and he liked what he called *"classic rock"*.' She scoffed. Monday, we met at the site and went back to his and had sex. Tuesday, after the meeting we went drinking. Johno had to go out, I think he was meeting someone but then he came back to mine and he was in a very good mood and we smoked a lot of drugs and he had pills too. Wednesday, ugh, we found out about Gus and that was an awful day, just horrible. We met in the Whistling Haggis and he had a lot of cash so we had a lot of drinks. Nice ones. Expensive. Then we went to his and we sat outside, looked at the stars and talked and had sex. I asked to go to the secret cave again but he said no. He seemed weird about going back. Then on Thursday it got odd.'

'Odd? How?'

'We had an argument. We were in the Whistling Haggis. Something had happened to make him jumpy, you know, agitated. We normally didn't meet on a Thursday because Johno and Rory always went out but Rory was busy. I don't know if Johno was pissed that his best friend had stood him up, but something was upsetting him. I went to the bathroom and when I came back I saw him with a necklace. It was a silver Berkano rune.' She saw Amelia's questioning expression and explained.

'It's a symbol from the Elder Futhark runic. It's like a pointy capital letter 'B'. The necklace was beautiful, engraved on a hammered pewter disk and a silver chain. I thought he'd bought it for me but then he jammed it into the pocket of his shorts and said he'd found it. I then asked Johno if he had another girl he was going to give it to. He said no, it wasn't like that.'

Maja took another deep drag of her joint and exhaled slowly then turned to look at Amelia with a frown.

'He was not like the Johno of the other days. He was tense, on the edge, you know? We drank and had food. It was busy in the pub and Johno didn't want to talk. Then Drew and his dad came over. Drew was also in a bad mood because his girlfriend was busy and his dad, Andy, was waiting to pick up his boss from a meal out or something. No one seemed very cheery. I got drunk and starting winding Johno up and asked to see the necklace again and Johno told me to be quiet and stop going on about it and I got angry and stormed out. He followed me and apologised and said he had a lot on his mind. We went to his SeaShack. We had sex but then, straight after, he said I had to go and he'd meet me there on Saturday before the parade. And that was it. I never saw him again. The police knew about our argument. Luckily I was in the beer tent all of Saturday with dozens of witnesses.'

Maja offered Amelia another draw of the joint and she took it, thinking over what the woman had told her.

'Do you have any idea what could have caused Johno to be so tense?'

'No idea. He was usually a laid-back person. All the drugs and sex I think. Even when Gus was having a go at him, Johno still never got that angry.'

'What did Gus say to Johno?'

'He always liked to remind him I'd had sex with Gus too. Big mistake.' She rolled her eyes. 'He wasn't good. Not like Johno. Gus teased Johno about the secret cave. He knew about it.'

'How did he find out about it?'

Maja gave Amelia a very cynical smile. 'Gus had a way of finding out lots of things and then used them to his advantage.'

'Blackmail?'

Maja thought before she answered. 'No, not as obvious. Not for money. He liked knowing things about people. I think it made him feel big and powerful. He must know things about Isobel because she never said anything when he was late or took time off. She didn't used to be like that with him. But not long after we got here, she started to let him get away with murder.'

'Did you ever find Gus's yellow notebook?'

'Ah, you know about that! Isobel has searched everywhere, but it must be gone. Gus was always off doing his own little projects on site and now Isobel and Tim have no way of finding out what it is.'

'Do you know what it could have been?'

Maja laughed. 'Gus never told me anything. He just bored me by going on and on about this wreck he'd found when he went diving.'

'A wreck? Near here?'

Maja nodded. 'Yeah, I think so, I didn't really pay much attention. He said it was interesting and he'd found treasure. But the way he said it I don't think it was gold doubloons, you know? He always had his eye on the main chance, is that the saying? To be honest I'm not surprised Gus ended up dead. There was only so long he could play everyone. He meddled too much.'

Then Maja stood up and slung her little backpack on again.

'Do you know anyone who deals drugs around here?'

'Um, no. Sorry.'

Maja frowned. 'Johno liked his pot and Gus always seemed to have a never-ending supply of everything. And I don't know how I'll cope without my benzos at night. I can't sleep with all this shit going on.'

'Maja, runes have meanings, don't they?'

'Oh yes.'

'The necklace, the Berkano rune, what does it signify?'

'It can have more than one interpretation. It stands for female fertility, also secrecy and sanctuary. But at its most basic, the Berkano rune represents birth and motherhood. Maybe Johno got someone up the duff,' she said with a little shrug before striding off towards Glencarlach.

Amelia walked slowly back to the Jeep.

'Amelia Adams! Did I see you smoking?' Gideon said accusingly the moment Amelia got in and put on her seat belt.

'Just a couple of puffs,' she said, turning the key in the ignition, looking in the rear-view mirror at Maja's retreating figure.

He leant over to sniff her hair. 'And I'm guessing it wasn't a Marlboro Light you were sharing.'

'Don't worry, I didn't inhale,' Amelia replied.

Gideon narrowed his eyes for a moment, obviously trying to work out if she was serious, but then curiosity got the better of him. 'So, what did you find out?'

Amelia signalled and pulled out onto the road again. 'Johno had a lot of sex.'

TWENTY-EIGHT

After her shopping trip, Amelia dropped Gideon at Stone Manor then doubled-back into the village to go and find Lily to pass on Rory's message. The estate agents didn't normally open on Sunday, but Amelia could see the lights were on and someone inside when she drove past. She parked and got out.

Lily looked up as soon as Amelia opened the door. Make-up free, wearing tracksuit bottoms and an oversized fleece, Lily looked very different from her professional, well-groomed office persona. The red eyes and runny nose also weren't her usual look.

'Hi, Amelia, I'm sorry, we're not actually open at the moment,' Lily said, tying up her unwashed and unbrushed hair into a ponytail.

'I just wanted to pass on a message from Rory. He said you're not to worry and he wouldn't say anything about the two of you.'

Relief flooded Lily's face. 'It's okay, he called me just a few minutes ago. He's on his way home. No arrest or anything like that.' She took a tissue out from the sleeve of her fleece and blew her nose. 'These are tears of relief. The silly fool could have been in so much trouble by not telling the police that I was with him. But I phoned as soon as I heard he'd been taken in after the police found something in his harbour-master's shed. I spoke to Dabrowski.'

'Were you able to give him an alibi?'

'Yes. We met up on the Saturday before the parade.' She looked away, her cheeks flushing pink. 'After you saw us we decided to go somewhere more private and have lunch. We made our way back to Glencarlach just in time for the handfasting ceremony. I let the DS know where we were and at what time. She's going to have to follow it up but it will check out. I can't believe Rory was going to risk getting arrested just to protect me. Rory was sure I'd go back to Drew. He couldn't get his head round the fact I'd much rather be with him. Now, all I really feel is relief. I hated feeling guilty all the time.'

'And Drew knows?'

Lily nodded. 'He seemed to take it okay, didn't actually appear that bothered when I told him. He seemed more distracted by his phone than me telling him I was leaving him to be with his brother.' She walked to the back of the office and picked up a large cardboard box that had an umbrella sticking out of it. She brought it back over and sat it on her desk.

'I thought I'd come here and collect my office things. I needed to get out of the house, to be honest. I'll go back later and pack up my clothes and move out.'

Lily opened her top drawer and lifted out her laptop and charger and put it in the box then dropped a set of headphones on top.

She opened another drawer and removed a make-up bag, unzipped it and looked inside, then she bent down to rummage through the open drawer.

'Damn, I can't find my good Charlotte Tilbury concealer or my contour stick anywhere! I thought they'd be in here.' She slammed the drawer in annoyance then went into the kitchenette and returned with a Take That mug and some photographs that had been pinned up on a cork noticeboard. Amelia saw they were of Lily and her friends, obviously taken on nights out. One of them also had Big Davey in it holding up a yard of ale. Amelia remembered that night, when the Whistling Haggis had celebrated Oktoberfest. Big Davey in traditional lederhosen costume was a sight Amelia was not likely to forget in a hurry.

Lily went over to a filing cabinet and brought down a spider plant and she gently put it in the box, the fronds spilling out over the top.

'Drew isn't good with plants. He even killed a cactus once.' Lily stopped and stared into the box for a moment before looking back up at Amelia.

'I didn't set out to hurt anyone or have an affair, you know. I just fell in love with Rory. It kind of happened gradually. I suffer from insomnia, you see, especially when I'm stressed or worried. And I have been very stressed recently. I don't want to make excuses but Drew and I haven't been getting along for a while. When I first met him he owed serious debt due to gambling. He managed to clear it but... he's been so secretive lately, out till all hours, taking long lunches in areas I know have betting shops, then coming back to work in a bad mood. I'm sure he's started again. And losing money. Or it could simply be that he's seeing someone else.'

'I can see why you were stressed. I'm sorry for walking in on you the other day when you were arguing.'

'Don't worry, I'm surprised you ever came in when we *weren't* arguing. So, anyway, when I can't sleep I usually go for a walk and I'd often find myself down by the harbour. I like looking out at the sea, it calms me. I'd been doing this for almost a week, then one night, it must have been about one in the morning, Rory came out of his boat with a flask of hot chocolate. He usually worked late getting the boat ready for his cruises and he'd noticed my night-time wanderings. That night was colder than usual, and he felt a bit sorry for me. It became a bit of a habit after that; we'd meet up on the wall and talk and drink hot chocolate. Then one night, it started pouring which turned to hailstones and we had to run to his boat to take cover and then that became our meeting spot. We'd listen to music and swap books... we talked.'

Amelia knew how small the covered bit of the *Amber Dram* was and could imagine how much more intimate their meet-ups became.

'For a long time I tried to convince myself I'd found a great new, platonic male friend. I mean, as Drew's brother, I always got on with him. But now, it felt different. Like we were seeing each other as people, not just having Drew as something in common. I would get so excited at the thought of seeing Rory. And I realised rather than my insomnia keeping me up, the thought of meeting with Rory was keeping me from sleep. I know you'll find it hard to believe but the first time we actually even kissed was after he had crashed his car.'

'Wednesday? Just a few days ago?'

Lily gave Amelia a small smile. 'Yes, luckily he doesn't make a habit of crashing. He was really shaken after seeing that creepy pagan-type figure. He messaged me and I suggested we meet up.'

Amelia remembered Rory's mobile going off in the Whistling Haggis and him leaving immediately.

'And, well, things happened and it turns out he feels the same as I do. We both want to be together. I can't stay with Drew. Rory is worried Drew will see this as a complete betrayal. His own brother. With Johno being murdered, poor Rory is a wreck. And I need to be with him. The fact the police took him in for questioning is ludicrous. Rory adored Johno.'

Lily went back into the kitchenette and returned a moment later to add a bean grinder into her box. 'I almost forgot this. Drew always drinks rubbish instant coffee. The cheapest own-label brand he can find. No taste.' Lily pulled a face.

She bustled about, gathering a few more of her belongings to put in her box.

'I don't suppose you have any rooms vacant at Stone Manor?'

'I do.'

'Great. Can I book one for a few days? Maybe a week?'

'Of course. I can give you a lift back, if you like.'

'Thanks. I know Rory will ask me to move in with him but it's quite a big leap to go from admitting our feelings to immediately living together. He's had enough to contend with these past few days without me turning up on his doorstep looking for a home. I'd hate us to start out from some misplaced sense of duty or chivalry on his part. I'm sure I'll be able to rent somewhere nearby and I'll need to find another job...' Lily's face fell and her bottom lip started to quiver a little as she realised the enormity of her situation.

Amelia could empathise. She herself had once been in a similar situation; losing her boyfriend and job on the same day. Although within a week of those events occurring, Amelia had also discovered she'd inherited Stone Manor and her situation had changed completely, for the better. Life had a funny way of working out, sometimes.

Lily started snuffling and went to blow her nose again but the little bit of soggy tissue was woefully inadequate.

'I'll be back in a minute. I must look a right state!'

A moment later Amelia heard a fresh round of loud nose-blowing from the toilet.

Lily returned. 'Sorry about that,' she said. 'I need a drink. Drew keeps a bottle of vodka in his drawer.'

Amelia, who was closer, opened the top drawer and pulled out a bottle of Absolut Citron. Then she saw the edge of a little plastic tube. She moved a couple of papers and unearthed a concealer.

'Is this the one you've been looking for?'

'Yes!' Lily came over and rummaged some more and pulled out a contour stick. 'Why on earth did he have these? He knew I was looking for them. Bloody hell, he's so vain.' She slammed the drawer in annoyance and the vibration caused his computer screen to come to life on his events calendar.

'He normally has this closed down and password protected. Another reason to make me think he was up to something.'

Lily leaned over and clicked the mouse a couple of times on a date that was highlighted in red.

'I remember that night, he was out until about five in the morning.' Amelia looked over Lily's shoulder. The evening was blocked out with *take Prosecco to Molly's* typed in.

'Do you know her?' Amelia asked.

'I know one of the estate agents in Inverness has a secretary called Molly. I thought she sounded quite old on the phone, but who knows? Maybe he has issues after his mum walked out! Well, if he's been seeing her, it assuages my guilt a little.'

Lily came out of that screen and Amelia saw other days blocked out on the main diary, she recognised some as being the dates listed on Gus's receipt.

'Do you mind if I check something?' Amelia asked.

Lily took a step back to let Amelia nearer the computer. Amelia clicked on the dates that been listed. Drew was meeting Molly on all of them. Was Gus meeting her too or had he known about Drew and this was one of the things Maja alluded to when she told Amelia that Gus liked to find things out about people? Had Gus been holding something over Drew?

Amelia clicked on Monday 2nd, which was the next date written on the receipt. Once again, Drew had blocked in the time from nine o'clock that night and typed *chilling with Molly*.

Amelia wondered if this event was going to happen at the Hunting Lodge.

The door opened and Andy McAvoy popped his head around.

'Hi, Lily. Oh hello, Amelia.'

'Hi, Andy.'

Andy McAvoy came into the estate agents. 'I know what's happened. Rory called me. He's on his way home.'

'Yes, I'm so glad he's been released. I thought I'd box up all my stuff. I'll be heading to Stone Manor for a few days while I sort everything out.'

Andy nodded.

'How is it having your boss Hector back?' Amelia asked Andy, making polite chit-chat as Lily boxed up the last of her things.

Andy puffed out his cheeks. 'To be honest, I've worked there so long he just lets me get on with everything and doesn't get involved in the day-to-day running of the place.'

'I hear you both had a bit of a fright on Tuesday.'

Andy blinked at her.

'The person wearing the pagan robes?'

'Ah! Oh yes! I'd forgotten about that. Oh, it was just some silly Beltane nonsense.'

'I think Hector was a bit more freaked out.'

Andy nodded. 'He was very shaken up about it. I suppose after all that happened in the past, he's worried about being haunted by things like that.'

'What happened?'

Andy looked a bit unsure before carrying on hesitatingly. 'It was just rumour really... I heard he... followed in his ancestor's occult... *leanings*. Hector's father had to send him away. I think they were all worried about his mental health and him going mad the same way Samuel Bain did. All that dark magic he and Cameron carried out. It left a mark on him. I've often thought it's why he doesn't come back very often. Being close to where... everything happened... it sometimes sends him a little off-kilter.'

Amelia was a little taken aback at this. It wasn't how Hector came across. Nor was it how the others remembered him. But then... he was never back regularly, or for long periods of time. And rarely caught up with his old gang when he did. Amelia surmised that Andy was probably the one who knew Hector best.

'Right, shall we go?' Lily said, lifting the box.

'I'll let Drew know you've cleared your things,' Andy said as the three of them left.

Lily turned off the lights, locked the door and posted the keys through the letter box.

TWENTY-NINE

Later that evening, Rory came in through the front door of Stone Manor.

'Hey, Amelia!' he said. 'Lily messaged me to say she's here?'

'She is. How are you?'

'I'm okay, although hours of intense questioning is exhausting.'

He did look rough, Amelia thought. His pallor was accentuated by the dark bruising shadows under his eyes.

'Was it awful?'

He gave a rueful smile. 'It wasn't fun.'

Just then Lily came running down the stairs and ran into Rory's arms. They stood like that for a few moments.

'They let you go with no charges?' Amelia asked as Lily and Rory broke apart.

'Yeah. Thankfully the restaurant we went to remembered us and then, on the way back we stopped off at a garage to fill Lily's car with petrol and I went in to pay and it was time-stamped. The police are pretty sure Johno was killed late afternoon or early evening. I'd have had to have been Lewis Hamilton to have got back in time to kill him. But just to make sure, the police checked the road camera footage of me on the journey back and it fits with what you told them and that I arrived in Glencarlach with only half an hour before the handfasting ceremony. Thankfully, I had plenty of folk who'd seen me at that point on.'

'That's a relief.'

Rory nodded. 'It wasn't just that they wanted to question me over though. You'll never guess what they found in my harbour-master's shed; the thing they put in the evidence bag. It was a pagan robe!'

'What?' Lily said in puzzlement.

'Just like the one Gideon saw and the one the person was wearing who jumped out at me.'

And the one Hector and Andy saw, Amelia thought.

'Do the police think someone wore the robe and killed Johno and then stuffed it in your harbour-master's shed?'

Rory shrugged. 'I guess. Now, I really fancy a drink. Want to join me?' he asked Lily. 'You too, Amelia, if you're free, and Jack...'

'Does your invitation extend to injured actors?' Gideon said, as he poked his head out from the drawing room.

Amelia often marvelled at Gideon's bat-like hearing.

Rory smiled. 'Of course.'

'You guys go,' Lily said. 'I want a quiet night and a long soak in the bath. I'm going to call my parents and catch them up on everything.' She turned to Rory. 'It's no doubt all around the village by now.'

'Let them talk. I don't care,' Rory said.

'I know I shouldn't care either, but I'll be the one painted as a scarlet woman. I'll need a day or so to gather my strength over this, okay?'

Rory nodded.

Leaving Lily to go back upstairs, the others headed out to the Whistling Haggis, picking up Jack on the way.

On entering the pub, the little group walked straight up to the bar. Moira was sitting next to Archie and they both turned round to greet them.

Wee Davey looked up from pouring a pint. 'Hey, guys, what can I get you?'

'This round's on me,' Rory said. 'Whisky?'

'Sounds good, thanks.' Amelia nodded as Jack gave Rory a thumbs up in agreement.

'Gideon?'

'Soda and lime. With a side order of morphine if possible,' Gideon said, leaning heavily against the bar.

'I did say the walk was a bit ambitious,' Amelia pointed out.

'No one likes a know-it-all, poppet,' Gideon said airily. 'I thought the exercise would do me good.'

'Exercise, right. And nothing to do with not wanting to miss out on hearing about Rory's experience and drama at the police station,' Jack said under his breath with a raised eyebrow to Amelia.

Moira leaned forward on her stool. 'Davey, love! Can you get me a cup of boiling water from that fancy new tap your dad installed, please?' She then delved into her pockets and produced a little plastic bag and handed it to Gideon.

He took it, peering dubiously at the contents through the cellophane. 'What's this? I was only joking about morphine or other drugs.'

'Relax. It's dried willow bark.'

'It looks like it belongs at the bottom of a hamster cage.'

'It's to make willow-bark tea,' Moira explained, taking the cup of water from Wee Davey and sliding it towards Gideon. 'Pop a teaspoon of the bark into hot water and leave it to infuse for ten minutes, strain then drink. It's a natural painkiller and there's enough there for a few cups. Come find me when you need more.'

'I would normally just pop a Solpadeine,' Gideon said.

'I'm sure you would. But why not give this a chance first? It's also kind on your tummy.'

'I'm always up for a bit of kindness. Thank you, Moira,' Gideon said as he took off the elastic band at the top, shaking a teaspoon's worth of the bark into the hot water. 'You are quite the witchy woman, aren't you? You'll be suggesting we cavort round the woods next in pagan worship,' he added archly.

Amelia and Jack exchanged a wide-eyed look at Gideon's loaded remark, but Moira just winked and said, 'Only if you're very lucky.'

Gideon sniffed the tea suspiciously.

'It's lovely with a cinnamon stick and you may need to sweeten it with some honey as it can be a little bitter,' Moira said.

'As can I be, darling, as can I,' Gideon said as they took their drinks over to a nearby table.

'Is the incident room still set up over there?' Amelia said, looking out the window at the church, half expecting to see the DI standing in the doorway, looking over at them.

'Probably,' Rory said.

Amelia wondered about popping over to let him know about the Gosling's rum and the receipt with dates on the back. She didn't know what McGregor would make of them, probably nothing and he would tell her off for interfering. She had planned on telling him about it when they were all round for dinner, but the opportunity hadn't arisen, and then all the attention went to Moira finding the tarot card and message in her room.

Gideon narrowed his eyes. 'I don't think I can look McGregor in the eyes after what you told me.'

Rory raised an eyebrow questioningly.

'Jack and Amelia saw him cavorting in the woods doing some sort of pagan-like worship.'

'What, naked?' Rory asked, agog.

'No!' Amelia and Jack said in unison.

'See, I'm not the only one who wondered that!' Gideon said with a smug look, clearly feeling vindicated.

'Is that all?' Rory asked. 'I mean, it's Beltane, it often makes folk go a wee bit funny round here.'

'Rory,' Amelia said, changing the subject, 'you know that voicemail you got from Johno? He seemed worried and scared. Why didn't he go to see McGregor in the incident room?'

Rory rolled the base of his whisky glass on the table for a moment, before saying, 'He was probably wary of going to the police about anything. He liked to smoke a bit of hash, pop a pill now and then. He'd normally just keep it for himself but I think he'd got a bit more lately and was maybe selling a little too. I'd wondered if that was why he'd been so freaked out about the police going round to the SeaShack to question him about the diver. He could have had a few joints lying around and didn't want to risk the police finding them. Johno knew I wasn't into anything like that so he didn't really talk about it with me.'

That made sense, especially as he seemed to have a little extra money lately.

Rory exhaled. 'I hope to hell they find out whoever did this.' He raised his glass. 'To Johno.'

They all joined in the toast for their dead friend then fell silent for a few moments.

Rory ran his hand under the rim of his bucket hat and

exhaled, 'Oh bugger,' as the door opened and someone walked in.

Drew.

The estate agent stared at Rory.

Amelia started to feel uncomfortable and hoped there wouldn't be any trouble. Now she understood why Lily hadn't wanted to join them.

'Drew...' Rory started as Drew stood looking fierce.

'Don't you *fuck*ing dare say you're sorry.' Drew kicked the leg of Rory's chair, propelling his seat back a few inches. Without breaking eye contact with his brother, Rory slowly dragged his chair back to the table.

'We don't want any trouble,' Jack said evenly. 'We're trying to enjoy a quiet drink.'

'He should have thought of that before he screwed Lily.'

Rory stood up. 'D'you want to talk outside?'

Amelia guessed there wouldn't be that much talking as Drew had both fists tightly clenched at his side.

Rory wasn't as tall as Drew but he was compact and, given he worked outside throughout the year in hardy conditions, he was in good shape.

Without another word, Drew launched himself across the table, grabbed Rory by his T-shirt, held him fast and cracked a solid right hook on his jaw.

Jack immediately jumped up and hauled Drew away from Rory, who had staggered back on impact and fallen over a chair. Drew turned and took a swing at Jack, who ducked out the way.

'Come on! Fight!' Drew shouted as Rory got to his feet.

'I'm not fighting you,' Rory said.

Then the estate agent took a run at the captain of the *Amber Dram*, only stopped before contact by Big Davey, who'd marched out from the back and grabbed Drew by the back of his shirt and held tight.

'No fighting in my pub,' the landlord said in a dangerously low voice and shoved Drew towards the door. 'You, go and sleep off your anger and don't think of coming back in here until you've calmed down.'

Drew looked ready to go again but stopped himself. 'What'll Mum make of this when she finds out?' He touched the side of his eye and winced then slowly sloped out.

'I didn't touch him!' Rory said in defence. He then apologised to the landlord and got up to leave, but Big Davey pointed at his chair.

'Sit.'

Rory sat.

Big Davey hoisted up his belt. 'It's best you wait here until your brother's calmed down. He's spoiling for a fight. Word to the wise, Rory, I think you and Lily should lie low for a bit, until emotions stop being so raw. Drew's not a bad lad but no one likes their nose being rubbed in a shitty situation,' Big Davey said firmly as he went back behind the bar.

'Davey, lad,' Big Davey said to his son, 'best get Casanova over there an ice pack,' he added as he disappeared off into the back room again.

'That was all rather dramatic,' Gideon said. As soon as the trouble started, he'd scooted his chair against the wall, keeping himself and his cup of infusing tea out of the way of any trouble. 'Who knew Big Davey could move so fast!'

'I should have expected that,' Rory said, fingering his jaw.

'Are you worried Drew will be waiting for you?' Amelia said.

Rory gave them a rueful smile. 'This is not the first time we've been in a fight. I'm a bit surprised he's reacted like this to be honest. He didn't value Lily; took her for granted and didn't treat her well. But I guess it must be a pride thing for him.'

'And so speaks the foolhardy voice of love!' Gideon said

with a dramatic sigh before taking a tentative sip of his tea. 'I hope Lily's worth it,' Gideon said when he'd put the cup down.

Rory gave a lopsided smile. 'Aye, she is.'

'The things we do for love.'

'You may want to get some arnica for that if it starts to bruise,' Moira called over to Rory.

'Is that another of your strange potions; leaves of the arnica plant, collected at dawn on a new moon?' Gideon asked.

'Not quite, I tend to buy mine in tubes from the chemist. It's widely available,' she said with a smile.

THIRTY

The evening wore on and Amelia went up to the bar where Big Davey and Moira were chatting together.

Davey walked over when he saw Amelia. 'You caught us reminiscing.'

'Davey found some old photos.' Moira held up a sleeve of Boots' prints. 'It's of some random things as well as Cameron's eighteenth.'

'I remember it took me a while to get around to developing them. I just couldn't bear to see them for a long while, but I then worried the film would get damaged if I didn't take it out of the camera.'

'Those were the days, before all this Instagramming nonsense and digital cameras. You never knew what you were going to get when you picked up your photos.' Moira held one up, turning it all ways to try and figure out the image. 'Hmm, often just a blurry mess.'

Moira held another out to Amelia. It was of herself and Davey. Moira looked absolutely stunning with her long dark hair and pale face, made paler by gothic-inspired make-up. Davey was tall and skinny and had a mullet hairstyle.

'I remember the days when I didn't have to suck in my gut for photos!' He laughed.

'Here's Cammy.' Moira held up a photo of a very good-looking teenager, with dark curly hair and fine features.

And another one where Moira's brother was laughing uproariously, beer in hand, eyes screwed against the smoke from a roll-up cigarette.

Moira beckoned Amelia over and handed her the pack of photos as they looked through the rest.

Ray looked as fresh-faced and rosy-cheeked as he did now, just without the large, bushy moustache.

'Hector?' Amelia queried, pointing to a dramatic-looking boy with shoulder-length straight hair, eyeliner and a frilly shirt. He sported a monocle.

'Oh yes, his dress sense hasn't improved much!' Davey gave a snort of a laugh.

'And there's Elizabeth. So beautiful!' Moira said, pointing to a tall girl who could have been a model with her long curly hair, high cheekbones, straight nose and perfect skin.

'You can see us getting drunker as the night goes on!' Moira laughed as she plucked out one of Davey and Ray, arms around each other's shoulders, leaning towards the camera, Davey with his eyes half-shut. Beside them was a youth who could only be McGregor. Dressed in black jeans, black turtle-neck jumper and black leather jacket, with a cigarette dangling insouciantly out of the corner of his mouth, McGregor looked like a throwback to the Beatnik poets. Even with a long fringe flopping over one eye, Amelia knew that intense stare; she'd been on the receiving end often enough.

Photo after photo, it was a group of loving friends having a night out to celebrate Cameron's eighteenth birthday.

'Hector always played up to the camera!' Moira laughed. 'That bloody monocle. He thought he was so cool, remember?'

'Is that Archie?' Amelia asked as she honed in on a photograph, clearly taken in the Whistling Haggis.

'It certainly is, in his favourite spot at the bar; third bar stool from the left.' Big Davey peered more closely. 'Jeez, is that Andy McAvoy? I don't remember him being there that night.'

'We certainly wouldn't have invited him. Creepy wee bugger. Cameron might have let him come along. My brother always looked out for the waifs and strays,' Moira said to Amelia.

'Hector wouldn't have been happy, Andy being there,' Davey said.

'Hector doesn't like Andy?' Amelia said in surprise. 'But Andy works for him as his estate manager,' Amelia said.

'Back then?' Moira shook her head. 'Hector was very protective of Cameron and liked the group as it was.'

'That's what the big argument was about,' Davey said. 'Cameron thought we should be more welcoming and Hector lost it. Said he'd had to put up with a lot already but he wasn't about to let Andy McAvoy join them. I actually felt quite sorry for Andy.'

'What did Hector mean about already putting up with a lot?' Amelia asked.

Moira shifted on her bar stool. 'Well, the heavy-duty ceremonial things was always just Cameron and Hector. It wasn't for us. But then Elizabeth joined in. Hector wasn't happy. I think if it was anyone else he'd have put his foot down, but he adored Elizabeth, so he let it go.'

'Hector must be okay with Andy now, surely? He's Hector's estate manager,' Amelia said.

'I think it was Hector Senior that hired Andy. But yes, they're fine now. Hector probably felt a bit guilty about how he behaved back then. And, Hector's never back here anymore, so has very little opportunity to have direct interaction with Andy,' Davey said.

Moira let out a cackle of laughter. 'Oh God, here's one with the infamous pagan robes,' she said.

Cameron, Hector and Elizabeth stood looking faux serious, wearing their robes. There was another one with Elizabeth and Moira where Moira looked very much the worse for wear.

'How come Elizabeth's not looking as deranged as the rest of us?' Davey said.

'She wasn't drinking that night, remember. This is a gorgeous one of her.' Moira handed Amelia the photograph. It was a close-up of Elizabeth looking straight at the camera, a small smile playing on her lips, but it wasn't her beatific expression that caught Amelia's attention. It was the necklace she was wearing that made Amelia look more closely. Round Elizabeth's slender neck was a chain with a disc engraved with a pointed 'B'.

'That necklace!' Amelia said.

Davey looked. 'Oh yes, she always wore that, whenever I saw her. It didn't matter how many expensive necklaces Andy bought her, Elizabeth never took that one off.'

Amelia flicked back through the photos.

'She isn't wearing it earlier in the evening.'

Moira took the photos from Amelia and looked. 'You're right. Come to think of it, I don't remember her wearing it before that night.'

'Could someone have given her it at the party?' Amelia asked.

'I guess,' Davey said as he went to serve someone that had come up to the bar. 'I never really understood why she wore it, because her name didn't start with the letter *B*.'

But Amelia had an inkling. Moira said Elizabeth hadn't

been well on the lead-up to Cameron's party and that she'd not been drinking. And to be wearing the runic symbol that represented birth and motherhood and secrets...

Could Elizabeth have been pregnant?

THIRTY-ONE

Amelia was up early the next morning and drove the Jeep the few miles to the florists whose address had been typed on the card with the flowers left at Cameron's grave.

The shop front of E&E florists was delightful. Pale-pink woodwork had pastel flowers painted up the sides of the door, which looped and whirled onto the window which framed the dozens of buckets of flowers on display.

The door was open and Amelia was met with sweet smells of freesias as well as the heady aroma of lilies as she entered the cheerfully cluttered shop.

A woman stood behind the counter wrapping twine around a free-form bouquet of spring flowers. She looked up and gave Amelia a beaming smile.

'Good morning. How can I help you?'

'I was hoping to speak to Elizabeth.'

The other woman's face fell a little. 'I'm afraid she isn't here. I'm Emma, her business partner, can I help?'

'It was really Elizabeth I wanted to see. I live in Glencarlach and there's something I need to speak to her about urgently.'

Emma cut the twine and put the scissors and flowers down.

'If you live in Glencarlach, I'm surprised you don't already know she's gone,' she said kindly.

'It's just that she sent a bouquet of flowers recently, from here. It was for a gravestone in the church in Glencarlach. For a Cameron Ballantyne. I'd hoped that she still popped into work from time to time.'

Emma shook her head sadly. 'No, I haven't seen her in six months. I sent that bouquet on her behalf. She always sent flowers every year around that time. I didn't think she'd want to miss it.'

'Oh, did you do the arrangement yourself?'

'I did.'

Amelia felt a little deflated as suddenly the flowers seemed less meaningful.

'But I made sure to use the exact same arrangement as Elizabeth always did. She was very particular about choosing those flowers.'

Amelia smiled. She *was* onto something.

'Do you have any idea where she's gone?'

Emma shook her head.

'Did you have any idea she was leaving?'

'Oh yes. Elizabeth had everything planned. That was her all over, really. She wasn't the type to leave things to chance. She contacted our lawyers and insisted on temporarily signing over her half of the business to me, until she came back.'

'Did she say when she thought that would be?'

'She just said when things settled down. I thought it was just going to be a few weeks, not a few months.'

'Did something happen to make her decide to leave?'

'She fell in love.'

'Did you ever meet Paddy?'

'A couple of times, they were like teenagers together. He's a handsome man, clearly worships her. To be honest, I'd never seen her so happy as she was in the few months before she left.'

'Did she say anything else?'

'I know she felt guilty about her boys, but they're really grown men now. She'll have been in touch with them by now though, surely.'

'I don't think so.'

'Oh.' Emma looked a little taken aback.

'One other thing. Do you remember a necklace she wore, with a pointed 'B' engraved on it?'

'Yes, she always wore it. I once asked her if it stood for Beth, or Bee, but she said no, she was always Elizabeth. She laughed and said one friend got away with calling her Lizzie, but no one else dared shorten her name.'

'Okay, thank you.'

She was on her way out when Emma called her back.

'I don't know if you want to pass these on to her boys? She would get this delivery every month. It must be a standing order she's forgotten to cancel. The last few are backed up but I don't know what they are. It didn't feel right opening it.'

Emma went into the back and came out with a bag. Inside were six identically-sized small cardboard boxes.

'And if you do catch up with her, tell her to please get in touch. Not about the shop, that looks after itself now after so many years! But I want to know she's okay. As a friend. I miss her.'

After promising she would, Amelia left, holding the bulging bag. On the other side of the road, Amelia spied a welcoming-looking café. Leaving so early, she'd only managed a very quick shot of espresso and now she fancied a flat white with some kind of wickedly gooey cake to go with it.

Amelia crossed the road and gave the barista her order,

selecting a slice of lemon-and-passionfruit sponge with a thick coconut butter icing before sitting down at a table.

She opened up the bag Emma had given her and was about to open one of the boxes when someone else entered the café and sat down at the table in the window.

'Your usual, chai latte?' the waitress shouted over.

'Yes please,' the woman called back and when she turned, Amelia realised it was Isobel.

Now would be the perfect opportunity to say hello, sit down beside the archaeologist and try and find out what it was Maja suspected Gus knew about Isobel.

'Hello!' Amelia called out, giving her a friendly wave.

Isobel looked up and stared at Amelia for a few seconds before bursting into tears.

THIRTY-TWO

Amelia's order arrived as Isobel continued to cry and another waitress rushed over to make sure the archaeologist was all right.

Amelia got up and went to Isobel's table.

'Is everything okay? Has something happened?'

But Isobel just sat shaking her head.

The waitress brought over Isobel's order as well as Amelia's from her previous seat.

'Can I get you anything else?' the waitress asked, hovering for a moment.

Isobel shook her head and the woman left.

'So, do you come here often?' Amelia tried to joke.

Isobel nodded. 'I do, actually. A few times a week.'

'The cake must be good.' Amelia eyed up the big slab of her own.

'I'm sorry, I'm not normally as emotional as this...'

'It's been a very trying time.'

Isobel nodded again and sniffed and Amelia handed her a tissue from her pocket.

Isobel raised her head and looked over the road. Amelia

followed her gaze to see Emma placing a silver bucket full of bunches of daffodils outside the shop.

'Do you know Emma?'

'No.'

'Elizabeth?'

Isobel nodded. She looked up with a tear-stained face. 'I'm so desperate to find her. I can't believe she abandoned me. Again. I don't understand why she left. We'd been getting on so well, getting to know each other...'

And Amelia properly looked at Isobel, took in her tall, long-limbed frame. The straight nose, the features... She guessed Isobel was in her late thirties. And Elizabeth had the rune necklace that symbolised birth and motherhood.

'Elizabeth's your mother, isn't she?'

Isobel nodded sadly. 'Nobody else knows, now.' She grabbed hold of her mug, but didn't drink from it. 'I've not known her long, only traced her about eighteen months ago. My adoptive parents are wonderful and I had a brilliant upbringing. They've always been open about my adoption but I never really felt the need to seek out my birth parents. Until I hit my mid-thirties and suddenly thought the time left to find out answers was narrowing. It was a now or never moment. So, I contacted social work and it turned out my birth mother had it on record that she was open to me getting in touch. And we met. And it was lovely. She said she always wondered about me but didn't want to contact me in case I didn't know I was adopted and it caused problems so she was delighted that I'd sought her out. We talked about her being so young and how she kept it hidden and only her mother, my grandmother, knew.'

'How did Elizabeth manage to keep it a secret?' Especially in Glencarlach!

'She waited until just before the summer holidays which was when she started to have a bit of a bump, and she and her mum left. They said it was to go and visit a sick relative. She had me and then they returned to Glencarlach. No one guessed. But when we met, she said she wanted me to be a part of her life and she didn't want to hide anything anymore. And that's why I don't understand why she left.'

'Did you meet Rory and Drew and Andy?'

'No. Elizabeth wanted to tell Rory and Drew about me. She said it wasn't fair that we didn't get to know each other but neither of us wanted to rush anything.

'Elizabeth and I didn't meet up often as it was difficult for her to get away and neither of us were ready for me to come to Glencarlach. It was nice getting to know each other slowly. It felt special with it just being the two of us. I saw her at the end of October and we talked about me coming to Glencarlach in the new year. She planned on telling the boys over Christmas.'

Isobel sniffed loudly and Amelia handed her another tissue. The archaeologist blew her nose before continuing.

'And then she ghosted me. I tried phoning and emailing but nothing. And then I got wind of the possibility of the Pictish site and I moved heaven and earth to get here. I figured if I was there in an official academic capacity it would explain my presence and we could continue getting to know each other.'

'And then you got in touch with Hector Bain for funding?'

Isobel looked down at the tabletop for a moment before answering. 'It wasn't just for that. I'd wondered if he was my father.'

'Wow!'

'Well, possibly. He might be. Elizabeth mentioned bits about the past and confessed that my father was one of her friends in the group that all hung out together. There were seven of them and they called themselves the Watchful Wiccan, and they did tarot and spells and that sort of thing and she even wore a pagan robe. She gave it to me, thought it was fitting because of my archaeology speciality. So, I got in touch with Hector as he was the easiest person for me to track down and I had an excuse because the area of archaeological interest was on his land.

'And when I arrived in Glencarlach I found out nobody had seen Elizabeth for months as she'd left with Johno's dad. I'm trying hard not to take it personally but it's still hurtful. But I guess I just have to wait until she comes back. I spoke to Johno about his dad one day when he came to take Maja out. I asked him if he'd heard from him but Johno hadn't. He also said it had always been his dad's dream to sail around the world and that's what he thought his dad and Elizabeth were doing. Paddy had left Johno a letter saying he'd get in touch when he could and the next morning Paddy's boat, *Sundowner*, was gone. I guess there's not much internet connection in the middle of the Atlantic.'

'I'm sorry.'

Isobel stirred her chai latte. 'I tried to get friendly with Rory and Drew. Just to maintain some connection, subtly though, you know?'

'And then Drew mistook your friendship as a come-on?' Amelia remembered the evening in the Whistling Haggis when Isobel had freaked out that he rested his hand on her knee. Obviously he hadn't known he was her half-brother.

'Yes. And then I got really drunk and did a stupid thing.' She momentarily hid her head in her hands. 'The night of the meeting in the community hall, I put on the pagan robe and walked up to Gull Point.'

'You were the one Gideon saw in the Stone Manor grounds!'

Isobel nodded.

'And then you stood outside Hector's house.'

She nodded again. 'I hadn't realised he was coming back to

Glencarlach. It had been a bit of a shock seeing him and I wanted to talk to him, but there was someone with him and I got cold feet and ran.' She took a sip from her mug.

'And the next night you jumped out at Rory.'

Isobel put her mug down and leaned into the table, eyes wide. 'But no, I didn't. That wasn't me! That's what freaked me out, because clearly someone else had pagan robes too and people thought the pagan-robed figure was behind the murder. But I wouldn't ever do that, even though Gus found out about Elizabeth being my mum. God knows how, he had a knack for gathering information. I thought, because of the robes and Gus knowing my secret, I'd be a suspect. I was scared and got rid of the robes.'

Amelia remembered back to the Beltane parade. Isobel had bumped into her by the oyster stand with that bulky bag over her shoulder. 'You left them in Rory's harbour-master's shed.'

'Yes, and that made everything so much worse! I only put them there because they belonged to his mum. I didn't realise poor Johno had been killed and was only a few feet away. And I still keep coming here and waiting and hoping that Elizabeth will miraculously appear and make it all right again and she can confirm if my dad really is Hector Bain.'

Judging by the bouquet left at Cameron's grave every year, in an arrangement which symbolised romance and secrecy, true love forsaken by death, Amelia thought it far more likely that Cameron was Isobel's father.

Elizabeth really did say it with flowers.

'You're going to have to tell McGregor about the robes.'

Isobel hung her head, her shoulders deflated. 'I know. And I'll have to start at the beginning. And everything will come out.'

Amelia thought that might not be a bad thing.

'You're definitely sure Elizabeth has never been back to

Glencarlach?' Amelia thought back to the Hunting Lodge and that someone had been there.

'As much as I can be.'

'Did Elizabeth go into much detail about the Wiccan things she got up to, if she still practised the occult?'

'She said she left it all behind. Couldn't stomach it anymore. She only kept the robe because of sentimentality.'

Amelia took the information in before asking, 'Would you like a lift back to Glencarlach?'

'Yes please. Public transport takes forever round here.'

They finished their drinks and walked back to Amelia's Jeep. Getting in, she threw the bag of unopened boxes into the boot and together, she and Isobel drove back to the village.

Amelia and Isobel got to the church in Glencarlach by mid-morning. The doors were flung wide open as a welcome gesture to the congregation of Glencarlach. Taking it as an invitation, the two women stepped inside the vestry. Despite there being a table with a notepad and pen next to a board with a notice on it asking for any information pertaining to an 'incident' on Tuesday night, the area was deserted. Amelia had a quick peek into the main church where the sun streamed through the stained-glass windows, highlighting the dust particles in the air and casting a rainbow of colour onto the vacant pews.

No incident room there.

Another door led from the vestry into the room which was used for parish council meetings. Amelia slowly opened the door.

Bingo!

Two large tables had been joined together in the middle of the room to house computers and other electrical equipment, although none were switched on. A variety of chairs were positioned around the tables, but like the other areas of the church, the room was void of people. It looked like the investigation was being wound down, or possibly paused. At the other end of the room stood a magnetic dry-wipe board where photographs had been attached and words scribbled on. There were photographs of the exterior and interior of a small boat. There was also a photograph of a man, clearly Gus but taken a while previously due to fewer piercings and tattoos. Even from far off, it looked like a police photo to Amelia. Underneath the man's image she could make out the words *fatal stab wound to chest, head injury* and *defensive wounds. Let murderer into room/ already in room/ known to victim? Murder weapon?* then some smaller writing Amelia couldn't make out.

Underneath was a list:

Possession, intent to supply. Trafficking ring. Insider hit?

She was taking a couple of steps nearer the board to read the small print when a DC came out of the adjoining kitchen with a cup of tea.

'Can I help you?' he asked, putting his tea on the table and looking at her suspiciously.

Isobel took a step forward. 'I'm looking for DI McGregor as I have some information for him.'

'I want to talk to him too,' Amelia said.

'What would you like to tell me?'

Amelia jumped at the voice speaking directly behind her. She hadn't heard anyone approach.

She turned to see Detective Inspector McGregor.

'Although you'd better be quick as another team will be arriving soon.'

Isobel looked worried. 'Another team?'

'Yes, we were a joint teams investigation but it now seems it's not so much joint as taken over.'

'Why?' Amelia asked.

McGregor briefly glanced behind Amelia at the whiteboards then settled his unflinching gaze back on her, the muscle in his jaw clenching.

'Was Gus part of a bigger crime?' Amelia pressed.

McGregor gestured to the DC to turn the boards around then said, 'Ms Adams. I understand you are keen to be of help. But I have warned you about playing detective. Miss Aitken, do you still want to talk to me or would you rather wait until the other team arrives?'

Isobel hesitated a little before saying, 'I'd quite like to tell you. You see, there's a little bit of a personal nature attached.'

McGregor's eyes widened imperceptibly at this. He turned to Amelia. 'I'll let you be on your way. I would imagine a busy hotel like Stone Manor takes up a lot of your time.'

McGregor stood to the side to let Amelia leave.

Amelia felt quite dismissed. She'd only been trying to help! She left the church and crossed over Main Street.

It was only when she got to the Whistling Haggis did Amelia glance over her shoulder and saw McGregor standing in the church doorway, watching her.

THIRTY-THREE

Later that Monday, Amelia came out into the hotel reception area to find Rory hovering in the drawing room.

'Hi, Rory, are you waiting on Lily? She said she was popping out.'

'It's actually Isobel I'm waiting on. She messaged me and said she had to talk to me. No idea why but it sounded quite urgent though. Is it okay to wait in here?'

'Of course. How are you? How are things with your brother?'

Rory gave a rather lacklustre shrug. 'Drew's walking around with a massive shiner. I could have sworn I didn't hit him. But, wow, it's a bruise all right. Dad's just keeping his head down and working and trying not to take sides. Luckily Lily is amazing.'

'You must miss your mum at a time like this,' Amelia said.

'Aye, I could do with a good old chat and cup of tea with her. She always manages to put things into perspective.'

'And you've no idea where she's gone?'

'Nope.'

'I heard she sent you and Drew a Christmas card. Is there a postmark on the envelope?'

'The card came direct from one of those internet sites, with our name on the front to make it personal. A note or visit would have been far more personal.' He gave Amelia a rueful look.

'And there's been nothing else?'

'Not since November. It was fifth November, Guy Fawkes night. While we were all watching the fireworks my mum and Paddy were running away together. Like daft teenagers. Drew keeps saying Mum would be raging at me, but I don't think she's got a leg to stand on when it comes to falling in love with someone else.'

'Had Johno heard anything?'

Rory looked stricken. 'God, I've just realised, how will Paddy find out about Johno...? Oh this is awful.'

'I'm sure the police will be trying to track them down now.'

Rory nodded sadly. 'No, Johno hadn't heard. But his dad's boat, *Sundowner*, was missing the next morning, so looks like they're living out their dream and sailing the world.'

'Did it make things weird for you and Johno? With your friendship?'

'No, it was nice to talk to someone who was going through exactly the same thing. In fact, Johno and Drew had even gotten more friendly over the last couple of months. Drew had always thought Johno was a bit of a waster, but we can't all be high-flying estate agents, can we?'

'Rory, was your mum doing this out of character? No one had a clue?'

Rory took a moment to answer. 'You know, at first it was a shock. Everyone around here felt it, people all said Elizabeth McAvoy was a doting wife and mother. Involved in the community, why did she leave, blah blah blah, but see... there's something about Mum. Like you can never get the whole of her attention. While talking, she has a look on her face, like she's ninety-five per cent with you but the other five per cent is preoccupied with something else, like she's wondering if she's left the stove on, or if she's replied to an important email, or running through a list of the flowers she needs for her next trip to the market. I always thought it was because she was so busy, but looking back, was it? Was there someone that has a bit of Mum that she doesn't want to share?'

Amelia wondered if it was the knowledge of Isobel that affected her.

'And I don't mean I thought she had lots of affairs,' Rory continued. 'She's not the sort to do something without meaning or to be frivolous. She obviously fell in love with Paddy. I don't believe leaving would have been an easy decision. For either of them. She planned everything, from signing over the business, to the letters she gave me, Drew and Dad. She's thorough, I'll give her that.'

'The letters? How did you get them?'

'She'd put mine in my boat and Drew's through the estate agent's letter box. She'd left Dad's by the cereal boxes. He's a daily bowl of All Bran kind of guy. Although turned out Dad was actually the last to know. Hector had got him busy on a new project and he'd been up really early and missed breakfast. Drew and I went to talk to him the next morning. He'd not found the letter at that time. He thought we were joking at first. That was a difficult conversation.'

'Are you angry at your mum?'

'No, definitely not. I really hope she's finally happy.'

'Finally?'

'Well, I mean... happy. If she'd been looking for something else, you know?'

'Did your mum and dad get on?'

Rory scratched his head, a little at a loss before saying, 'I thought so, but clearly not well enough. They weren't like love's young dream. Since Mum went, I've been questioning a lot of things. I suppose Drew and I selfishly thought Mum was only really there for us. And she was brilliant. I never questioned her and Dad's relationship until a few months ago. Mum once said, she'd only ever gone out with him at the start because she felt a bit sorry for him. He always tried to do everything for Mum but the more he did the more she pulled away. Like when he bought that stupidly expensive necklace for her birthday a few years ago. He wanted her to take that old necklace off but she refused. He was really upset about it, it was like he couldn't understand why it meant so much because it wasn't worth anything. And after that Mum got quite distant with him. I don't think it helped that Hector started Dad on a whole load of extra projects around that time. Dad was always out. I think Hector was very demanding. I guess Mum just had enough, got together with Paddy, and left.'

'All from that necklace.'

'Possibly. Mum has a stubborn streak.'

At that moment, Isobel walked into the drawing room. On seeing Rory, her cheeks flushed scarlet.

'I'll leave you two to chat,' Amelia said as she left the room. 'Everything okay?' she asked Isobel in a low voice.

The other woman nodded. 'McGregor ended up being very nice to me, which I didn't expect.'

'Any word on who will be taking over the investigation?'

'It's some team from Europol or something like that.'

Amelia wondered who she'd tell about the rum now, and if it was even important if reading about the drugs link and it being an insider hit on the whiteboard was anything to go by.

'Can I bring you anything?' Amelia asked.

'No thanks, but Rory may need a double brandy for shock, in a bit.'

'I'll be right outside.'

Amelia squeezed Isobel's arm and left, closing the door behind her to give them some privacy. James was on the phone behind the reception desk, scribbling something down on a notepad.

'That's lovely, yes. She's here now, I'll let her know, thanks, Christine.' James hung up and handed Amelia the little bit of paper. 'The citronella candles came in.'

'That's great, I'll go get them now.' She looked down at the note, at the top, James had written down that day's date – May 2nd.

'Everything okay?' James asked as he watched Amelia.

'Yes, just thinking.' Amelia recalled the list of dates Gus had written down on the back of his receipt, the next of which was May 2nd. The date Drew had blocked out on his electronic diary for his possible rendezvous at the Hunting Lodge...

This time it was Biffy Clyro blasting out of the speakers when Amelia entered the outdoors shop.

'Hello there, Amelia.' Christine McGuthrie looked up from reading a leaflet, putting her glasses on top of her hair.

'Hi, Christine. James said you called to say the candles were in.'

'I've got four each of the triple-wick and torch-type ones for you. Although, rain and high winds are forecast so I doubt you'll have anyone sitting outside tonight.'

'They're good to have just in case.'

Christine lifted up a big bag and put it on the counter. 'I've also got a special on at the moment. Buy a Deet spray and you get a half-price tick remover and a free hurricane whistle.'

Amelia had recently read an article on Lyme disease and did not fancy getting a bacterial infection courtesy of a tick. 'Sounds good.' She pulled one of each out of the basket on the counter and as she did her eyes fell on the poster Christine had been looking over; advertising that evening's wildlife society meeting in the Whistling Haggis.

Christine came back over with the candles and noticed her studying the poster as she put them in a bag. 'Fancy coming along? We're on the lookout for new members. I suggested to Andy he get Drew involved. The lad'll have more time, now he's split with Lily.'

Amelia managed to keep a straight face at Christine's rather cynical take on Drew's new-found single status.

Underneath the leaflet was a petition for those to sign if they were against the archaeological dig.

'How do you feel about the excavation site now you know it'll hopefully have minimal impact on the environment?' Amelia asked.

'I don't mind, to tell you the truth. In fact, I see the advantage of the excavation, but one of us had to be the spokesperson for the group and it couldn't really be Andy as he's a local councillor and has to seem impartial.'

'Andy's against it?'

'He hates the thought of badger sets being destroyed and the destruction of hedgehog travel routes being interfered with. But he's in a tight position as his boss is also the one financing it all. In fact, it's odd that Hector Bain's all for it. What with his background in all that weird pagan stuff. Andy told me all about *that*, you know. Andy thought Hector would have wanted to preserve the sanctity of the site. Still, I suppose Hector Bain needs to be seen as a great benefactor. Although, now I wouldn't be surprised if it all gets cancelled anyway. Any connection with a murder will put people off.'

Christine popped the Deet spray, whistle and tick remover into a little paper bag, which Amelia put in her pocket. Hoisting up the bag full of the lemony scented midgie repellents, Amelia headed back to the Jeep.

THIRTY-FOUR

'Is this becoming our place?' Murray asked as Moira walked up to the abbey ruins, next to the excavation site, just before five that evening.

'It could be. I like it here. There's something restful about it.'

Murray had been sitting on one of the low walls of the ruins and he stood when she arrived.

Moira looked behind him and saw a tartan picnic blanket as well as a couple of glasses and a bottle of Macallan whisky. There was also a Tupperware box.

'Cheese and oatcakes,' Murray said. 'I remember the last time you were here you talked about missing a good cheddar.'

The last time she'd been here.

'Nearly twelve years ago.'

Murray nodded. 'Your dad's funeral. I remember you were quite overcome by how many were there.'

'Yes. He was a good man, my dad. It was nice so many wanted to pay their respects.'

'Everyone wanted you to stay on for a bit, but you were adamant you were only there for a night. So imagine how surprised I was when you followed me home.'

Moira felt her face flame. She remembered it keenly. His arms around her. The passion. The feeling of security...

'That was some night. And I really believed you when you said you wanted to stay. With me. But then you were gone. Vanished off back to France.'

'I wondered if you'd come and look for me.'

'You didn't leave a forwarding address.'

'Well, I thought, being in the police you might have had some sort of way to look me up.'

'Ah, and that's why you were angry with me all those years. Honestly? I didn't think you'd want me to find you. Running away is usually a sign a person's not happy. And well, let's face it, you had form.'

Moira's heart was racing wildly. She knew they'd have to have this conversation at some point. It had been the massive elephant in the room every time they'd seen each other since she'd returned a few days ago.

'I'm not leading the case anymore,' Murray blurted out.

'Whyever not?'

'Got word Gus was involved in something a lot bigger. It's a Europol matter.' He walked over to the picnic blanket and poured two glasses of whisky.

'And I think it's for the best. I'm too close.'

'But you didn't know Gus.'

He handed her a glass. 'Not to the victim. But a suspect.'

'Me? I'm a suspect?'

He smelt the whisky, savouring the aroma before saying, 'Not seriously, but what with the tarot, and you staying where the murder happened... and, well, there's another thing. The night of the murder, everyone remarked how lucky it was I was so close to the area. It was nothing to do with luck. I'd heard you were back and I knew where you were staying and I'd been sitting in my car at the end of the drive for the entire evening wondering how I could come and talk to you. I must have fallen asleep. It doesn't look good that a murder happened under my very nose and I saw nothing.'

There was a lot to unpack with what Murray told her.

Of all the questions she could have asked, she said, 'Why did you want to see me?'

'It seems I'm a glutton for punishment, doesn't it?'

'I wish we could go back to that night, to Cammy's eighteenth. And make it different. We could have stayed home. Or drunk less and that way no one would have argued and Cammy wouldn't have gone off on his own. And he wouldn't be dead and we wouldn't all have had our lives irrevocably altered from that day.'

'I've often wished that myself. Although I do have some fond memories of that night,' Murray said softly. 'I remember how you bummed a cigarette off me, and stood like this sexy screen siren while you got me to light it and I remember my hands shook. But you didn't notice, mainly because you were three sheets to the wind and weren't too steady on your feet. And you accused me of being too engrossed in my new Depeche Mode album to notice you. Then you pushed me against the wall and snogged the face off me before handing me back the cigarette and disappearing off into the night. I see a pattern with us, Moira,' Murray said, a faint trace of humour in his voice.

'I was testing the water to see if you liked me.'

Murray laughed. 'Oh, Moira, I was besotted by you. And terrified of you.'

'What!'

'You were this amazing free spirit. You had opinions on things and spoke passionately and had causes and didn't take nonsense from anyone. You were so cool.'

'*You* were the cool one. Detached like you didn't care about anything. I jumped through hoops trying to get you to notice me.'

'Until that night I never thought I had a chance with you. I would have done anything for you.' He sighed, running his hand through his hair. 'Still would if I'm being honest. And that's the problem. You, the past, all that, it was skewing my view on the case.'

'I didn't know. Well, I thought you maybe liked me; that's why I launched myself at you as I was fed up of waiting for you to make the first move. I'd drunk so much to give me Dutch courage. Too much, because Elizabeth had to drive me home and I was sick in a hedge. And I remember she was just getting over her sickness bug and said she felt sick too.'

Murray smiled. 'Aye, her sickness bug...'

'And the next day, it was all about trying to find Cammy. And you and I...'

'And everything else faded into the background,' Murray said.

'Nothing mattered after that. Not us. Not college. Not those stupid fallings out, not that godawful row Hector and Cammy had. Those things didn't seem important in the midst of our grief.'

They lapsed into silence for a moment.

'I had Isobel come see me today. She's–' Murray's phone rang. 'I'm sorry, I have to answer this.' Murray turned away and spoke to someone for a moment.

A moment later he came back. 'I need to go. Want a lift back?'

'I'm okay for now, thanks, I'm going to finish this, soak up the atmosphere for a bit before I wander back.'

'Sounds idyllic.'

'Be safe,' Moira called out.

'Aways.' McGregor smiled. Then jogged over to his car.

THIRTY-FIVE

Later that evening, Amelia pottered around the Stone Manor kitchen while Jack and Gideon played billiards and Toby checked the produce in the polytunnels. With no dinner reservations that night the kitchen didn't have the usual frenetic energy. Amelia took a rare moment to sit and have a cup of tea whilst listening to the relaxed banter of sous chef Ben as he prepped dishes for the next day.

Amelia was washing her mug at the sink when the back security light came on. Leaning forward to peer out of the window Amelia couldn't see who, or what, had triggered it. The wind had picked up and she hoped none of the garden furniture had blown over. The light also showed large raindrops splatting on the patio stones.

Wiping her hands dry on a dish towel she headed through to the little hallway which connected all the storage areas and pantry, and opened the back door.

Moira, who was walking past, gave a little start and quickly shoved something behind her back.

'Amelia! I didn't expect to see anyone!'

'I, um...' Amelia lost her train of thought as she was fixated on what appeared to be smoke emanating from the top of Moira's head.

Rather sheepishly, Moira brought her hand round to show Amelia what looked like the weirdest-looking cigar she'd ever seen. It produced a rather strange odour and Amelia wondered if it was possibly the weirdest joint she'd ever seen.

While Amelia was still working out what on earth the other woman was in the process of smoking, Moira explained.

'It's sage.'

'Sage? I never knew you could smoke it. I always thought it was for adding to stuffing to go with a Sunday roast.'

'I'm not smoking it, like inhaling it; I'm burning it around your property.'

'Um... okay,' Amelia said, still none the wiser.

'It's to help cleanse the area and dispel negative energy and protect everyone inside,' Moira explained. 'I thought it would be a good idea after what happened to Gus. And Johno. Just be thankful I'm not burning asafoetida. That stuff stinks to high heaven, like liquorice and rotten garlic. Keeps everyone away, not just demons and other unsavoury entities.'

'Did you also paint the symbol on the back door of the Hunting Lodge?'

'I did. Many years ago. The crossed spears is for protection. It blocks conflict.'

'And these?' Amelia pointed to the wreath on the back door.

'Yes, I put up those. And I've got some High John the Conqueror if you fancy carrying some around with you.'

'High John the what?'

'Ipomoea Jalapa. Also known as High John the Conqueror.' Moira delved into her pocket and brought out a small brown lump that could have been an animal dropping.

'It's a root and once it's dried you carry it in your pocket for protection.'

'You think we need protection?'

'Doesn't hurt to have a little bit of defence.' She gave a laugh. 'My maternal side of the McDonald lineage are all like this. We also have a bit of an intuitive and fae bent. A couple of relations even had second sight. I've got a wee touch of it, a bit of extra perception, picking up on vibrations and feelings. And dreams.'

'Did Cammy?'

'Not so much. He got annoyed with me because it seemed to come easily, he had to work at it. I think that's why he liked doing the ceremonial Wiccan stuff as it channelled his power more. I had no choice. I would get dreams and things would come to me when I did the tarot. Like little visual bursts. I still get that.'

'Is it not strange?'

'I don't always like it but I suppose I'm used to it. It's what drew me back here, Amelia.'

'Are you glad you came back?'

Moira thought for a moment. 'In many ways, yes. It's lovely to be with the old gang again. Despite a few grey hairs and wrinkles we're all the same folk we used to be, just a bit older and... I was going to say wiser, but maybe not so much. I just wish Elizabeth was here.'

'What's she like?'

'A beautiful mix of passion, love and stubbornness. Or she was, until...'

'Cameron.'

'Oh yes. We all changed after that, but none so much as Elizabeth. She left that summer, she and her mum went to visit a sick relative. I think she needed the break from this place. She was gone months. It was long before we had mobile phones or Instagram or Facebook so I didn't have any contact until she came back. And when she did, there was something different.

She was quieter, softer. She had almost an air of defeat about her. We'd all lost something but with her it seemed to go deeper. That's when I realised she and Cammy had been in love. I'd had my suspicions, but they did well to keep it hidden from the rest of us.'

'Why do you think they did that?'

'Hector had quite a soft spot for Elizabeth. She adored him too, but platonically. Cameron wouldn't have wanted to rub his best friend's nose in it.'

'And then Elizabeth got together with Andy?'

'Yes, but that was after I'd left to go travelling. Otherwise I'd have had something to say about that!'

'You don't like Andy?'

She wrinkled her nose. 'It's not that I don't like him, but he's just a bit... backgroundy, you know? Always so eager to please and to try and get in with us. Cameron was the only one who gave him the time of day. But when I heard Andy and Elizabeth were together, I thought she could have done a lot better. And clearly, so did she, eventually!'

There was a sound of someone running over gravel and an out-of-breath Toby appeared holding his trug basket in front of him.

'Ah, my hunter-gatherer brother's back from raiding the polytunnels. You get everything for tomorrow?' Amelia asked.

'Yes, and something else I wasn't expecting.'

'Are you okay?' Amelia asked, realising Toby had gone a sickly grey colour.

'I need to call McGregor. Or Ray, or *some*one. I think I've just found the murder weapon.'

Toby pulled back a dish towel from the top of the basket and lying on top of freshly cut chives and parsley was an ornate dagger, whose blade and handle were covered in a mixture of dried blood and soil.

THIRTY-SIX

'I know you're not on the case anymore but I didn't know who else to call,' Toby said to Detective Inspector McGregor a little while later. The two of them along with Amelia, Moira and Ray looked at the weapon which McGregor had placed in an evidence bag. Gideon and Jack arrived back from the billiards room.

'What's that?' Gideon asked then gave a little shriek when he saw what they were all looking at.

'Looks like you found the murder weapon,' Jack said. 'Where was it?'

'Embedded in the soil by the herbs. I realise I should have left it there but I'd already touched it. I thought it was one of the little trowels and pulled it out without thinking.'

'And it now has your fingerprints all over it,' Gideon said, worriedly.

'It's a very strange shape,' Amelia said, looking at the wavy blade.

'It's an athame,' Moira said faintly. 'And I haven't seen that particular one in over thirty years!'

'It's yours?' Gideon said.

Moira, Ray and McGregor all exchanged an uneasy glance. 'Cammy and I were given it by an old aunt who was a bit of a white witch. It's a ceremonial dagger. Cammy used it when he and Hector cast circles and invoked energy, nothing sinister. It's one of four elemental tools.'

'I remember,' McGregor said. 'And the others are the wand, the cup–'

'And the pentacle,' Moira finished off hollowly. 'Back to the tarot.'

'Back to the tarot,' McGregor agreed grimly.

'What the heck is going on?' Moira said. She pointed at the dagger. 'Where has this been all these years? And why, if you want to hide a murder weapon, only leave it a few yards from the murder scene?'

'Maybe the murderer panicked and hid it, planning on coming back to remove it further away at a later date?' Jack said.

'It wasn't exactly well hidden,' Toby added. 'It was only a matter of time until one of us here stumbled upon it.'

'Unless the murderer wanted it found?' Amelia said. 'And possibly wanted to incriminate you, Moira? The tarot cards, the note. Now this.'

'Jesus,' Moira scoffed. 'The murderer doesn't give me much credit! If I had wanted to get rid of it, surely I'd have the brains to get it further away than the garden at Stone Manor, where I'm staying. I'd have thrown it in the loch. That thing is deep enough to hide all sorts.'

'But then it wouldn't be found,' McGregor said. 'Amelia's right, the murderer wanted it to be found.'

Moira pushed her long hair back from her forehead dramatically. 'I don't understand any of this.'

'You know we have to hand it in,' McGregor said.

Moira let out a frustrated wail. 'Why is this happening?'

'If we knew that, we'd be a whole lot closer to solving this crime,' Ray said sagely.

'But the other force from Amsterdam is in charge now,' McGregor said.

'Amsterdam!' Gideon said excitedly. 'Is there a connection due to those Black Devil cigarettes? Remember the ones we saw in the Hunting Lodge! They're from Amsterdam.'

McGregor frowned. 'You've been in the Hunting Lodge?'

'Yes, but not just us! Other folk have been hiding there too,' Gideon quickly backtracked, mouthing 'sorry' at Amelia.

'People always find a way in. Remember when we'd shimmy in through that dodgy window?' Moira said.

'I couldn't do that now,' Ray said, patting his ample stomach. 'And obviously *wouldn't* do that now,' he added in an officious tone.

'Hector's father had turned a blind eye to us using it as a den and carrying out those Wiccan ceremonies, but he boarded that place up after Cammy died. He changed the locks and banned us all from going back, even threatened us with trespassing,' Moira said.

'Yes,' Ray said. 'Hector Senior was worried his son would be attacked for bringing up all the bad feelings from before with Samuel Bain and the occult links, or worse, he'd follow the same path as Samuel Bain. He didn't understand we were just using it as a place to drink cheap cider and smoke and muck about. The ceremonies the others were doing, well, it was hardly slaughtering goats!'

McGregor frowned and turned to Amelia. 'How did you get into the Hunting Lodge?'

'It wasn't difficult, as I'm rather nifty with a Swiss Army knife,' Gideon said with quite an air of bravado.

'I really shouldn't be hearing this,' Ray said shaking his head.

'Anyway,' Amelia said, keen to move on from the breaking and entering incident. 'We found evidence that someone's been in there. Recently. The coffee and biscuits were well in date. There was a bottle of rum, the same type Gus had got from the Whistling Haggis. And of course the Black Devil cigarettes, which as Gideon mentioned are popular in Amsterdam.'

'Not the only thing that's popular over there! The drugs! When I was over in Amsterdam filming, they were rife. I remember there being a big news story about a smuggling ring being found and how that country is still one of the biggest MDMA producers.'

'The street name of which is Molly!' Amelia said joining the dots.

'Yes,' Gideon said, 'along with others including Smartees, XTC, Adam... I had quite a confusing conversation in a bar over that.' He gave a little laugh and looked around at everyone. 'Which is clearly a story for another time.'

'I know something is likely to be happening in the Hunting Lodge tonight,' Amelia said.

'Why am I not surprised?' McGregor said. 'And *how* do you know?'

'Drew had blocked out his electronic diary for tonight with an entry that said he was meeting Molly at 9pm. I have a hunch this will take place at the Hunting Lodge.'

'Molly! Drugs! *And* Lily told me Drew likes cheap coffee,' Gideon added. 'There was a jar of supermarket own brand there.'

'I can hardly lock him up for grievous bodily harm to tastebuds,' McGregor said. He looked at everyone. 'I cannot check this out on nothing more substantial than a hunch over nasty coffee and a virile imagination. What if it is a romantic assignation between Drew and a woman called Molly? And if it is a drugs deal, who's to say he won't be armed?'

'Can you seriously see Elizabeth and Andy's boy being armed and dangerous?' Moira scoffed.

'He does have quite a mean right hook,' Gideon pointed out.

But all further discussion was pointless when a second later, James came into the kitchen. He looked flustered.

'There's a bit of a situation out front. Drew McAvoy came here to see Rory and Lily. He saw the detective inspector's car out front and is insisting on speaking to you.'

James was pushed aside as a distraught-looking Drew hurried into the kitchen.

'If I confess, will you protect me?' he asked McGregor.

'What exactly are you confessing to?'

'I don't care! Anything. Just as long as I'm safe! Put me in police custody. No, make it witness protection.' Drew held his arms out, wrists together, awaiting handcuffs. 'I need witness protection.'

THIRTY-SEVEN

'Witness protection?' McGregor said in bafflement. 'Who do you need protection from?'

'The folk that are going to kill me, just like they did Gus and Johno! I was due to meet them tonight and I was terrified, but then they sent word that they're not coming now, the weather's too bad. But I know I've merely postponed my execution until next time.'

'Fair-weather criminals?' McGregor muttered under his breath. 'Bloody snowflake millennials.' He gave Drew a measured look. 'Witness protection isn't as simple as heading off to a safe house in the woods in a new country, you know. You need to tell me everything. From the start.'

Drew dropped his arms. 'It was Gus's idea. Well not even an idea. He came in with a plan as he'd obviously done all this before and he made it all sound so easy. And it was, until he ended up dead.' He ran his tongue over his dry lips.

'He knew about my gambling debt. I don't know how he found out. He asked if I wanted to do something that would help clear it. Of course I did. Gus had connections in

Amsterdam. I don't know how Gus did it, but he even knew about the weird secret cove.'

'Secret cove?' McGregor said.

Drew nodded. 'Where Shuggie's tunnel is.'

'And who, dare I ask, is Shuggie?'

'Archie's ancestor,' Amelia piped in. 'He won the bit of land around the Hunting Lodge in a card game. He built a small house there and smuggled whisky out to evade the excisemen.'

'When was this?'

'1740-ish.'

'Or thereabouts,' Jack added.

At this point Rory came into the kitchen and stood staring at his brother in bewilderment. 'What the hell are you doing?'

McGregor looked back to Drew and bade him continue.

'So, just after Gus got here, with the other archaeologists, Gus was out diving and discovered the cove and followed the tunnel up to the Hunting Lodge. He knew it was on Hector's land and found out my dad was the estate manager. That's when he must have done a bit of digging on me and found out about my gambling debts as a way in. Anyway, I managed to get the key to the Hunting Lodge, cut a spare and returned it without Dad finding out.'

McGregor looked sceptical. 'Gus coordinated all this?'

'Isobel said this was just like Gus,' Amelia said. 'He managed to find out things about people and used it to get his way.'

Drew nodded. 'He joked that he was a collector, but of information as well as artefacts.'

'So, what did he do once he had this spare key?'

'Gus's mate berthed up a boat, near but not conspicuously so, then Gus would swim out to the boat, pick up the... packages, and swim them back to the Hunting Lodge where they would stay until they were moved on. Then I got a cut. It seemed easy money.'

'And Johno?'

'One of the nights, something happened to a bit of Gus's equipment. I have no idea about diving and all that so I pointed him Johno's way. They obviously got talking and next thing I knew, Johno was on board.'

'I wondered at you and Johno suddenly becoming so pally,' Rory said. 'You got him into this!'

'He gladly came!' Drew protested.

'And what's in these packages? Exotic cheeses? Wellington boots? Flat-screen television sets?' McGregor asked dryly.

Drew looked confused. 'Televisions? No! The water would screw up the electrics.' He glanced back briefly at his brother before asking the DI, 'Do you really need to know?'

'Aye, I do.'

Drew stayed quiet.

'Well, it's drugs, *obviously!*' Gideon blurted out. 'The meetings with Molly were code for MDMA!'

'I just needed confirmation,' McGregor said in exasperation.

Drew nodded. 'Yes, it's drugs. You knew?'

'What's the name of the Amsterdam contact?' McGregor cut in.

'Ruben. I only know his first name.'

'How did you communicate with Ruben?'

'He spoke English, I don't speak Netherlandish or whatever.'

McGregor gave him a withering look. 'I mean, communication from mobiles, burners, email, smoke signals, carrier pigeon?'

'Oh right. Mobile. But it was always done through him and Gus on a burner.' He pulled out a mobile and handed it to

McGregor. 'It's how they let me know they're not coming tonight.'

'Tell me about the Glasgow connections. Who were the drugs passed on to and how?'

Drew shook his head. 'I have no idea. That was something Gus organised. They sat in the Hunting Lodge for a few days until Gus got the go-ahead and then he took the drugs down to Glasgow. He then got money. He gave Johno some drugs as part of his cut. I just wanted the cash.'

'So I'm guessing you had one of these meetings arranged last Tuesday? I need you to tell me everything that happened that night.'

'Do I have to?'

'Now is not the time to play coy! You can't cherry-pick your confession, son.'

'Well, I need to know what's on the table before I go into any more detail.'

'This is not an American cop show!' McGregor said in frustration.

Drew thought for a moment then started talking. 'It kind of went down like normal. But after Gus brought the gear back he said he wanted to make it more often. As well as the MDMA and hash and all that, Gus said there was an appetite for prescription medications. You know, benzos like diazepam, temazepam, zolpidem and nitra... something.'

'Nitrazepam,' McGregor said. 'It's a hypnotic.'

'For hypnotising people?' Gideon asked in disbelief.

'No, usually for sleeping disorders. They're all used for that.'

'Yeah, Gus said there was a huge market for those, especially around here. So, Johno seemed happy with it all but I didn't want to. I wasn't really comfortable with any of it, to be honest. But Gus wouldn't take no for an answer. Started laughing and said I didn't have a choice. I got majorly pissed off.'

'Did you often argue?'

'No, this was the first time. We'd always got on fine. Mainly talked about women and football. Trash-talking each other's teams. And darts. We both like the darts. Had a side wager between Gary Anderson and Michael van Gerwen in the latest match.' Drew's face fell. 'I owe him a tenner, but I guess he won't need it now.'

'Tuesday?' McGregor prompted.

'Anyway, he was such a cocky bugger we ended up having a bit of a scrap.' Drew's hand automatically went to the bruising on his face.

'I didn't cause those bruises then!' Rory said, 'I knew I didn't touch you!'

'And you used Lily's make-up to hide it,' Amelia jumped in. 'It was that which got accidentally smeared all over the property schedule you gave me. Then, when Lily removed all her belongings from the office you couldn't access her make-up so you had to manufacture a fight with Rory to explain the bruising on your face.'

'I'm sorry. And I'm really not that pissed off about Lily. I mean, it's a blow to my pride that she'd go for a waster like you,' he gave his brother a wan smile, 'but we all know she's much better off with you, Rory.'

'Back to Tuesday, please,' McGregor urged.

'Yeah, so we had the fight but we sorted it. Gus had some rum and a packet of those weird black cigarettes. And the three of us sat and drank and smoked and we were good. He was a bastard but a charming bastard and could talk his way out of a whole load of shit. He left with me thinking it was a really good thing to up the drug deals. When he left us he was alive, I promise you that.'

'What time was that?'

'Late. Probably around midnight.'

'Do you know if he was meeting anyone else?'

Drew shook his head. 'I've no idea. When I heard about Gus I was shocked, but guessed he must know a lot of bad people. But then, when Johno was murdered I figured someone must be after us all. Tying up loose ends, kind of thing. Can you help me?'

McGregor looked serious. 'All I can do is pass this on to the team that's taking over the investigation, but you know I need to take you in.'

Drew nodded.

They all trooped through to the reception area where Isobel was hovering in the doorway of the drawing room.

Rory patted Drew on the back. 'See after you're charged, if you manage to get back out on bail or whatever, you and I need to have a family talk, all right?'

Drew nodded and Amelia noticed Rory turn to Isobel and give her an imperceptible wink. She smiled back.

'And tell Lily she doesn't have to look for another job if she doesn't want to,' Drew said. 'I'll probably need someone to hold the fort for a while now, anyway.'

'I'll let her know.'

'The one thing I *am* glad about is not having to be in that awful place for long periods on my own,' Drew said. 'The Hunting Lodge gave me the creeps. It's obviously haunted. Dad said you lot hung out there years ago. How did you cope with all the weird ghostly noises; the wailing and the banging?' Drew asked.

Amelia looked at Moira, who shrugged.

'We must have been playing our music too loud to hear any ghosts.'

Leaving a defeated-looking Drew on his own for a moment,

McGregor came back over to the others. 'I'm going to alert those higher up to send out a team to watch the coast although I think Drew's right, the weather's too wild for a boat to get near tonight. And, lovely as it is to catch a cog in an international drug trafficking ring, it doesn't exactly point to who is behind Gus and Johno's death.'

Amelia began to think out loud. 'Obviously Gus was linked with drugs and there may have been internal arguments and possibly someone wanted Gus removed. But can you really see international drugs traffickers going into small details of leaving tarot cards and trying to implicate someone else? They wouldn't care if people knew it was them. Whoever murdered Gus and Johno wanted to make it look personal. Why leave the note on Moira's bed? Why use a knife that belonged to Moira and her brother?'

'You are a very astute young woman, Ms Adams. However, as I keep mentioning, this case has been taken out of my hands.'

'But that just means a double murderer is walking about Glencarlach. And who's to say they won't strike again?'

'That's what I'm worried about,' Ray said.

'Especially if I'm being implicated in this!' Moira added. 'I'm just back and all this starts happening. And the tarot, and the dagger? It looks bad.'

'If it's any consolation, Hector's just back too,' Gideon pointed out but Moira didn't look that relieved.

'I'll be in touch,' McGregor said as he and Constable Williams escorted Drew down the steps and out to the waiting car.

'The weather seems to be getting much worse,' Isobel commented when Amelia went into the drawing room a little while later to make sure the fire was lit. The archaeologist was sitting on one of the wingback chairs with a heap of books on a small table in front of her.

Amelia agreed as the rain lashed against the windows. She noticed the book on the top of Isobel's pile had a bright yellow cover.

'You found Gus's notes!'

'Yes, Drew gave it to me before he went to see McGregor. Gus had left it at the Hunting Lodge last week and Drew had taken it home, thinking he'd hand it back the next day, but then obviously Gus was killed.'

'Did you let McGregor know you have it?'

'No, I didn't.' Isobel looked stricken. 'I was so pleased to have it back for Gus's academic research I didn't even think of it from an evidence point of view.' She stood up, looking flustered. 'I'll need to take it to the Detective Inspector.'

'We can message him and let him know it's here.' Amelia looked at the glossy cover. 'Although, we could have a quick look first. In case there's something important.'

Isobel opened the book. There were two loose pages folded and inserted next to his last entry.

'This is a plan of the section of ground the abbey's on,' Isobel said. 'He's circled this area by the longest abbey wall. Hang on, let me call Tim, he's better at deciphering Gus's abbreviations and squiggles.'

Tim, who had been sitting with Moira in the bar came through, carrying a pint, Moira also followed, her interest piqued. Tim sat his drink on a table as he perused the papers.

'He'd been talking about a phase two excavation. I'd told him to just concentrate on the main one, but you know what he was like. Looks like he wanted to get a proper geo survey done on this section. He's noted some ridge and furrow here too.'

He flipped back a few pages. 'He's made an entry.' Tim

skim-read the paragraph. 'He doesn't think this has anything to do with the Pictish dig. Thinks whatever's here is recent. Very recent. He took up a metal detector. Something set it off.' He looked up. 'So whatever it is can't be too deep. Oh, looks like he found this.' Tim turned the notebook around and showed them.

It was a rough sketch of a necklace; a silver disc with the pointed runic 'B'. Like the one Elizabeth wore. And that Johno had then gotten hold of.

Tim carried on reading. 'Says he found it on the road, here.' Tim pointed to a rough drawing of the village and Gus had marked an 'X' on the section of road leading from the village up to Gull Point.

'What is Elizabeth's necklace doing there? She must have dropped it,' Moira said.

Amelia nodded. 'Johno had it. Maja saw him with it on Thursday, two days before he was killed. He told her he'd found it.'

'Where is it now?' Moira wondered. 'Did Johno still have it when he was murdered? If so, it'll probably be in an evidence bag or something. Murray will need to release it as Elizabeth will want it back,' Moira said.

'Gus also found some other things,' Tim said. 'He bagged them up, doesn't say here what they are, just that they're disappointingly recent.'

Tim removed the other piece of loose paper and on unfolding it they saw it was an enlarged copy of the shoreline of Glencarlach with whorls, loops and spiralling circles printed on it. Amelia guessed it was the map Gus used for diving. And plotting out the drug-smuggling routes.

Amelia could see Gus had drawn in symbols and little arrows. He'd also circled one small area in red pen and written *Sundowner*.

Sundowner was the name of Paddy Davis's boat. Amelia

suddenly started to get a bad feeling. Maja had said Gus had found a wreck.

'What's Gus's last entry?' Amelia asked.

Tim cleared his throat, and read, "'Drop done. D&J on for more. Ruben happy. Lost necklace, cigs and keys(!) – dropped at HL? Luckily left Lib door open. Will check wreck site tmw. Interesting! Abbey 2nite (late), speculative excav at high metal part. <u>Def</u> post pict and abbey. Abbey wall – Smth hidden/buried? Too big for animal. Human?".'

'I don't like the sound of that,' Moira said.

'Isobel,' Amelia said, 'I know it's a horrible night, but would it be possible if we could see what Gus found with the metal detector?'

THIRTY-EIGHT

A very windswept and water-logged Amelia and Moira returned to Stone Manor a short while later. Together with Isobel and Tim, they'd started up to the excavation site but Isobel insisted they turn back due to the torrential rain and the wind that had picked up.

'The site will be treacherous in the mud. We're insured but neither of you are. Gus was pedantic about filing and I'm sure Tim and I will be able to find what he logged,' Isobel had said, before she and her colleague hurried through the night.

'Are you okay?' Amelia asked Moira as they now stood, dripping, in reception.

'I'm fine. It's just this weather; it reminds me of the storm the night of Cammy's eighteenth.'

Moira shivered.

'Go sit in front of the fire and warm up,' Amelia said.

'I'm not cold. I just had a goose walking over my grave.'

At that point Betty and Gideon walked out from the bar. Betty lifted up a pair of folding opera glasses to her eyes to get a better look at Moira.

'I see the weather's turned. The pair of you are like drowned rats,' Betty remarked. 'A night fit only for ducks! Come on, Gideon, let's get that game of Scrabble.'

'Only if you stop using filthy words to get a triple-word score!' he remarked as he hobbled after her into the drawing room.

'So, Gus thought there could be a body buried up there?' Moira asked.

'Yeah.'

'That's more recent than the Picts.'

'That still covers quite a few centuries,' Amelia said.

'True. And it's hardly like a dead body can just be gotten rid of. I mean Glencarlach is a small place. Someone must have seen something.'

And possibly someone had.

'Davey,' Amelia called after their night porter as he headed into the dining room to set out the tables for the next day's breakfast. She hurried over to him. 'Have you got the number of your friend, the one that went up to the Hunting Lodge and saw a dead body?'

'Eddie? Don't be taking him seriously!' he scoffed.

'I'd like to talk to him.'

Wee Davey got out his phone. 'Okay, I'll forward you his contact. But he is a bit odd. None of us ever believe anything he says.'

Amelia's phone pinged.

'Thanks, Davey.' Amelia got her phone out of her pocket. Her phone's charge was less than half so she plugged it in before calling the number. Moira huddled close so she could hear the conversation.

'Hello?' a suspicious voice asked on answering.

'Hi, is that Eddie, Davey's friend?'

'Yes.'

'I'm Amelia. I own Stone Manor, I wanted to ask you something, if that's okay?'

She took the gaping silence to mean that it was, indeed, okay.

'Davey told me about you going up to the Hunting Lodge a few months ago. He said you think you saw a dead body?'

'Oh man, are you just gonna take the piss outa me?'

'No! I wanted to ask you about it.'

'No one believes me. But I know what I saw!'

'Can you tell me what you saw?'

'Are you gonna laugh?'

'I promise I won't.'

'Well, it was a few months ago. Fireworks night.'

Amelia clutched the phone tighter. That was the night Elizabeth and Paddy left.

Eddie continued. 'Everyone knows how the Hunting Lodge is haunted and cursed. I'd had a few bevvies and thought I'd go see for masel'. I got there late, after eleven, or maybe it was closer to midnight. I cut through the woods and I saw there was a pickup truck outside.'

'Outside the Hunting Lodge?'

'Yeah, just by the front. And the back edge bit of the truck was down and there were all these covers bundled up and I saw an arm come loose and kind of fall out and dangle in mid-air.'

'Could you tell if it belonged to a man or woman?'

'Naw! I didn't hang about to check. I got out of there speedy-like.'

'Did you tell anyone?'

'Just my brother. He told me I was havin' him on. I told him I wasn't and we went back. But there was nothing there. No truck, no body. Nothing. But I know what I saw.'

'Can you remember anything about the truck?'

There was a very long pause before a quiet, 'Aye. But I don't think I can say.'

'Please. I believe you. I also think there was a dead body there that night. And I need you to tell me anything you remember, no matter how small.'

'This isn't small. I didn't see anyone there, right? But the truck had the Bain estate logo on it. But it wasn't the mucky ones that the estate guys go around in. This one was shiny and clean. Like Hector's own one.'

'But who would use that if he wasn't there?'

'But Hector *was* there that night. There was a big hullaballoo of him having flown in that morning so he could be the one to light the bonfire.'

THIRTY-NINE

Amelia hung up. Moira looked confused. 'It won't be Hector.' She looked at Amelia, shaking her head. 'And whose dead body would he have?'

'We know of two people who left on Guy Fawkes night that no one has heard from since,' Amelia said.

'You think Hector would hurt Elizabeth?'

'Probably not intentionally, not if he adored her...'

'But he may have been angered if he thought she was leaving with another man. And I suppose he wouldn't feel the same love towards Paddy.'

'You all know Hector well. Do you think he could do something like this?' Amelia asked.

'I wouldn't have thought so, but then again, I haven't seen Hector in over thirty years. People change.'

Another ping indicated a text message.

Amelia read the text. 'It's Isobel. She's got the bags. She's sending photos of the contents.'

She and Moira looked at the first couple. A special limited edition year Y2K Mickey Mouse keychain and a silver troll necklace.

'I can't see Elizabeth with either of those,' Moira said with obvious relief.

Amelia's phone pinged again. Another photo.

'It's a silver ring; two hands holding a heart.'

'A claddagh,' Moira said, taking the phone from Amelia, her hand shaking.

The phone pinged again.

'There's an inscription,' Moira whispered. 'It's the date " 1st May 1986, love from Mum and Dad".'

Moira held the phone back out to Amelia. She screwed up her eyes and gripped the edge of the reception desk.

'That was Cammy's eighteenth birthday present. It was a bit too big for him. He needed it resized but wore it that night, anyway. But I don't understand. We weren't at the abbey that night. How could Cammy's ring get there?'

'Could he have gone there after everyone else had left?'

A gust of wind made the front door of Stone Manor rattle as the rain drummed down harder on the glass cupola.

Amelia had a horrible thought. 'Moira, you said the weather was like this on Cameron's eighteenth? If it was this bad, would Cameron really have gone for a walk along an exposed coastal path?'

'Not normally. But he'd been drinking. And he may have wanted to have cooled off after his row with... Hector. Oh God, their argument... What if they continued their argument and... I need to see Hector.'

'Wait until McGregor comes... what if...' She was about to say 'Hector killed all the others' but Amelia left the rest of the sentence hang unspoken as Moira turned and ran out of Stone Manor.

Amelia had to stop Moira before she did anything rash. She quickly disconnected her phone from the charger and raced after her, reaching the other woman as she was getting into the little red hire car.

'You can't stop me.'

'I know, Moira, but least let me come with you. It could be dangerous.'

Moira gave a curt nod of agreement and Amelia had barely got in the passenger side when Moira pulled out of the car park.

Ringing the large bell at the front of Hector's house at Gull Point didn't seem to have any effect and Moira resorted to banging her fists against the solid wooden door. The rain was now lashing down horizontally, carried by the ferocious wind.

A few feet behind, Amelia looked up at the imposing stone façade which was in complete darkness.

Moira dashed down the front steps and beckoned Amelia to follow as they ran round the back of the house where a light was on in the kitchen.

As they got closer to the back door, Amelia could see Hector's housekeeper moving about inside, stacking plates into a dresser. Moira banged against the glass but still the housekeeper didn't turn round. That's when Amelia noticed the two little wires dangling down from the woman's ears. She was listening to music.

Moira tried the handle; the door wasn't locked and before Amelia could stop her Moira barged inside just as the housekeeper turned around, letting out an almighty scream and dropping the pile of plates.

'I'm sorry, I didn't mean to scare you,' Moira said as the other woman clutched her chest.

'Oh no! Look what I've done.' She removed her

headphones. 'These are the good plates with the crests. They've been in the Bain family for generations.'

'Where's Hector?' Moira demanded.

'I suppose I can glue the bigger bits back to–'

'Hector! Where is he?' Moira demanded again.

The housekeeper looked up from the broken pottery.

'Gone.' She blinked. 'Sorry, you are?'

'Moira. An old friend.'

'Oh yes!' The woman's face broke into a delighted smile. 'He told me how thrilled he is you're back. Said you being here brought back lots of memories. And you're Amelia, who owns Stone Manor, aren't you? Hector had a lovely time at your place the other night. He told me all about the delicious dinner.'

'Lovely,' Amelia said.

'So, where is Hector?' Moira repeated, clearly not in the mood for small talk.

'Back to London, I suppose.' The housekeeper looked out the window into the darkness. 'Although I'm worried about him taking off in the storm. In fact, I wouldn't have thought a helicop–'

'When did he leave?' Moira cut in sharply.

The housekeeper looked less cheery at the rude interruption.

'I'm sorry,' Amelia said, trying to smooth over any awkwardness, 'we don't want to be rude, it's just very important we speak to Hector. It would be very helpful if we knew when he left.' She gave Moira a look which she hoped conveyed the message to let the older lady speak. If they appeared too impatient Amelia feared the housekeeper could clam up and they'd learn nothing.

The woman seemed mollified. 'I'm not sure. I came back and found a note to say he'd been called away on urgent business. That's why I was putting all the good china back. I only bring it out when he's home.' She looked back to the floor with a worried expression. 'Oh, do you think this'll be fixable?'

It was clear from Moira's face that she didn't give a flying frig about the crested dinnerware but didn't say anything. Amelia nodded and said, 'I got a wonderful tube of glue from the hardware store in the village. I can't remember the name but it bonds china in seconds and worked a treat on a vase. And I agree with you, I think it would be too risky to fly in this weather.'

At the word 'risky' the housekeeper looked anxious.

Moira turned to Amelia. 'I guess he could have driven to Inverness. Or even Glasgow or Edinburgh to catch a flight. Points on his licence or a driving ban wouldn't exactly matter if he needed to get away, would it?'

There was a dramatic crash of thunder followed closely by a flash of lightning and the housekeeper clutched her chest again. 'I hate storms. That's why I put my music on until it stops.'

'When did you find the note?' Amelia asked.

'When I came in from lighting the fire in his study. He likes to sit and look through his emails before dinner, you see. It was going to be steak and kidney pudding with my cauliflower cheese tonight. It's one of his favourites. He would say, "Mrs Cuthbertson, I've travelled the globe and nothing I've eaten anywhere compares to your magnificent cauliflower cheese". He did call it that, you know, "magnificent". I always use whole milk and a good strong cheddar but the secret ingredient is the mustard, you see. I put two types of mustard in my cheese sauce. English mustard powder and Dijon, just a quarter teaspoon, that's all you need, but it totally lifts the dish. So it must have been something very urgent to have called him away from that. Especially in this storm. And it's a waste of good firewood too, it's blazing away with no one to benefit from–'

'Mrs Cuthbertson,' Moira cut in. 'I'm sorry, but I really need to speak to Hector, it's *very* urgent. I need to know what *time* you found the note.'

'It would have been just before six. I'd been in the kitchen and the note wasn't there, then I'd gone to make the fire and when I returned the note *was* there! Right next to the kettle. He knows I like a cup of tea around then.'

Amelia exchanged a glance with Moira. That was over three hours ago! He could be anywhere now.

'Thank you, Mrs Cuthbertson!'

'Do you think he'll be okay?' the older woman called anxiously from the doorway as Amelia and Moira left.

'Sorry, but I couldn't handle that woman prattling on any longer!' Moira said, stomping round the side of the house towards the car.

They drove all the way back to Stone Manor in silence.

'He could be anywhere by now,' Amelia said as they walked back into Stone Manor.

'I know.'

'We need to let McGregor know. And to let him know there's a very strong suspicion that there's a body buried by the abbey walls.'

'I know. Amelia, do you think you could alert Murray and Ray to this? I need to go and have a bit of a lie down.'

'Of course, can I send anything up?'

'I think I'll take a bottle of red with me.'

Amelia went through to the bar and returned with the Côtes du Rhône she knew Moira had had a couple of times and liked.

She watched as Moira trudged up the stairs before she went into the office to make the calls.

FORTY

Moira sat on the end of the bed, holding the bottle of wine. Although sorely tempted to open the damn thing and pour herself a very large glass, she didn't. Her head was too full of everything that had happened that day. She looked at her tarot cards, where she normally took solace in times of uncertainty but realised she wasn't at all uncertain. She didn't need guidance as she knew what to do: find Hector.

Leaving the bottle on the bed, Moira went downstairs. There was no one in reception, but even if there had been she didn't want to stop and chit-chat or let anyone know what she was doing.

If anything, the weather was even worse now, as Moira felt herself being pushed by the ferocity of the wind as she hurried back across the car park. It was a relief to get into her little hire car.

The visibility was dreadful and Moira drove at a snail's pace, her windscreen wipers on full. She could feel the side of the vehicle being buffeted with the bigger gusts as she left Main Street behind and drove out of the village using the top road.

Driving up the road she had a flash of something. In her mind's eye she saw a woman in white, with long dark hair covering her face. She raised a hand...

Damn! Of all the times to get one of her visions!

Not now.

Moira shook her head and the vision was gone.

A large SUV passed her at speed, its beams on full and Moira was momentarily blinded and had to swerve a little to avoid it on such a narrow road. She skidded and nosedived into the verge. She stalled. Hitting the steering wheel and swearing loudly made her feel a little better. She put the car into gear and... nothing. The wheels spun uselessly in the mud. She pressed down hard on the accelerator.

Still nothing but the high-pitched protest from the engine.

She swore again.

Then she turned off the engine and got out of the car. Clutching the edges of her jacket together, she walked, struggling for breath as the wind grabbed it from her. After twenty minutes, Moira came to the turning and followed the path towards the Hunting Lodge. Why hadn't she thought of coming here first?

The trees creaked ominously as she made her way down the drive. The sound of rushing leaves was almost deafening as she screwed up her eyes against the little particles of grit and foliage that blew up into her face as she hurried along.

And there it was before her. For some reason she was surprised to see it in darkness. She'd half expected to see a candle lighting the window, a sign to beckon and invite her in.

Regardless she walked round to the back door.

It was ajar.

There was another deep roll of thunder and Moira automatically found herself counting the seconds before the lightning. She only got to three when bright jagged white rented through the black. It lit up the sky long enough for her to glance someone in her peripheral vision. She was turning to see who it was when she felt something hit her on the back of her head.

And then she saw nothing at all.

FORTY-ONE

There wasn't much anyone could do the next day apart from wait.

Amelia had called McGregor and updated him on everything from the night before. He'd arrived first thing that morning to collect Gus's yellow notebook and listen to Isobel and Tim discuss their findings.

McGregor tried to locate Hector Bain but with no luck.

The area near the abbey wall was now covered by a large police tent while the forensic archaeology team began to excavate whatever or whoever was buried there.

Around mid-morning, Amelia had tentatively knocked on Moira's door to keep her abreast of everything that was going on but there was no answer. Amelia figured the poor woman needed to be left alone.

She walked downstairs to find Gideon loitering in reception. He'd now stopped using two crutches as he'd found an antique walking stick, which he'd taken to wielding when he was making a point.

'Where are you going?' he asked when he saw Amelia reach for the Jeep's keys.

'I thought I'd go into the village. It feels really odd here at the moment.'

'I'll come and keep you company. I tell you, that tea of Moira's is an absolute marvel! I must make sure I get some more of it before she goes.'

They crossed over the car park. The torrential rain of the night before had lessened to a steady downpour, but the wind still had some strength behind it.

'Would you mind if we stopped at the cottage so I can get more of my things?' Gideon asked. 'I think I'll get you to pack a couple of cases this time.'

'Let me check there's space,' Amelia said as she opened the boot and peered inside.

There was a can of de-icer, a couple of yoga mats, still unopened and in their original packaging, three odd woollen gloves, a deflated beach ball and the bag Emma the florist had given her.

'There's plenty of room,' Amelia said, pushing everything to the side, her hand hovering over the bag the florist had given her.

'I need to make a quick stop on the way. I need to hand something in for Andy McAvoy.'

'You know where he stays?'

'Nope, but I can leave it with Rory in the harbour as I doubt he'll be running his cruises in this weather.'

'And I'd quite like some of my fluffy throws and big cushions to make it feel more like home here,' Gideon added as he put on his seat belt.

Amelia started the engine. 'Do you think you might be able to move back soon?'

Gideon's face fell. 'Do I have to?'

'No, you don't *have* to, I thought you'd want to.'

Gideon was very quiet as Amelia pulled out of the car park.

'To be honest, poppet, I don't like being on my own very much. That's why... I know I said you couldn't move away because Toby would miss you, and he would, obviously... but I'd hate it if you went. You're my best friend and I adore you and I couldn't stand it if you were more than a five-minute drive away.'

'Oh, Gideon,' Amelia reached over and squeezed his hand affectionately, 'if I'm being completely honest, I'd hate to leave you too.'

They smiled at each other.

'And I suppose I've grown to consider Jack as... being far less annoying than he used to be,' Gideon added.

Down by the harbour, Amelia pulled in behind a Bain estate truck and she and Gideon got out, taking the little bag from the florists with her.

'Oh, Amelia! Helllooo!'

'Why is there a little old lady trying to break the hundred metre sprint in a bid to get hold of you?' Gideon asked with interest as Amelia turned to see Hector Bain's housekeeper, Mrs Cuthbertson, running towards her.

'I'm so glad I caught you. Did you manage to contact Hector?'

'I'm afraid not.'

She clutched her chest in anguish. 'I couldn't get hold of him and the police are also trying to contact him. I didn't get a wink of sleep last night for worrying about him in the storm. And I was going over everything in my head when I remembered something. Moira thought he might have driven to an airport, well, he couldn't possibly have!'

'I know, he has points on his licence.' Amelia seriously doubted Hector would baulk at driving illegally when he'd already murdered a few folk.

'What! He never has points, so he hasn't!' Mrs Cuthbertson

scoffed. 'Hector can't drive. He would say to me, "Mrs Cuthbertson; I can sail, fly, ski and horse-ride, but I never got to grips with this driving malarkey". And then he'd laugh and say, "Although I do know how to manoeuvre a tank, but can you imagine the uproar if I drove a CR2 down Main Street!" And we had such a laugh together about that.' Mrs Cuthbertson laughed uproariously at the thought.

'How do you think Hector left Glencarlach yesterday?' Amelia asked.

'He'll no doubt have had one of the estate hands drive him wherever he wanted to go. They're awfully good like that. Cheerio!' And off Mrs Cuthbertson went, pulling her tartan shopper behind her.

'I suppose if an estate hand drove Hector, it will be easy for McGregor to find out where they took him,' Gideon said as they continued their way down to the jetty, with Gideon commenting on the boats as they passed them.

'I'd quite like to learn how to sail. I can just see myself behind the wheel of a boat. Even better, I could just hire someone to sail it for me. Toby and I on the high seas with the wind in our hair and a tang of brine in the air. Glorious.'

Ahead of them, Amelia could see Rory and Andy talking together by the *Amber Dram*.

'Hi, Amelia,' Rory said as he tugged on his denim bucket hat. 'Everything okay?'

'Yes, it was actually your dad I wanted to see.'

'Me?' Andy McAvoy blinked a couple of times.

'Yes, it's a very long story, I'd popped into your wife's florists, got chatting with Emma and she mentioned a little parcel arrives every month for your wife. Emma thinks it must be a standing order Elizabeth hasn't cancelled. Anyway, Emma asked me if I could give them to you.' She held out the bag to Andy.

'Oh, okay, thank you.'

Andy went to walk past.

'Dad!' Rory said incredulously. 'Are you not going to open them? It might give us a clue where Mum is.'

Amelia and Gideon exchanged a glance. Neither wanted to say there was a possibility of Elizabeth being buried next to the abbey walls.

'Oh, right okay. Yes, yes.'

Looking slightly mystified, Andy opened up one of the boxes inside the bag. He then gave a little laugh.

'It must be a face cream,' he said, holding up a little tube, before dropping it back into the bag.

But from the quick glance Amelia got, she saw it wasn't face cream. It was a little tube of arnica. Arnica. That rang a bell...

She watched as Andy McAvoy headed off to a little boat and hopped on.

Just then Amelia's phone rang. It was Constable Williams.

'Amelia, sorry to bother you, but have you seen Moira recently?'

'No, I haven't seen her since last night, after we got back from looking for Hector. She took a bottle of wine up to her room.'

'It was lying on the bed, unopened. She didn't stay at Stone Manor last night as her bed wasn't slept in.'

'Oh. I'm in the village at the moment, I'll keep a lookout. What about Hamish and Sally's place, could she have stayed with them?'

'I've already called them. And some of the other family too.' There was a pause before he said, 'We found her hire car. It was in a ditch at the side of the road, at the edge of the village.'

Amelia could hear the worry in Ray's voice.

'Any word on the forensics up by the abbey?'

'They're making progress. They've confirmed it's a body.'

Amelia felt faint. 'Elizabeth?'

'They don't think so. It seems more historic than that.'

'Oh, so is it old, like eleventh-century-abbey old?'

'Not as historic as that. They're thinking a few decades old. Male. Wearing a silver buckle belt on his jeans, that I remember seeing...' Ray's voice cracked a little.

'Cameron?'

'It looks a very distinct possibility. We need to find Moira.'

'What about Hector?'

'Nothing yet.'

'Okay, well, I'll keep a look out for Moira.' They said goodbye and Amelia hung up the phone.

'Are you okay?' Gideon asked her.

'Moira's missing. And it looks like it might be Cameron's body that's been buried there.'

'But didn't someone see Cameron by the cliffs?'

'It was an anonymous caller. But, can you really see someone walking their dog, a beloved family pet, somewhere dangerous very late in the kind of weather we had last night? As Betty said, that weather was only fit for ducks.'

'And I suppose it's easy enough to scatter some belongings and embed a bottle of vodka in the ground,' Gideon added. 'But would Hector have killed his best friend? And where is Elizabeth?'

Amelia wondered if Elizabeth was in the bottom of Loch Carlach, in the wreck of the *Sundowner*.

'Hector seems such an affable chap.'

Amelia agreed. And she suddenly had a wave of doubt about it being Hector. She'd only known him a very brief amount of time, but she found it increasingly difficult to believe he could have done any of the atrocities. If he had killed Cameron all those years ago, would he really have buried the body? He was the sort of person whose father would throw money to sort out an incident like that. Amelia stared at the water beside her, trying to make sense of everything.

But then again, she didn't know him at all. Some were better than others at keeping up a façade.

Rory came over to them. 'Thanks for giving that bag to Dad. I know he didn't look that fussed, but I'm sure he is, deep down. It's amazing how he keeps on going.'

'He must miss her.'

'Yeah, he must, although he never talks about her. But he absolutely worshipped her when she was here. Always buying her things, taking her on weekends away. Even got all those stupid books on the occult, just to impress her. Evil things.'

'As Moira once told me, the occult just means hidden knowledge.'

'I wish they had stayed hidden – I opened one once and it scared the life out of me. All about animal sacrificing and resurrection and all worshipping Satan. I much prefer the fluffier kind of pagan-lite that's celebrated at Beltane.'

'Maybe he just went along with it because of your mum?'

'Oh, these weren't Mum's. No, she said she'd put all that behind her. She called it silly nonsense. I think that really pissed my dad off.'

'Rory, do you think your dad ever tried to get in with your mum's group of friends?'

'Yeah. One night, not long after Mum left, Dad got way too drunk, he's not really been a big drinker at all usually, but this night he started on about the past. How he'd tried for years to get in with Mum's group of friends. He'd read up on it, all this magic stuff, done incantations and all that kind of thing. Someone in the group said he could join in, I think. So, he'd planned something spectacular as an initiation, something to impress them all but then one of them said no. And that was it. Dad still sounded really bitter about it, all these years later.

Anyway, I'd best go. See you later.' Rory loped off back to the *Amber Dram*.

Amelia watched as Andy untethered the rope from the metal cleat on the dock.

'Ooh, I think I need some more of that tea,' Gideon said, leaning down to rub his ankle. He pulled up the end of his jeans to inspect the bruising.

'Arnica!' Amelia blurted out.

Gideon looked up. 'What?'

'Of course!' Amelia said. 'Arnica was the cream Moira mentioned to Rory in the Whistling Haggis. She said using arnica would help reduce the bruising.'

'Oh yes! Have you got some?'

'I don't but Elizabeth did. And she must have had a hell of a lot of bruises if she needed a regular monthly supply of the cream. I don't know much about what being a florist entails but I don't think it's a particularly hazardous career.'

'No, I would have thought cuts from the thorns of roses would be more usual.'

Amelia quickly tried to process everything, but putting Andy square in the suspect role.

Andy had wanted to join the Wiccan group. Cameron and Hector had argued over it the night Cameron died. Andy had been in the Whistling Haggis the night of his birthday. Andy didn't want the excavation dig. Elizabeth was leaving him... Elizabeth's necklace. Paddy's boat possibly lying at the bottom of Loch Carlach... Andy had driven Hector to Stone Manor the night they all had dinner and he could easily have slipped upstairs and left the tarot card and note on Moira's bed. Everyone had been so quick to think it was Hector because of the robe and the ceremonial dagger and that he'd argued with Cameron and adored Elizabeth... but if Andy was desperate to join the Watchful Wiccan group, he'd have read up about those things too...

'Andy,' she called as she ran over to his boat. 'One thing. Did you happen to drive Hector anywhere last night or this morning? It's just the police are looking for him in connection with the murders.'

Andy tapped his fingers on the back of his head. 'Um, yes, yes I did as a matter of fact.'

'And Moira was with him, yes?'

'Yes.' He nodded.

'Where did you take them?'

He paused for a moment before saying, 'Up to where Hector moors his boat. A few miles from here. He and Moira were keen to go for a sail.'

'In that weather?'

'I did say, but Hector was going to wait until the weather calmed before leaving. They both seemed very keen to go.'

Amelia doubted that very much, what with Moira suffering from seasickness. The last place she'd want to go was on a boat, in *any* weather.

'And I have to go now, goodbye, thanks for the boxes.' Andy smiled and ducked into the front of the cabin.

As Andy's boat slowly puttered away from the jetty, Amelia saw something.

A silver necklace hanging down from one of the levers. A beautiful little bashed pewter circle, with an engraving of the Berkano rune symbol.

'It's not Hector the police should be looking for, it's Andy!' Amelia said to Gideon in frustration as they watched Andy's boat get smaller as it sailed into the distance.

Amelia got out her phone and to her dismay saw it was completely dead. Of course, she'd grabbed her phone last night to follow Moira then forgot to charge it again when she returned.

'Gideon, call McGregor and Ray. Tell them I don't think it's Hector, I think it's Andy McAvoy.'

She began to run along the jetty to the Jeep.

'But, Amelia... you should wait for them.'

'No time!' she called behind her. 'I think Andy has Moira.'

'But where?' Gideon shouted.

There was only one place Andy would be heading to.

'The Hunting Lodge!'

FORTY-TWO

Amelia drove as fast as she dared on the road. She kept glancing down towards the water and could see Andy's boat below her. She worked through possible timings in her head. He'd have to get to the secret cove, drop anchor, then walk up the smuggler's tunnel to the Hunting Lodge.

She knew she'd get there first but that was where her plan started and finished.

Turning into the drive Amelia bounced down the track, wincing at the toll it was taking on the Jeep's suspension.

Her stomach went a little watery when she turned the last bend and saw one of the Bain estate trucks in front of the low stone wall.

She parked at the farthest end which she hoped wouldn't be visible from the Hunting Lodge, and got out. She checked the back of the Bain estate truck. Empty, apart from cloth sacking which had a dark-brown patch which Amelia feared was blood.

Feet pounding a matching rhythm with her heart, Amelia caught herself counting as she flew over the bracken and weeds and rough ground towards the ruined stable block. One count for every three steps. She headed straight, keeping the stables to the left as she hurtled forwards, her breath coming in ragged bursts. She needed the sequence of numbers, a list in her mind to allow her to focus. She feared if she didn't have some sort of order, she'd come to a stop and scream.

She ducked down behind a tall section of the stone wall, her body zinging with adrenaline.

She couldn't stay where she was as the stable ruins were too exposed.

As she weighed up her options, hands darted out from behind her, covering Amelia's mouth and pinching her nose. As Amelia tried to struggle free, screams dying in her throat, she heard a voice.

'Shh! It's me, Moira, you're fine!'

Amelia turned and Moira lifted her finger to her lips for a second before grabbing Amelia's hand and pulling her away. Keeping low, they ran along the edge of Shuggie's house foundations, dangerously close to the cliff edge as they circled wide and headed towards the Hunting Lodge.

Then Moira stopped, tugging on Amelia's arm for her to do the same. They jumped down onto a slightly lower piece of ground then rolled flat against the back, hidden from sight.

'Are you okay?' Amelia asked.

'I've got a lump on my head the size of Ailsa Craig, but I'm alive.'

'What happened?'

'After I left Stone Manor last night I came here. It was the only place I could think of to come. I'd barely left the village when the car got stuck, so I walked here. And as I was walking I was thinking about Hector doing all those terrible things and I realised he's just not the type. If he was really upset about Elizabeth, he'd have gotten drunk on some ridiculously expensive top-growth claret, listened to The Smiths, had a mope for a day or two then gotten on with life. He has a low attention span and I just can't see him pining for the same woman for over thirty years. He's not the type of man to dwell. And I was thinking all that when I got whacked on the head. And you'll never guess by who.'

'Andy McAvoy,' Amelia said.

'Yes!'

'From what Rory told me, Andy *is* the type to dwell, letting feelings of being hard done by fester for decades.'

Moira nodded. 'And then, when I came to, I found myself in the Hunting Lodge, bound and gagged. I used some of the broken glass from the bookcase to cut through the rope. I didn't even check to see if Andy was still there. I just let myself out through that old window that luckily no one had thought to fix. And that's when I saw you leaping across to the stables.'

'Andy's heading here by boat.'

'Shit.' Moira looked to the side. 'The smuggler's tunnel comes up close to here.'

'We need to run. I've got the Jeep.'

'I can't leave Hector. He's in there, tied to a chair. There's a bloody gash on his head too but he's alive if not responsive. I also think Andy's drugged him as there was a pack of those zolpidem tablets that Drew was talking about. And there was a lot out of them.'

'Damn. Lily mentioned Andy needed sleeping tablets. She said to Drew that the GP had stopped prescribing them and I bet Gus supplied them. Can I use your phone? Mine's out of charge.'

'I don't do tech. You do know that everything is recorded on your phone? And don't get me started on 5G, with goodness knows what being emitted out on waves, making people ill. I don't trust any of it.'

Amelia rested her head in her hands.

She was stuck in a remote area with a murderer on the loose.

Hector was tied up and unconscious and there was no way of calling for assistance, and Amelia's only hope was a conspiracy-theorist white witch. She liked to think she was a look-on-the-bright-side sort of person, but even Amelia was struggling to find a shard of optimism within their current situation.

'I asked Gideon to call McGregor, let's hope he has.'

'We need to rescue Hector.'

Amelia agreed.

'Moira, one thing. The body by the abbey wall. They think it might be Cameron.'

Moira sat still as she processed this information. Then she gave a slow nod. 'I kept getting drawn to that place since I came back. That makes a lot of sense. And did Andy kill Cameron?'

'I think so.'

'But why? He was the only one who gave Andy the time of day. And did he kill Gus?'

'I think Gus got close to finding out about Cameron's body being there and Andy killed him. And if Andy needed prescription medication for sleeping tablets, maybe Gus was using that against him too.'

'Andy must have been walking around like a zombie every day.'

Amelia remembered that's what Lily had said too. What Amelia couldn't understand was how alert Andy seemed to be after taking so many.

'Why Johno?' Moira asked.

'It must be because he found Elizabeth's necklace and was starting to piece it all together.'

Moira's eyes suddenly widened and she lifted a finger to her lips.

Above them, only a couple of feet away, Amelia heard twigs snapping as someone walked by and a moment later the sound of the Hunting Lodge door opening.

'We need to get back in there. We won't have long before he realises I'm missing.'

Amelia felt funny at the thought of entering the building with Andy inside.

'Can't we just lie in wait and hit him over the head when he leaves?'

'We've got the element of surprise! I don't suppose you know any martial arts?'

Amelia had once pondered doing an evening class in Krav Maga but ended up changing it to coil pottery at the last minute. She now wished she hadn't. 'No, sorry.'

Moira scrabbled around the earth and pulled up a heavy and viciously pointed rock. 'This might help.'

'Are you sure you'll be able to hit him with it?'

'Trust me, I have a lot of pent-up hatred for that man. It'll be stopping hitting him that'll be the problem.'

'Okay.'

They pulled themselves up and out of their hiding place and crept silently towards the Hunting Lodge.

The back door was ajar.

'Hector's in the main room,' Moira whispered. 'Count to sixty then go in, that'll give me time to get back in through the window and sneak up from behind.'

'Okay. Good luck.'

Moira squeezed her hand. 'You too.' And she ran off, disappearing round the side of the building.

It was both the slowest and quickest sixty seconds Amelia had ever endured.

As soon as she finished counting she let herself quietly in through the back door. Hardly daring to breathe, she moved silently through the house.

The door to the main room was slightly open and Amelia could make out Hector tied to a chair. Slightly beyond, Amelia's knees went weak when she saw a double-barrelled shotgun propped up against the wall.

It briefly crossed Amelia's mind she had no idea what she'd say when she opened the door. It seemed a bit ridiculous to say *hello*.

Amelia took a deep breath and opened the door wide. 'Stop!'

FORTY-THREE

Andy looked up at her and stood straight, a small smile playing at the corner of his lips.

Amelia's mouth was dry. No Moira came running through, wielding the stone.

'Stop!' Amelia repeated, far more loudly.

'Or?'

Amelia licked her lips. Hector stirred slightly and his head rolled back. He'd been gagged.

Andy held his hands up in amusement and looked behind him in an overly dramatic way. He turned back.

'Oh, are you expecting Moira to come running to your aid? I'm guessing your plan involved you causing a distraction while she hit me over the head with a blunt instrument.' He gave a little chuckle. 'Always annoyingly tricksy that one. Couldn't abide her when we were young. I should have realised she'd have escaped. Fool me once, shame on you, fool me twice...' He gave another chuckle. 'Don't worry, we won't be bothered by Moira. I modified an old hunting trap I used to use on the estate. When a pad is pressed on the window ledge, an arrow is released. Quite unsophisticated really, but clever in its simplicity. After she escaped, I came back and set it. Just a matter of pulling back a bit of string and holding it taut until... *twang!*' He made the motion of pulling back an arrow.

'I can now imagine Moira has been impaled through the centre of her chest and is bleeding out onto the bare floorboards.'

Amelia said nothing. She couldn't hear any noise coming from anywhere else in the Hunting Lodge.

She felt sick.

Hector began to stir, his eyes flickering open as he struggled to focus. His head snapped up when he caught a glimpse of Amelia. Eyes now wide, Hector thrashed in the chair, arms pulling at the rope around his wrists, the flesh of which was raw.

'Don't worry, Hector. Amelia and Moira came to rescue you!' Andy mocked.

He walked over to the wall just a foot away from his rifle. Amelia would have to get past him to make a run for it. She didn't fancy her chances against a bullet.

'It's quite a change having the upper hand for once,' Andy said in a disarmingly cheerful way.

'I know you wanted to be a part of their group for years,' Amelia said, hoping to stall for time.

'I did. Cameron had promised me I'd be part of their gang. I even bought a robe, just like theirs. And I'd been practising my words for the initiation. I was pathetically desperate to be part of the Watchful Wiccan all those years ago.' He leant down by Hector's ear. 'You were a bunch of narcissistic entitled arseholes. Watchful Wiccan? Oh, the irony as none of you had a clue what was going on, you were so wrapped up in yourselves. But I saw everything. I was the one who was watchful. I followed you and studied you. I spied you through the window to see what you were doing. I learnt all about the tarot. Got the same ones Moira and Cameron used. I would sneak in here and read about all the spells and the ceremonies.'

'Do you know they've found Cameron?' Amelia said, still glancing at the door behind Andy in the hope Moira was going to come through it.

Andy nodded thoughtfully.

'It was only a matter of time. Gus knew. He was clever. Too clever. That's why he had to die. Do you know, right up until the Tuesday night I hadn't known how exactly. And then that idiot turned up outside Hector's land in one of those pagan robes.' He slapped Hector on the back. 'Your face was a picture. So scared! Hector was clearly terrified Cameron had come back from the dead, ready to haunt him. I knew about their last row, you see. Cameron had wanted me to join their group but it was Hector who wouldn't allow it. He was already angry that Cameron let Elizabeth into the inner sanctum, but Hector so loved Elizabeth he forgave them. Do you know Hector used to creep to Elizabeth's house at night and peer through the blind to sneak a peek?'

'You killed Cameron because you were jealous?' Amelia said.

Andy looked genuinely surprised. 'No. I didn't think of Elizabeth like that. Not then. All I wanted was to be part of their group. It was only later, after everything was over that I thought about seeing her. It was simple then. She was broken. I felt powerful stepping in, knowing everything had been done by my hand. She'd lost Cameron. And the baby.'

Hector made a strangled noise and tried to turn round in his chair.

'Oh yes, Hector, Elizabeth was pregnant with Cameron's baby. She put it up for adoption. Her family had great ideas of her going off to college. But she didn't have the heart to stick at her course after everything. Elizabeth never guessed I knew. But

I'd found the adoption papers and the little hospital band that she kept. It's a shame Moira never got to find out she had a niece. She had conversations with her and never knew.'

Hector looked at Amelia, his wide eyes questioning.

'Isobel,' she told him.

'Gus knew,' Andy carried on. 'Gus and I were very similar. He liked to find things out and so do I. I wonder if he'd have worked anything out had I not wanted the sleeping pills. It was his *in*. He realised I had a weakness and he went out of his way to discover what it was. Oh well, I guess we'll never know.'

Andy stood behind Hector, resting his hands on his captive's shoulders.

'Meanwhile poor Isobel is still wondering who her father is. Elizabeth hadn't quite got round to telling her that. She thinks *you* might even be daddy dearest.' Andy slapped Hector on the back again.

'So, Gus found out there was a body there?' Amelia said, hoping to keep Andy talking. 'You tried to shut the excavation down but that didn't work, did it? So you waited for him?'

'It was more a chance encounter. I'd gone to find who it was dressed up in the pagan robes and stumbled across Gus at Cameron's grave. He'd already started to dig. I grabbed a spade and hit him over the head. I thought he was dead. I'd gone to my truck for the ceremonial dagger but as I got back Gus was up and running. He was slow because of the cumbersome dry suit but he still managed to get all the way to Stone Manor before I caught him up. But this was even better. I'd already seen Moira in the village hall that afternoon and that's when it came to me. I was going to get rid of Gus and frame Moira and Hector at the same time. I'd gone home to get the dagger I'd taken from Cameron all those years ago. And when Gus ran, he ended in the very place where suspect number one was staying. It was all so perfect. He already had bruising on his face and it looked as if he'd been in a fight earlier that evening. The tarot cards were just a little finishing touch. A flourish.'

'But why did you kill Cameron?'

Andy looked pensive for a moment. 'That was unfortunate. We'd arranged to meet at the Hunting Lodge later that night. I was so angry when he said he wasn't able to get me into the group. I wanted to prove to him I was worthy. I was convinced I could do a resurrection spell. I told Cameron this, but he said no, there was nothing he could do. I got quite desperate, we argued. He started to walk away and I grabbed the ceremonial knife and ran after him and caught up with him outside, near the stables and slit his throat.'

Hector let out a cry through the gag.

'I sometimes wonder if I did it hoping I could bring him back so he would tell everyone else how powerful I was, but other times I think I was so angry I wanted to kill him. I buried him, which took far longer than I expected, digging that hole by the abbey.'

'Why did you bury him there?'

'I didn't think anyone would ever dig up sacred ground, you see. Oh the irony of it being his daughter that came back to excavate the area!' He rolled his eyes. 'I placed Cameron's belongings on the coastal path and made an anonymous call. It was all so easy. But with everyone searching for him I had no time to go back and try the resurrection spell. So I'll never know if it would have worked or not.'

Amelia could see a tear roll down Hector's face.

'And Johno? He'd found Elizabeth's necklace, hadn't he?'

'My God, you are very annoying sticking your nose in where it really doesn't belong! You know, she was so ungrateful for everything I'd done for her? I was prepared to share her affection with a dead teenager, after all, he was no real threat.

But when I found out she'd been with someone else?' Andy shook his head. 'I needed to get her back.

'She left me a note by the cereal box. I know I wasn't meant to find it until the next morning, but I was ferrying Hector around everywhere and I didn't have time for dinner so went to grab myself a bowl of cereal. It didn't take long to find her. She and Paddy had arranged to meet by the abbey ruins. So poetic that it was by the grave of her first love. Not that she knew it of course. Well, not then. When my gun went off everyone thought it was just another firework.'

Hector let out a wail.

'Gus found Paddy's boat too.'

'I wonder if he looked inside?' Andy gave a high-pitched giggle. 'Imagine his surprise if he did!'

'And you were in the Whistling Haggis on the Thursday night and you saw Johno with Elizabeth's necklace?'

'No, I didn't see anything. It was his silly bint of a girlfriend who kept going on about this necklace. And Johno's expression. He kept glancing to me and Drew. And of course, when I checked, I realised it was gone. That was my carelessness.'

Amelia wondered how he could have checked. If Elizabeth lay in a watery grave in the wreck of the *Sundowner*, had Andy gone diving to see...?

Amelia glanced once again to the door but Moira wasn't there. She started to lose hope for the woman still being alive.

Now she had to hope Gideon had reached McGregor and Ray.

'You turned Johno's shop over.'

'Yes, looking for that blasted necklace. I knew if I didn't get it, it could catch me out. But of course, it wasn't there. On the Saturday, I overheard Johno making his call to Rory, obviously Johno was too stupid to work it out but I knew Rory would and I couldn't risk Johno telling him. I basically followed him down there, slipped into the water.'

'Did you dive, with scuba equipment?'

'No. I don't scuba-dive. I just pulled myself along by the front of the boats so no one would see me from the harbour. I then swam round the *Amber Dram* and went up the side. I killed him. Blows to the head with a Prosecco bottle. This time I made sure he was dead. He had the necklace, I took it back and then I went to my boat and changed into dry clothes before I went back up to the party, sat in the beer tent and talked to everyone. It's amazing how gullible drunk people are when you tell them you've been with them all evening.'

'Did you not worry that Rory would be blamed because Johno was found on his boat?'

'I did feel a little bad about that although I knew the police didn't have enough evidence to charge Rory with anything. Rory did get a bit of a rough deal.'

'Clearly you didn't care that much as you jumped out at him wearing the pagan robe and he crashed his car.'

'Yes. I wanted to push the pagan idea, especially as I had an alibi as Hector was with me that first time. It meant I could concentrate on framing Moira.'

'But not anymore, not if she's dead in another room.'

'But people think she's with Hector on his boat. A little bit of staging and *voilà*! Another tragic boating accident.'

'Just like *Sundowner*? It's not going to look like an accident when it's discovered Elizabeth and Paddy have been shot.'

'Paddy was shot,' Andy snapped. He looked lost for a moment before he began pacing. 'I thought I'd only have one body to dispose of today. Two is tricky, but not insurmountable. Three, an absolute pain but, I do like a challenge! It'll get my creative juices flowing.'

Amelia glanced at the floor and saw the blister packs of the zolpidem he'd drugged Hector with.

'What will you do for sleeping tablets now Gus and Johno are dead? And with Drew facing prison...' Amelia trailed off as she saw Andy's face turn red.

'He's a stupid idiot. So much potential and he had to use this hallowed beautiful place, to carry out those drug deals. I heard them talking you know. And I thought what a disappointment he'd turned out to be. And I'm sure Elizabeth felt the same. But *enough* of this chit-chatting.'

He turned and struck Amelia across the side of her face and she fell to the floor. There had been no hesitation, no doubt before he hit her. Oh yes, Amelia now knew why Elizabeth had the standing order of arnica.

Amelia knew she had seconds before he reached for the gun and shot her. She felt inside her pockets just in case there was something... anything she could use that would help in her current predicament. The Deet spray. No, she'd have to lean in very close to him to spray it and she didn't want to take the risk of the nozzle not working or him grabbing her wrist. The proximity issue was the same for the tick remover. And she wasn't even sure where she could stab him with the flimsy bit of plastic that would have any effect. There was a pack of travel tissues and some gum but she didn't think even the ingenious *A-Team* could pull together a weapon with those. Then her hand curled around the hurricane whistle. She had no idea how loud it would be but hoped the element of surprise would give her time.

It was also the only option of a weapon in her very poor arsenal.

Andy picked up the gun, and turned, the barrel pointing towards her.

Amelia put the whistle to her mouth, pressed her lips together... and blew.

It was loud.

So loud, Andy hunched his shoulders up towards his ears, face contorting in pain as the noise reverberated inside the room.

And the gun went off.

FORTY-FOUR

Andy stood dazed, looking at the bullet hole in the wall. A split second later, seizing the moment, Hector managed to stand, and, still with the chair attached, ran at Andy, headbutting him in the stomach with momentous force, knocking him to the ground.

Andy lay, winded, gasping for air as the door burst open and police swarmed in.

'Sorry I'm late,' a shaky voice said from the doorway. Amelia turned. Moira stood slumped against the woodwork, an arrow embedded in the soft flesh under her clavicle, blood staining the front of her top.

'You're alive!' Amelia said.

'I am that,' Moira said, managing to raise a small smile.

'Andy said the arrow was rigged to hit you in the chest.'

'And it would have done had I not snagged my skirt and stooped down to free it.'

McGregor marched in and looked around. He pointed at Andy. 'Take him away.' He looked over at Moira. 'Paramedics! *Now.*'

Amelia was aware of police radio static and words like

'armed response team' and 'secure the area' and then Jack was there, pulling her close and enveloping her in a hug and Amelia was grateful for the comforting warmth and solidity of his arms around her.

Constable Williams came over. 'Are you all right, Amelia?'

She nodded, although she could feel her legs starting to wobble.

'Divers went down and found the wreck of the *Sundowner*. Paddy was inside. Looks like he was shot, then tied to the wheel.'

'Elizabeth?'

He shook his head.

'Then I don't think Elizabeth's dead,' Amelia said as McGregor came over. 'Andy said he heard Drew talking and was disappointed in him and Elizabeth was too. It was like they'd been together and heard.'

'But where could she be? How could he have hidden her, alive for six months?' the DI asked.

'Drew had all these sleeping tablets. Everyone kept saying how amazing it was he remained alert. The GP stopped prescribing them and he had to resort to smuggled ones. I think Andy's been drugging Elizabeth.'

'But where is she?'

'Drew said whenever he was here he heard noises that creeped him out. And when I was here with Gideon and Jack, we all heard a strange thud too.'

DS Dabrowski came over and spoke to McGregor. He nodded and turned back to Amelia. 'The rooms have been checked and they're all clear.'

'She must be here, somewhere,' Amelia said.

Jack clicked his fingers. 'Archie told us about one of the myths of Samuel Bain when the locals thought he was some magical shapeshifter because the villagers had his house surrounded in a ring while the minister prayed and he suddenly walked up behind them. Everyone fled in terror. Obviously, it wasn't magic, but some sort of hidden exit.'

'Everyone start looking for a hidden room or exit,' McGregor said.

'What if there's a cellar?' Amelia suggested. 'What's beneath that?' Amelia pointed to the Persian rug in the middle of the floor. 'This is the only room that isn't just bare floorboards.'

Together, Jack and Constable Williams began to roll up the rug. It was old and heavy and full of dust.

'Look!' Moira shouted.

There was a hatch, with a wrought-iron handle.

Jack managed to pull the heavy wooden door up. Stairs led down. The room below glowed with flickering candlelight.

Amelia followed McGregor down. There, tied to a chair in a similar way Hector had been was a woman with her head slumped forward, long brown hair covering her face. She was in a white dress.

'Oh my God, I've had visions of her, standing on the road. She was telling me,' Moira cried. 'Oh, Elizabeth!'

'Jesus!' McGregor said softly as he looked around the room and the paramedics went to Elizabeth.

Amelia saw, on a nearby table, the many blister packs of sedatives.

'She must have managed to escape at one point, got to the road and scared the wits out of Jean Maddox's cousin before Andy got her back. But she must have dropped the necklace Cameron gave her for someone to find.'

'Cameron was protecting her,' Moira said.

There was a noise above them as Hector, now freed, clattered down the stairs.

'Oh, Lizzie!' Hector cried when he saw his old friend. He gently held her hair back from her face.

Elizabeth's eyes opened slightly. She smiled as she tried to focus.

'Hector, it's been a while,' she slurred. 'And you need a haircut.'

FORTY-FIVE

Murray knocked gently on the door and without waiting on an answer came into the hospital room, smiling tentatively at Moira. Elizabeth and Hector, who were sitting either side of Moira, turned to greet their old friend.

With no spare seats, Murray perched on the edge of Moira's bed. 'I wasn't sure I should come but it seems there's quite the party going on.'

'The dress attire leaves a lot to be desired,' Moira said, glancing at the hospital gowns she, Elizabeth and Hector wore.

'It might be a bit of an improvement from some of Hector's more eccentric pieces,' Elizabeth said as Hector let out an offended cry.

'I'm just glad everyone is in one piece.'

'Despite Andy's best efforts!' Hector snorted. 'We should get Davey and Ray along, then it'll be a proper party.'

'There'll be plenty of time for all that,' Elizabeth said. 'I need to get home and see my boys. And my girl.'

'And I can't wait for a proper reunion with my niece.' Moira grinned at Elizabeth.

'You concentrate on getting better,' Elizabeth said as she

stood up. Although still a sickly pale colour and painfully thin, Moira could tell a little of her friend's spark was back.

'Come on, Lizzie, I'll escort you to your room and then we can see about splitting from this gaff. Mrs Cuthbertson has promised me a splendid welcome home dinner. I hope it's steak pie and cauliflower cheese as I missed out on that when Andy clobbered me over the head and dragged me off in the back of a bloody truck! There'll be plenty for you and the boys and Isobel, all of you. I'd like if we could spend more time together. This has taught me true friendship. I'll never forget that you came back for me, Moira,' Hector said as he walked out with Elizabeth, patting Murray on the shoulder as he passed.

Murray moved to sit in the chair Elizabeth had vacated.

'Hector is in *mother hen* mode,' Moira said as she tried to sit up a little, using the arm that wasn't in the sling to push against the mattress. 'He's insisting that Elizabeth stays with him until she's better.'

'How is she?'

'Relieved. Angry. Emotional. She's strong and she'll recover physically but that poor woman will need a whole load of therapy. Paddy was killed in front of her and Andy confessed to killing Cameron too when he had her held captive. She's been through six months of terror. I think she'd be fine to have Hector fuss over her for a while.'

They lapsed into silence.

Now it was just the two of them, Moira didn't know what to say to Murray. She had so much to get off her chest but at the same time, had no idea where to start. It didn't help that she was still a little groggy from her operation.

'Are you here in an official capacity? To take my statement?'

'Nope,' Murray said softly. 'I'm here to check you're okay.' He reached over and took Moira's hand in his. 'Are you okay?'

'I will be. Once they stop pumping me full of drugs and let

me out. I've told them I'm not staying a minute longer than I have to.'

Murray smiled. 'The nurse told me as much. And do you have a plan after you leave here?'

'Hector's steak pie sounds pretty heavenly, I have to say.'

'And after that?' Murray pressed.

'I suppose I'll head back to Stone Manor, possibly have a drink in the Whistling Haggis, but I can tell by your look you want my slightly longer-term plans.'

He nodded, giving her the ghost of a smile.

Moira took a moment before she answered, listening to the buzz of people in the corridor outside. A porter passed, whistling cheerily as he pushed an empty wheelchair.

'When I arrived back in Glencarlach, I had a feeling... that it would be my last visit. If I'm being honest, I thought it was because my time was up, my last stop. The end. And I suppose I went back into the Hunting Lodge to get Hector with that sense of finality.'

'It very nearly was,' Murray said quietly.

'Oh, I know. If that twisted psycho Andy had had his way, I wouldn't be here.' Moira paused, trying to form the right words before she spoke.

'But I did survive. And sitting here, jacked up on painkillers, I've come to realise, I had that feeling of it being my last visit because now I'm here, I'm going to stay, so I won't be *visiting* anymore, I'll be *living*.'

Murray looked at her solemnly before saying, 'Is this just until you get out of here and change your mind again? You have done it before.'

Moira shook her head, trying not to wince at the movement.

'I don't need to run away again. Remember Cameron talked about leaving? Turns out he and Elizabeth had planned to run away and have the baby and do all that. When Elizabeth told me this, just moments ago, I thought what typical naive teenager behaviour and it hit me, *I'd* done exactly that! And I was *still* doing that! I had to give myself a quick reality check and remind myself I'm not a teenager anymore. I want to stay. And I'd really like it if we could be...' she searched for the least cringy word, '...friends.'

Murray raised an eyebrow. 'Friends?'

'Dear God, man, don't make this any more difficult for me.'

'I'd like us to be friends too.' He grinned.

'Now you're laughing at me.'

'Maybe.'

'If I wasn't attached to this drip I'd lamp you one!'

'That's not very friendly.'

Moira started laughing. Partly from embarrassment, partly from relief, and partly from feeling the giddiness of a future in Glencarlach. With Murray.

She remembered back to the last tarot reading she'd done when The Lovers card came up. How right they'd been.

'Ah, I see someone's recovering well,' a nurse said, bustling into the room.

'Laughter is the best medicine,' Moira said as Murray stood up to let the nurse do her observations.

The nurse looked down from studying the monitor and winked at Moira.

'Our timing hasn't been the best in the past, Moira, but maybe it was meant to be like this,' Murray said. He headed towards the door. 'I'll let you rest. Phone me when you need picking up.'

They smiled at each other and Moira knew she was finally home.

FORTY-SIX

Later that evening Amelia was sitting in the Gatehouse's living room nursing a large Lagavulin whisky and being fussed over by Jack, Toby and Gideon, when there was a gentle knock on the front door. A moment later, Jack showed Constable Williams and Detective Inspector McGregor into the room.

'Sorry to bother you, but we thought you'd appreciate a brief update,' McGregor said after they'd declined the offer of a cup of tea, which was fast becoming Gideon's go-to remedy.

'It looks like Andy had that room in the cellar built for a while. Possibly even before he knew Elizabeth planned to leave with Paddy. It was fully set up with chemical toilet, bed, sofa, some kitchen equipment. I think Andy knew he was losing Elizabeth and planned on keeping her there.'

'I know it's possibly a *little* soon, but didn't I tell you?' Gideon said with more than a touch of smugness.

'What?' Toby asked, looking slightly concerned at whatever Gideon was about to say.

'Didn't I say that the Hunting Lodge was just the sort of place to be a serial killer's lair and would have rotting corpses in the cellar! I said those *very* words.'

'Yes, you did, Gideon,' Amelia agreed. 'But luckily we managed to get to Elizabeth while she was still alive. How is she?'

'Fragile. As you would imagine after being drugged and held captive for six months. I spoke to her earlier and she knew Paddy was dead as Andy shot him in front of her. And Andy told her about Cameron. She had tried to escape, around the time when the GP reduced Andy's sleeping pill dosage. She found a way out through an old hidden tunnel that linked up to the network of smuggler's tunnels. She's now being well looked after by her boys and Isobel.'

'And Hector,' Ray added.

'How's Moira?' Amelia asked.

'Surgery went well and she's now winding up the hospital staff by insisting they use some herbal tincture instead of co-codamol.' Although he sounded gruff, McGregor was unable to hide the smile of relief. 'And she's delighted to find out about Isobel. It's quite a touching family reunion.'

'And Moira's planning on staying. With the DI,' Ray added.

McGregor turned a little red.

'What about Andy McAvoy?' Jack asked.

'He'll be going away for a very long time.'

Ray nodded solemnly as McGregor continued.

'It would seem you have a knack for attracting drama, Ms Adams. I mean this in the nicest possible way, but I hope I don't see any of you for a very long time.'

'I feel the same. But please keep Stone Manor in mind if you ever need a wedding venue,' Amelia said.

The DI gave a slight laugh and turned even redder as he and Constable Williams headed to the front door, Jack following to see them out.

'I'm going to put the kettle on and make a big pot of tea,' Gideon said, leaving Amelia with her brother.

'I need to know, with everything that's happened, are you still keen on moving into the Hunting Lodge?' Toby asked.

'Honestly? No. I don't like the mounted stag heads.'

'*That's* what you don't like?' Toby said incredulously as Jack came back into the room and sat beside Amelia.

'Okay, not just that,' Amelia said. 'I don't mind a bit of mystery or the odd alleged ghost but I draw the line at living in a place like that.'

'I suppose we can manage in the Gatehouse a little longer, until the perfect place turns up,' Jack said.

'What about extending the Gatehouse?' Toby suggested. 'Or building somewhere on the vast acreage of grounds. I'm sure you'd find the perfect spot.'

Amelia and Jack looked at each other. Neither of them had even considered that.

'That sounds like a plan,' Jack said.

'And,' Toby continued, 'for the next wee while is there a chance you could lay off the sleuthing, finding dead bodies and putting yourself in perilous danger? Do you think you can manage to live a quiet hotelier's existence?'

Amelia smiled. 'I can try.'

'I've got an even better idea,' Jack said, just as Gideon returned with the tea. 'Why don't we put all our energy into planning our wedding. It would be a nice, murder- and mystery-free way to spend the next few months.'

'That sounds a great idea,' Amelia agreed. 'Let's plan a lovely calm and incident-free wedding with no drama at all!'

'Perfect,' Jack said.

'I'll say cheers to that,' Toby added and they all clanked their mugs together in agreement.

THE END

ALSO BY LAURA STEWART

The Murderous Affair at Stone Manor

Mistletoe and Murder

———

Twelve Labours of Love

ACKNOWLEDGEMENTS

I would like to thank a few people. A big shout-out to everyone at Bloodhound Books, especially Betsy, Fred, and Tara, for your superstar qualities. And thank you, Ian, for your brilliant editing; your attention to detail is fabulous and your advice spot-on.

Thank you, Helen, for generously giving me your time to answer questions on police procedures in Scotland and to go over hypothetical scenarios. Any inaccuracies are down to me.

And thanks, Jen, for showing me your drysuit and not thinking I was weird when we worked out the practicalities of running whilst wearing one and how various methods of murder and blood loss would be impacted by neoprene. And thank you, Kaye, your passion for diving is wonderful, even though I never, ever fancy donning a scuba suit; snorkelling in the shallows of warm crystal-clear waters is as far as I'd be willing to go.

Also, thank you, Robin, for not minding me quizzing you about boats and harbours. Looking through the photographs of our sailing trips around the north-west of Scotland was a delightful trip down memory lane for Pete and I. Those sunsets! The enthusiasm with which we shouted 'Whale!' only for it to turn out to be a puffin. Your mum's baking. The great idea of filling up the little fridge with delicious cheeses, only to have the boat stinking of ripe Époisses after only half a day. The Scissor Sisters album was the soundtrack to our first trip and I am transported back to that summer whenever I hear it. I do seem to recall I was far better at making the gin and tonic sundowners than being entrusted to do anything nautical. Probably for the best.

A NOTE FROM THE PUBLISHER

Thank you for reading this book. If you enjoyed it please do consider leaving a review on Amazon to help others find it too.

We hate typos. All of our books have been rigorously edited and proofread, but sometimes mistakes do slip through. If you have spotted a typo, please do let us know and we can get it amended within hours.

info@bloodhoundbooks.com

Printed in Great Britain
by Amazon